NIGHTMARE
The unfolding of a world crisis

DONOUGH O'BRIEN
& LIZ COWLEY

Donough O'Brien, before turning to writing, enjoyed a successful career in Europe and the US. His illustrated history books include: *Fame by Chance* – looking at places that became famous by a twist of fate; *Banana Skins* – the slips and screw-ups that brought the famous down to earth; *In the Heat of Battle* – those who rose to the occasion in warfare and those who didn't; and '*Who?': The Most Remarkable People You've Never Heard Of.* Also co-written with Liz Cowley was *Serial Damage* and *From One Hell to Another.*

Liz Cowley had a long career as an advertising copywriter and creative director, working in several of the world's leading agencies. A long-time fan of poetry, she enjoyed success with her first collection, *A Red Dress*, published in 2008; and her second, *What am I Doing here?*, published in 2010,which were made into a theatrical show in Ireland and the UK. Two poetry books for gardeners, *Outside in My Dressing Gown* and *Gardening in Slippers*, are selling well. *Pass the Prosecco, Darling!*, a humorous book about cooking disasters, was followed by *Serial Damage*, a murder novel co-written with her husband, Donough O'Brien.

DEDICATION

To those who think it might never happen.

A CIP catalogue record for this title is available from the British Library.

978-1-912031-18-4 hardback
978-1-912031-17-7 paperback
978-1-912031-16-0 eBook
978-1-912031-15-3 Kindle

 GB Publishing Org, www.gbpublishing.co.uk

ACKNOWLEDGEMENTS

Paul Lewis, stockbroker
W.M. Keck Observatory, Hawaii, USA
Neil Hudson, psychologist
Dr John Akeroyd, botanist
Timothy ffytche, surgeon
Major-General Sir Robert Corbett
Melody Douglas-Henry, nutritionist
Katy Young, Beauty Director, *Harpers & Queen*
Mukesh Prajapati
Spokane, Washington, City Council

PART ONE

PROLOGUE

June, 2027

'Sorry, I just don't feel like it.'

'You never do.'

'I do.'

'When? I can't remember.'

'Look, I've had a pretty tough day.'

A long pause, and then his wife spoke. 'Don't you want a kid any more? Or me, come to that?'

'Yes, but…'

'What?'

'I just don't want sex at the moment.'

'You need to see someone. It's not normal.'

'It's perfectly normal. Lots of guys at the office are going through the same thing.'

'*What?* You discuss our sex life at the office?'

'No. It's just that all of us seem to have gone off it.'

'And you discuss that at work? Great!'

'Look, just shut up and go to sleep. We'll talk about it in the morning.'

The same conversation was going on in bedrooms all over the world.

CHAPTER ONE

Yorkshire, England

The whole thing seemed to have started four months earlier and three thousand miles away, with a row on the telephone between two Royal Air Force officers.

'Why the *hell*, Jim, didn't you tell us?'

The urgent and rather rude call was mystifying.

'What do you mean, Sir?'

'Something entered our airspace two hours ago, trailing fire like a meteorite and hit the sea west of Ireland. Didn't you see it?'

'No, we've tracked nothing unusual, nothing like that. Just the usual airline traffic.'

'Well, everybody *else* saw it. You only had to look at the night sky. It's already all over the television and YouTube. I *can't* believe you detected nothing.'

The ultra-sensitive radars under their great domes at Fylingdales on the Yorkshire moors should indeed have detected any large object entering Britain's airspace. The threat of aircraft or missiles had never entirely gone away, with potential terrorists now replacing conventional old enemies like the Soviet Union and Russia.

The Duty Officer at the RAF's Command Centre at Naphill continued. 'It must have been quite small, about the size of a bus. Otherwise we'd have had a tsunami already and some real damage. As it is, it's created a huge cloud of water vapour, miles in the air. It's drifting back across Ireland with the wind – blocking out the sun. God knows what it was. The cloud will cover Britain tomorrow and then, I suppose, the continent. Please watch out for anything new.'

A few hours later, American morning television picked up the mysterious story from Britain, but typical of the rather insular attitude of the US media, it was given just a passing mention.

That changed dramatically the next night, when the people of Chicago saw their own fireball in the sky. Whatever it was, it appeared to strike land, or rather water, right in the middle of Lake Michigan. A small wave, two foot high, was recorded in lakeside cities like Milwaukee. Much more dramatic was the huge cloud that mushroomed tens of thousands of feet into the air. What had been forecast as a clear, sunny day all over Illinois, Michigan and Ohio turned out to be grey, dark and misty.

Three hours later it was the turn of California, when something hit the Pacific a few miles off Los Angeles. Then one near San Diego. And Seattle. And San Francisco. Over the next few days, a veritable meteorite shower bombarded the world with projectiles striking the Atlantic, the Mediterranean, the Indian Ocean and the Pacific. One hundred and twenty nine were finally counted. Strangely, they all arrived at night, all of them hit water and not one was detected by radar.

Only one hit land, just on the shoreline of the Black Sea. A group of fishermen saw it extinguish itself in the dark. The Russians quickly sent a team from the Crimea to investigate.

With mist and cloud covering the globe, now the world's media could talk of little else. Pundits on television speculated endlessly about the possible similarities with an asteroid that probably destroyed the dinosaurs sixty-five million years ago by creating a dust cloud blanketing the world for enough years to wreck the food chain.

Stock markets plummeted. Social media jammed the ether.

But, gradually, after just a few days, the clouds of vapour dissipated like early morning mist and the sun came out.

The world seemed to return to normal and the media turned to other things.

CHAPTER TWO

Washington, D.C.

Ann Hearst backed carefully out of her driveway. Her new electric car was eerily silent. She raised a hand to Sergeant Donovan in the car behind.

'Mommy, guess what I'm doing today?'

Ann looked in the mirror at her six year old daughter, Tricia, and smiled. Blonde and blue-eyed just like her. But with so much of her father in her. Stubborn. Strong-willed. Very much with a mind of her own.

'I don't know, darling. Why don't you tell me?'

'Well, we're going to do a painting class, and I'm going to paint Daisy.'

Daisy was her doll, strapped in the seatbelt beside her. Ann suddenly realised why she had insisted on taking her favourite toy to school. Toys and dolls weren't normally allowed.

'Oh how lovely! Make sure you bring the painting home and we'll show it to Daddy.'

'And next week, my friend Marty's having a party. Can I go?'

'Of course you can. I've already talked to her Mom.'

'And what are you doing today, Mommy?'

'Oh, nothing much, just work.'

The car fell into silence. Tricia was looking out of the window as she always did when they neared the school, hoping to see her friends out of the window.

Ann helped her out of the car and watched her meet her friends, waved goodbye, and then drove off on to the busy Interstate 495 Beltway circling America's capital, Washington, D.C. She occasionally took a look in the mirror to see if the two guys in the Secret Service detail were still keeping position. Not that she drove fast, especially in this new electric car.

It was an easy and short drive to work in Fairfax from Alexandria where she lived with her husband Ted and Tricia. Ted, recently promoted to Lieutenant Colonel in the US Marine Corps, also had an easy commute to the Department of Defense. He'd been on active service in the Middle East two years ago, so Ann had stayed behind and devoted herself to helping her father on his long campaign

11

trail, from the Primaries right up to the thrill of his Inauguration as President of the United States. It had been so satisfying and encouraging to be reported by the media as a great asset, filling in for her mother whose arthritis was making it increasingly difficult for her to appear in public. All the hard work had been worthwhile, and so had her own widely reported academic successes, which helped give her much-needed confidence when in the public eye.

So far, President James Morrow had enjoyed a reasonable first two years in office, with the Senate and the House fairly on side and world events not causing too many problems. Muslim extremism was at least contained, North Korea had become a democracy and was joining the South, and Iran had turned firmly capitalist.

Ann turned off the Beltway on to I-66 and drove to the Fair Oaks Business Park at Fairfax, guiding the car into the parking lot of Genecorp Inc, the genetics research company. She got out and plugged in her car's battery. The driver of the Secret Service team waved and they drove off. There was no need for their protection in the Genecorp building. Security there was tighter than in the Pentagon.

At least she was helping with one world problem, she thought – the eight billion mouths to feed. Because of climate change and increasing temperatures worldwide, there was less land with adequate water to grow crops. So, but for the genetically modified crops, especially the drought-resistant ones that she was helping to create, starvation might be stalking many more parts of the globe.

She enjoyed her work and the occasional foreign travel, especially when she went to visit her colleagues in the research station at Rothamsted in England. Thank goodness the Europeans had woken up at last and backed off their knee-jerk unscientific opposition to GM. Even Prince Charles, before he became King in old age, had admitted he had 'gone a bit too far'.

There was only one cloud in the sky of Ann's life. Ted seemed to have totally gone off having sex with her, even though they wanted another child. She hoped it wasn't another woman, one of those pretty and ambitious staffers and secretaries in a bureaucratic city with not enough men. Or maybe he was just tired.

Probably only temporary, she thought.

CHAPTER THREE

New York City

It started with women, in the social media. And it became a clamour almost instantly. Within days, thousands of Twitter and Facebook groups were created, talking about the overnight problem. On Twitter there was soon a popular hashtag – #impotence – and others that people thought were more funny. Very soon the world began to realise that it was not funny, not funny at all. And it did not take more than hours for television, radio, newspapers and magazines to make it *the* story. It was not as if you could avoid the momentous nature of what was going on. Nor the fact that male journalists and presenters were affected just as badly as their listeners and readers.

For the same reasons of immediacy, the medical profession rapidly took note and doctors' blog pages were soon trying to solve the problem with natural remedies. And almost inevitably, hundreds of people also started trying to sell fake cures via advertising on social media.

For the millions of men who were experiencing the symptoms, completely unexpectedly, it was not funny at all. Hot flushes and sweats, intense fatigue, total loss of libido, erectile dysfunction even when taking Viagra, sudden muscle weakness, loss of self-confidence, depression, lethargy, anger, anxiety – doctors' surgeries were overflowing with confused and frightened men, also angry about how long they'd had to wait for a consultation at all.

And the agony of sitting in a crowded waiting room didn't help. These days they seemed to be crammed with worried-looking men avoiding eye contact, and even without the heart to read magazines. Probably because many of them were full of articles about men with exactly the same problems.

Most of them had already taken a test to check for low, or even no testosterone levels, having reported no libido, sudden impotence and muscle weakness, and were coming in to discuss the results.

And most of those waiting had been told to take the test before breakfast, because testosterone levels change throughout the day, peaking in the early morning, and affected by food intake, stress and fatigue.

And all of them were hoping to be referred to a hormone specialist, an endocrinologist, having seen no improvement whatsoever in their sexual interest and performance.

But doctors were beginning to be seriously concerned that their testosterone replacement therapy was no longer working, even when used with a PDE-5 inhibitor like Viagra. What's more, reports of erectile dysfunction were rising to such a high level, they simply didn't have the time to address the problem more than they were already, not with all their other patients. Pregnant mothers (lucky them). Sick children. Geriatrics. People on crutches, or in wheelchairs. Waiting lists were quite long enough without this sudden onslaught of newly impotent men.

Many of the patients had been there for hours. Losing patience. Losing money, depending upon their jobs, many of which wouldn't pay for two or three hours off, or more. Losing dignity. Losing hope. And losing, in some cases, the love, respect and patience of their wives. And more with every day this went on.

Already the medics were working far longer hours. And it wasn't as if the male doctors didn't have the very same problem and worries themselves.

What on earth was going on?

*   *   *

Nobody believed it, however scientific were the explanations connecting it to the plumes. It had to be a blip, something in the air, something to do with global warming, airborne gases, dangerous emissions, sudden uncharted and unexpected earth movements, climate change, or some irresponsible country – or indeed industry – emitting, but not admitting, some catastrophic pollution. In many primitive societies, it was put down to evil spirits or the will of the Gods.

It wouldn't last. It *couldn't* last. Of course it was a total shock, and horror, to find out that impotence, and just as important, male infertility were not local but worldwide problems. But with this, as with everything else, there would surely be an answer, such were the massive advances in medical and scientific knowledge. There *had* to be a solution. Surely the drug companies, the clever scientists or the World Health Organisation would come up with something? It was only a matter of waiting. *Surely?*

New York Stock Exchange

Monday had been a torrid and very unpleasant day. Anyone with a historic bent would have compared it, unfavourably, with the 'Black Tuesday' of the Wall Street Crash of 1929.

As the sun dipped behind the skyscrapers, the Partners of the firm gathered in the conference room to try to analyse what had happened and work out what on earth the future held for the trading in stocks. Everyone was exhausted. They had all come to work even earlier than usual, alerted by Bloomberg on tablets iPhones and watches that a World Health Organisation briefing had triggered huge falls in Europe. And this was after three weeks of falls all over the world, ever since the first health rumours.

The partners were tousled, tired and shaken, having then spent the day rushing round the room, looking over the shoulders of their shouting traders in front of screens almost entirely full of red. Down on the floor of the Exchange it had been worse, with signs of panic only too like those in 1929.

Leon Lerner, the Senior Partner, was a white-haired veteran of the stockbroking business. His partners were all much younger. Before asking the heads of the various teams to review the stocks in their sectors, Leon did two things. First he sent out for some whiskey and vodka. Then he reviewed the situation.

'This is completely unprecedented, my friends. And I've been around Wall Street for forty years. If we believe the media and our own experience, something has stopped us men being interested in sex. That's tragic enough, but worse is that no sperm can be produced. So, no more children. And, therefore, a steadily declining and aging population. This morning's WHO announcement, admitting the problem may be permanent, put the boot in. You saw on our TV link what our people in London looked like by lunchtime. Shattered. The markets ain't stupid and, even if you allow for the usual knee-jerk panic, they've quite sensibly marked down the stocks that have a reduced or even no future. Some we have seen today literally have no buyers at *any* price, so-called 'air-pockets', just like in '29. Last week, stop limits and the banning of high frequency and dark pool trading by the SEC cut out the volatility a bit, but only a bit. The currency markets don't seem to know where to go. There may not even be *certain* currencies soon.

As usual, the retail markets have tanked, especially if people are on margin. All those old men in Shanghai, betting their own money, they'll be wiped out. Some of the exchanges that closed last week may not re-open – ever.

We think that world trade will inevitably decline, and millions, tens of millions, will be thrown out of work, and their pension incomes devastated. There could be civil unrest as well in some countries.

All of us here have personally lost a fortune and the firm has too. It's worse for our clients and catastrophic for many of the corporations out there.'

He poured himself quite a glass of Bourbon, not caring if people noticed how large.

'Now, can we look at things in detail? Nice and short, please. We all need to get home. Might as well use the alphabet. So, aerospace. Bill?'

'Down, Leon, perceived drop in air travel, due to reduction in business and tourism, and long-term,

just fewer and older people. So, fewer planes needed.' Bill Eustace, also poured a much-needed drink.

'Banks, Sarah?'

'Down. Declining prosperity and reducing customer numbers. Down, too, are investment trusts. But, worse, we think that some of the banks exposed to derivative products may go under – and quite quickly. A whole lot of Lehman Brothers.'

'Commodities, Jay?'

'A surprising positive spike in the soft ones; wheat, cattle, pigs. Chicago knows that even with artificial insemination, the numbers will go down and the prices up. But hard commodities are down, as Al and Conor will report.'

'Construction, Ethan?'

'Down. Lower future population means declining worldwide demand for houses and apartments and for business premises. And, by the way Leon, property prices have crashed – halved, or worse. All over the world, but especially places like London, where the very high prices were inflated by lack of stock and speculation by foreign buyers – who are about to go broke.'

'Engineering, Tony?'

'Mostly down, but mixed. A positive spike in freezer companies, probably anticipating freezing the fewer stocks of meat.'

'Food, Axel?'

'Mixed picture. Baby and kids' food have plummeted, of course. No more babies in a few months time. Some others are holding up, but I'd expect them to slide too, eventually. With fish unaffected, fish food companies have held up, so far.'

'Insurance, Paul?'

'Disaster. All down. Some nearly out. People realise they are like legal Ponzi schemes, relying on future contributions that won't come. 'Act of God' clauses may help insurance companies not to pay out, but that doesn't help if nobody pays in. And the pension side will be wrecked by the stock collapse.'

'Media, Sally?'

'Another disaster. There'll be a huge drop in advertising, in the vulnerable sectors, which are the lucrative ones. So, I'm afraid lots of newspapers and magazines will fail, in our view, and TV and radio stations. We think Twitter, Facebook and even Google are also vulnerable. People will want to talk to each other okay, but the advertising is what's really holding them together. And the big ad agency groups like WPP and Omnicom, they'll be in trouble too.'

'Mining, Al?'

'All down badly. With less construction, there's less need for steel and copper and anything else used. The Australians and Africans are in real trouble. China's trying to flood cheap steel back into the market.'

'Oil and Gas, Conor?'

'Same again, Leon. Fewer people. Less heating, air-conditioning and the use of cars and trucks.'

'Pharmaceuticals, Cynthia?'

'Mixed picture. Some are actually *up*. I suppose they're hoping science and research can solve the problem. Restrictions on cloning may go, so those stocks are up. But others are wiped out, like contraception companies. Who needs condoms or the Pill?'

'Sure' grunted Leon. 'Retail, Liz?'

'Down. Fewer people, less spending power. Anything to do with sexual attraction, like fashion and beauty, is right down, and of course, kids' and toy shops.'

'Telecoms, Dan?'

'Down. Fewer people, less money. Less traffic. Plus they're too dependent on ads on cells now.'

'Transport, Jim?

'Down. Less people, less travel, less money.'

'Leisure, Charlie?'

'Down. Fewer people, less use of clubs, holidays.'

Leon Lerner looked up, and nodded gravely round the room.

'Thanks, everyone. So, a pretty disastrous picture, and it'll get worse. I think there will be a general feeling of depression – which will *also* get worse. Why wouldn't it? We may get protectionism, the collapse in the value not just of stocks, but even of money. We may end up bartering cabbages, for Christ's sakes! At the very least, the aspirational world we know can't help but change. Why bother with smart cars, expensive clothes and new devices? I've got a nasty feeling people will just stop bothering.'

He topped up his drink, before adding more bad news.

'For you partners in this firm, there's another thing. As you know, we've been discussing merger plans with Kenny and Stein. I talked to Jack Kenny just a few moments ago. He agreed with me that neither of our firms is currently worth a red nickel. So the merger won't happen. Sad but inevitable

With the collapse of stock prices, the reduction in earnings and, in many cases, with the destruction of the actual companies themselves leading to a black hole in dividends, I'm afraid our pensions will be worth a fraction of what they were. We may join the millions of pensioners out there who'll be suddenly broke. And that's a Doomsday picture.' He topped up his Bourbon again, again not caring what his colleagues thought.

'Thank God it's Friday, as they say. I've also just realised that it's the hundredth goddamned anniversary of the '29 Crash. Christ!'

His cell phone buzzed. A text message. He looked up with a resigned smile.

'That was my wife in Westchester. Apparently, there's been panic buying in our local Walmart.

They had to call the police and close the store. She says she can't buy any food for dinner.'

He downed the last of his drink.

'Have a nice weekend.'

CHAPTER FOUR

Washington, D.C.

Barbara Schroeder, the United States Secretary for Homeland Defense, listened aghast.

Barbara, a big, confident, blonde woman from New Jersey, who after years in business had turned to politics, was presiding over a conference room of scientists and White House staffers. There was no good news.

The Chief Scientist addressed her, looking tired and worried. 'Madam Secretary, our scientific team has concluded that those so-called meteorites of a few weeks ago, and the vapour plumes, have triggered some unexplained, massive and ubiquitous chemical effect or virus. The invisible poison, all round the world, only lasted about a month, but that was enough.

Let me explain, perhaps in very personal terms. I have a son, Hal, aged ten. Normally, in about two years, Hal would be experiencing the first effects of puberty. You all know those effects – deepening voice, growth of facial and body hair, the creation of sperm and interest in sex. We think that none of that will now occur, for Hal, or any other human males – or even male mammals – at least not unless a miracle happens. Something has shut down key functions of the cerebral cortex and the limbic system, together with the production of sperm and the hormone testosterone. Hal will never have children, nor will his pals or anyone else.'

He introduced his Chief Endochronologist, John Aitken, who went into detailed scientific data, ending on an equally grim note.

'We had hoped that the women who were pregnant during the events would have given birth to normal boy babies. I'm afraid that isn't the case. You remember how we used to worry about getting the mumps as adults. Well, it's as if all the men in the world had got it.'

There was a stunned silence in the room. After what seemed at least sixty seconds, but was in fact a tenth of that, the Chief Scientist cleared his throat and continued.

'We've been flat out focusing on the tests and we've not even started to figure out the consequences of all this – but they'll be massive. And not just for humans, although that's terrible enough. As far as animals go, it seems to be only mammals that are affected. Birds seem okay, and fish, except for dolphins and whales, of course.

But the bottom line is that only those humans and mammals with protected sperm and with some operational artificial insemination system will be able to procreate.'

Another shocked silence.

A Department of Agriculture official raised his hand to interject. 'There is a tiny bit of good news, at least on the animal front. Here in the US, we already have 75% of cattle and 85% of pigs being raised through AI. We're checking the sperm bank status. AI with sheep is much more tricky. But, of course, from a *world* food perspective those figures only apply to the US and other advanced countries. I'm afraid everywhere else will soon have no meat.'

No meat? Another stunned silence in the room, from an audience which included no vegetarians.

A State Department official added. 'As for humans, the AI rate would be *much* lower, of course. And, anyway, whole swathes of the world are against AI in principle. The huge populations of Muslims and Catholics. And in poorer countries, with ballooning populations and lower resources, they'd scarcely have bothered with AI.'

The meeting turned to the peculiar and suspicious aspect of the meteor shower. They seemed to have arrived in regular waves, about fifteen at a time. 'As if someone had fired a giant shotgun at us', said the man from Princeton, morosely.

The meeting had fallen silent, with some thinking the unthinkable.

The delegate from M.I.T. added more suspicion. 'And they all arrived at night, and almost as if carefully placed all over the world. All but one hit water, creating those plumes. And not *one* showed up on radar.

What's more, the Black Sea one that hit the shore. That landed only a few hundreds yards from the water – like a very near miss. Still pretty accurate when you consider that it probably came from hundreds of thousands of miles away. Darned good shooting, if you want to put it that way.' His mild sense of humour did not raise a smile.

General George Johnson, from the scientific department of the US Air Force, lifted his hand.

'Here's another thing. The Russians, suspicious as always, at first wouldn't confide in us, but they now tell us they've found no evidence of rock impact at the Black Sea site, just an unexpectedly tiny crater with some fragments of burnt-out green substance. They have no idea what it is. They're still trying to analyse it. We've offered help, but they haven't responded yet. We're still waiting.'

After much discussion and speculation, the Homeland Secretary wound up the meeting, 'Whatever happens, we've got to protect what sperm we have. We may have to control all those women rushing to AI centres, desperate to have children. And there may be some men who have *not* been affected. Haven't we, and others, got a handful in space? And several countries have some submarines that may have been under water with their crews unaffected.' Everyone knew that would be a tiny number.

Gathering her papers, looking haggard and worried, Barbara Schroeder got up.

'OK, I've got to go brief the President.'

As she walked to the door, her cell phone buzzed.

It was a text from her broker. Apparently her stocks had just lost $300,000 while she had been in the meeting.

CHAPTER FIVE

Even though US Space Station Zebra was comparatively roomy and luxurious, its crew members were quite excited to be going home. After all, they'd been up there, 220 miles above the earth, for nearly a year and were now really looking forward to seeing their loved ones. Especially as communications with earth had become very limited in the past few days.

The shuttle with the replacement crew was due at any time and the team carefully prepared for the docking procedure. They turned on the outside lights.

'What the hell is that?'

Mary-Ann Estevez was staring out of a porthole. Without any kind of radar warning from the Trajectory Operations Officer on the ground in Houston, another spacecraft had just appeared no more than 300 metres away, very steadily drifting towards them. Reflecting their lights, against the black of space it seemed to be sort of silver and dark green. It was not very large and, strangely, it was rolling end over end very slowly. It certainly was not the expected spacecraft with the crew coming to relieve them.

Any speculation about what it might be was interrupted by something much more urgent.

'Jeesus,' whispered Hank Lennox their senior commander, 'If it keeps going, it's goddam going to hit us!'

There was no doubt about it. The strange craft, with its mysterious motion, was getting ever larger.

'We'd better brace ourselves. God knows what's going to happen. Shit! What the fuck is it? It don't look like anything of ours.'

The youngest crewman, Chuck Wilson, peered out. 'It don't look like anything.'

They waited, strapped in, in full spacesuits and helmets, in case the hull was ruptured. For all of their years of training, they were, frankly, terrified. A year in space, now maybe to end in a crash.

But there wasn't a crash. The impact was soft, like being hit by a jelly or a sponge. The strange craft slid past them, covering one of the portholes with a green film. And with helmets off, the crew members floated over to the portholes. They watched it drift off, still rolling and apparently out of control. In a minute it was gone, lost to the blackness of space.

They quickly checked for damage. There appeared to be none. All systems seemed to be working and apart from the green-slimed window there was no evidence whatsoever of their strange encounter. In the panic, nobody had thought to take a photograph.

'We have to report that.' Mary Ann announced. 'Straight away. And ask TOPO why we had no warning.'

'I'm not so sure,' responded Hank. 'That was seriously weird. We don't know what it was or whose it was. And if it was, let's say, unfriendly, I figure we should not tell the world we saw it.'

'But ....'

'No, I mean it. We'll be back on earth within hours now and we can then report it properly – without anyone out there listening.'

Hank was the senior officer, and, for all the friendly, democratic banter that had built up over the months, on something like this his orders had to be obeyed.

'I'll tell you what though, we'll get the replacement crew to take a walk outside and send a coded message about what the hell that green stuff is.'

Six hours later their portholes filled with the more welcome sight of the replacement crew's spacecraft. Docking went smoothly and half an hour later the new crew, two men and a woman, entered the station through the airlock. But their usual greetings seemed muted, even tense. Their crew leader, Bill Stanton, had trained at NASA with Hank, and their families lived quite close together outside Houston. But now, unsmiling, he handed Hank a sealed envelope and asked his friend to read the contents straight away.

'I don't *believe* it!'

The rest of them turned to stare at Hank.

'Mary-Ann is going home but Chuck and I are staying on – for three goddam months. Tell me they're shitting us, Bill. What the *hell* is this all about?"

Bill Stanton had, of course, been ready for this explosion. He had been fully briefed before they had blasted off from the Cape.

'I'm afraid, Hank, you've been kept in the dark a bit. A lot's been happening since you've been up here. Remember those meteorites nine weeks ago? We now think they did something to the world, something very bad. More than bad, catastrophic. Fact is, no men on earth seem to be able to get it up, or to produce any useful sperm. So, no more children, or at least none born normally. Me and Jim here – the same.

It didn't happen all at once. It was sort of gradual. There were some who could still do it and they had a field day with the women. In Houston they even boasted and called themselves 'Woodies'. But even they lost it after a few weeks. And their sperm turned out to be infertile anyway.

The top brass have figured out that you two, a couple of the Russians, four guys on the International Station and the Chinese Tiangong 3 up here, plus some submarine crews may be the only ones unaffected. But we have to make sure, to protect you.'

Stanton allowed a pause to let the shocking news sink in.

'So two or three months getting bored up here may be balanced, old pal, by your wives being the only ones able to have natural children. And you two becoming world heroes for still being able to beat off. Or rather you won't be heroes, because apparently it's all got to be secret.'

Juanita Gonzalez, the new girl, winced. She was not quite as used to the men's coarseness as Mary-Ann had become. And childless, she was thinking of her own situation.

Silence fell in the craft as each crew member struggled to take in the news. It was broken by Hank reporting to the new team their own dramatic secret – the strange small craft that had blundered into them.

'That could be very significant,' said Bill Stanton, looking worried, 'Mary-Ann will have to go down and report that. We'll go with her. Juanita will take her place. You guys can return probably in three months, maybe less. We'll do our best. But we'll have to wait for the scientists to tell us there's no more pollution and that you won't get infected like the rest of the world's males.'

Chapter Six

Washington, D.C.

The President was still trying to adjust to what he had just heard from his Homeland Secretary about her depressing meeting with the scientists, followed by the very peculiar news hours ago of the US Space Station's encounter with another mysterious craft.

Jim Morrow was a slim, fit man of 56. He worked out, did not smoke, hardly drank and normally felt pretty good. But he was certainly not feeling like that now. He knew his world and everyone else's was about to fall apart.

Needing to think, he was eating a simple cold supper alone in the small President's Dining Room, created by Jacqui Kennedy on the second floor of the White House. He was by himself yet again because Elaine was away having treatment for her arthritis.

The phone rang. 'Hi Dad. Do you mind if I come over? I need to talk. I'll only be a few minutes.'

Jim hesitated, but only for a moment. He owed her so much. What else could he say to a much loved and loving daughter who had devoted two years of her life to getting him elected?

'Sure, honey. Come on over. But I'm afraid I can't be long.'

When she arrived, she seemed depressed, most unlike her. He poured her a glass of wine.

'Dad, I know there are horrific problems out there at the moment. I wouldn't normally discuss it, but it's just that, well, they've now affected Ted. And just when we'd decided to try for another kid. Is there *any* hope or news from anywhere?'

He sighed.

'Ann, honey, you probably know you're sharing that particular problem with about three billion other women.' He looked at her sadly. 'I'm afraid it looks as if there's very little to be done right now, or probably nothing except to try a fertility clinic.' He paused, 'Of course, it wouldn't be Ted's, but..' He left his words hanging in the air.

'Quite a decision, Dad. I've only just started to focus on anything like that. In fact, I've only *just* noticed that the problem's hit Ted and me, because I've been so tired myself. You know, absolutely locked into my sub-Saharan GM and RNA interference maize project. It's at a crucial stage. I even sent Tricia away for a few days to be able to concentrate and work really long hours.'

The President nodded. 'Well, as you can imagine, all this has changed everything. Not just socially, but economically and politically. All sorts of huge problems are piling up.'

'So what's happened? Tell me.'

The President felt he could confide certain things to his daughter because of her involvement in his politics and her security clearance. He ran through the terrible situation that was developing worldwide, and the scientific theories emerging, editing his words carefully.

Ann looked stricken, her eyes widening. She understood the implications in a flash.

Her father then told her the latest and secret development, the unexplained collision with the Zebra Space Station.

Absolutely focussed, Ann stared at her father, gathering herself together before asking several more questions. Having carefully heard her father out, she took a deep breath, 'This may sound far-fetched, Dad, but maybe we're under attack.'

'It *does* sound far-fetched, Ann. Attack by whom?'

'Well, nothing from earth. You say those meteorite things came from outer space. And so did that strange ship that hit the space station.'

'So?'

'Well, I can't believe I'm saying this. But it could be, well, what we used to call aliens.'

Her father lifted his hand to stop her. 'You've seen too many space movies.'

'No Dad, I've *never* believed in aliens. But this is different. Bear with me. As I see it, it could be something trying to destroy, or at least weaken the world's population. It certainly looks as if that's what's going to happen. So far, it's the only explanation for what's going on. It *really* doesn't seem random.

And that weird object, the one in space that hit the station. Suppose it was something that, luckily for us, just happened to malfunction. Suppose it was a sort of drone – and perhaps one of many. After all, our forces have been using them for long enough. Suppose they've started to watch us, to monitor our decline. They probably thought we wouldn't be able to see them. Like the meteorites, they seem radar-cloaked. It was only luck that one came blundering out of space and was seen by the Space Station, by chance, that gives us a clue that they're out there. Thank God, by the way, the crew waited to report it.'

Her father frowned. 'Why?'

'Because if our crew *had* used the radio, they might know we're on to their reconnaissance vehicles. Just the kind of thing we might have to hide.'

Was her father beginning to come round? Ann rose to her feet, fervently hoping so.

'Look, let me go home to my computer and be back here in the morning. I'll have something to show you.'

*   *   *

When Ann came back in with her laptop under her arm the next morning, it was obvious that her father was at least partly convinced, because he had been joined by his Homeland Secretary, Barbara Schroeder, as well as Patrick O'Neill, the Secretary for Defense, and David Hudson, the Secretary of State.

Patrick O'Neill had been a fighter pilot in the Gulf War years ago and was famous for his Irish wit. David Hudson was another veteran of the political scene. White-haired, he walked with a stick, and was highly respected on Capitol Hill. She knew all of them from both her father's long campaign trail and for the many Presidential functions since his election. They all smiled in a friendly way, but looked very strained, and wasted no time on formalities.

'Okay, Ann,' said the President, 'I've told my colleagues that you've come up with something pretty serious. Let's hear it, please.'

She set up her computer and connected it to a big screen.

'Let me start with the math of the situation.'

Click. Bar charts appeared on the screen.

'Assume, after nine months, no more births from then on. Then factor in a death rate of about 60 million people a year, but going up rapidly as health care deteriorates. I figure after twenty years the population will fall from 8 to 3.7 billion. Everyone will be over twenty, most of them older. The lack of male testosterone will mean reduced competitiveness and aggression – perhaps good for civilian life, but rotten for the military.'

She pressed a button. Click.

'Now, after 30 years we only have 1.7 billion, with everyone getting older and feebler – especially in defense terms.'

Click.

'At 35 years, we're down to seven hundred million.'

Click.

'After 40 years, it's just 400 million people, roughly the same as in the 15th century.'

'Except,' interjected the Secretary of Defense, who prided himself as a history buff, 'we'd have no warriors like Tamerlane rampaging around, or Henry the Fifth and his archers.' He grinned at Ann. 'Although I suppose we might have a Joan of Arc.'

Ann did not smile at the compliment, quickly continuing with her presentation. This was no time for wit.

'All things being equal, we'd have a pretty feeble world of old men and women. Now, if *you* wanted to take over that world, without having to fight for it or to dispose of a huge population, *you'd* wait a few years after your poison had done its work and then move, wouldn't you?

But you'd require reconnaissance. You'd need to watch the world carefully to see if things were working out to plan. Remember the vehicle that hit our space station – probably by mistake? That could have been some kind of recon ship.'

There was a serious and muted discussion about her evaluation. They respected her, remembering that it was some of her brilliant election ideas that had ensured that they were all in that room. Nobody seemed to be arguing with Ann's basic theory. Just conceivably, the meteor shower, the plumes and the consequences *might* have been natural events, but the strange spacecraft could not be so easily explained away.

'So, in a nutshell, you're saying we've had it' said the Secretary of State.

'Not necessarily. We *do* have artificial insemination, and wherever they are, they may not know about it. There *may* be just enough frozen and unaffected sperm to start to create a new world.'

Ann turned the screen back on.

'Now let's factor that in, and assume we have enough sperm for perhaps 50 million new births worldwide. I know that's quite an assumption. There are modern techniques that I may need to check out.

Now, after 20 years, the population is 3.75 billion. After 30 years, it is 1.9 billion because we can now include our 50 million AIs, plus perhaps 50 million up to ten year olds. Maybe more. Some mothers will have more than one kid, a few may fail to have any.

Click.

At 35 years we're down to 900 million, but that includes the 50 million AIs and 50 million 15 year olds.

Click.

At 40, we're at 700 million, but we have our 50 million AIs, still fit, plus 50 million aged 20, which is the average age of a soldier or airman. Plus 75 million younger children. Plus, very important, perhaps the first 25 million or so of the twenty year olds' small children. The world could then start to recover and the population could start to rise again.

Just as important, it may just have enough armed forces to be able to defend itself.'

She paused, and took a drink of water, aware of the shocked silence in the room.

'However there are two big 'buts'. First, there may *not* be enough sperm. And there certainly won't be if it's wasted. Forget those rich women who'll crowd into fertility centres trying to have children.' She paused ruefully. 'People like me.'

'No, our recipients have to be chosen, selected. Very carefully. They'd have to be committed, responsible. We need the mothers to create something like a breed of 'Janissaries' for us.'

The others looked at her blankly, not knowing the word, except the Secretary of Defense, who explained. 'You know, the captured Christian children that the Turks then made into their elite fighting force.'

The others nodded, as if they really knew all along.

'The second 'but' is how to do it all in secret. Whatever is out there must not detect that we have artificial insemination, or they may simply attack anyway before we're ready. They *must* think we have nothing but a dying world. And, by the way, that goes for male mammals too. Luckily, most cattle and pigs are raised by AI. And some sheep. There may be enough of their sperm to keep the food chain going. Most wild animals, I'm afraid, will just die out. Zebras, wolves, kangaroos and so on. But bizarrely, some of those that are facing extinction like pandas, snow leopards and rhinos may survive because organisations like Leonardo DiCaprio's trust have gathered and preserved the sperm for them.'

She turned to her father.

'So Dad, my suggestion is that you've got to call a conference of world leaders straight away. Face to face. No conference calls, no satellite use. And while looking like a crisis conference, you've got to use it to get them to all go along with an AI programme and its deception. It's the only chance.'

There was silence while her words were digested. The Secretary of State then voiced one immediate doubt. 'Supposing, just supposing, Ann is correct in all this. Convincing other countries just on her theoretical 'say-so' will be damn difficult. People like the Brits and the Germans might go along with it, but the others …?'

Everybody was thinking of the Russians and their usual suspicions.

The Secretary of Defense intervened, remembering the heat-seeking missiles in his Air Force past. 'We think those aliens, or whatever, can mask radar bounce-back. I wonder if they can also mask any heat emitted. We've developed infra-red technology way beyond what we used to bust tanks in the Gulf War. What if we tried to sweep space to detect any heat anomalies? Even a tiny difference in temperature would mean something was there. If there was, then you'd have something really impressive to show. That might convince them. Do you want me to try that?'

'Sure, go to it,' said the President.

*   *   *

It only took two days before they convened again.

An aide from her father's office had called and asked Ann to come to the White House. The same group was now gathered in the conference room, but Secretary of Defense O'Neill was now accompanied by a young Air Force Colonel with KOENIG on his name badge. Colonel Koenig turned down the lights and switched on a projector.

'We asked for the help of the Keck observatory in Hawaii, Mount Graham in Arizona, one in Tenerife and Dome C in the Antarctic. This is what they sent us.'

He began to show them a series of pictures of space. First, he pointed out some obvious sources of heat like their own and other countries' space stations and some government and commercial satellites. Then he turned up the magnification.

'Now, look there, and there and there. I think that's what you are looking for.' Distinct, small splotches of light showed.

'There should be nothing there. Visually, and by radar, we can see nothing. But those things are emitting a tiny amount of heat and we can just detect that.'

'How many have you found?' The President asked.

'Dozens, Sir, so far. We're trying to sweep the sky very slowly and methodically. These things are not evenly spaced, either. We've detected them mainly above countries with big populations. There are only four above Australia, and none at all above the North and South Poles. To state the obvious, no people to watch.'

Silence. Their fears were being only too amply confirmed.

The Secretary of Defense turned to the President.

'Jim, I think this would give you enough to convince the foreign leaders. So you could convene your conference. We also recommend that we send up a couple of satellites – apparently routinely. We could equip them with side-looking infra-red cameras and get a better look at what we are up against.'

The President nodded his approval.

When Colonel Koenig had left them, he turned to Ann.

'You'd better come with us too. If you've managed to convince us, I figure you could do the same with the foreigners. We'll take Koenig with us too, to show his infra-red material, and you can explain the population and AI issues. I'll try and convince them about the need for control and secrecy.'

By secure landline, I just called the Prime Minister of Great Britain, Peter Wilkins. Let's face it, they're still our closest ally. I haven't told him quite everything, but he gets most of the picture. And he's on side. He'll back us.'

However, I've been thinking. I figure, with some of those other countries we're going to have a practical and also a moral problem. We'll have to keep the AI ruse not just from what or who up there, but from some, maybe all, of the people down here.

I assume any supply of sperm is going to be very limited. Most is held in advanced countries that thought they had a need for it. Who do we share it with? Which of them will use it as we want them to?

Then we've got both Catholics and Muslims who probably won't have any sperm because they disapprove of AI morally. And there are lots of those African countries who – well, put it this way and not to go beyond these walls, if they treated the sperm like they usually treat foreign aid, they might just give it to their favourites, and families – or even sell it. Some of the South Americans as well. But are we to secretly doom whole regions or whole continents to wither away? I don't know. It's *really* difficult. In fact, inconceivable.'

He turned to the Secretary of State. 'I think you, David, should go off after our conference to visit some other countries, perhaps with the British Foreign Secretary, Mike Selway. And you should definitely visit the Pope in private to sound him out about his opposition to AI. And the problem with the Muslims, of course, is the one we've been facing over the terrorism for years. There's no one person, like the Pope, to give any kind of single lead.'

He stared at his notes, as if lost in thought, then stirred himself.

'You know, we may look back on this and realise that our knowledge is the equivalent of knowing that the Japs were coming for Pearl Harbor and having fighters in the air. Or knowing what those young men were doing before 9/11 and arresting them before they reached the planes.

Okay, then. Let's get the plans for that conference started.'

Washington, D.C.

Returning from the White House, and the discussion about a world leaders' conference, Ann found it very hard to look at the painting of 'Daisy', Tricia's doll, which she had brought back from school that afternoon. Surely love for a doll was an early sign of her daughter's natural maternal instinct, one that she now knew might never be fulfilled.

And what was she, or any Mom to say when their daughters were reaching puberty, which was getting younger and younger these days? That the monthly cycle was all about nature preparing them to have babies in the future? How could any mother say that, if despite all the great advances in medicine, there may never be future generations of children. At least, not unless a miracle happened. That thought – and the picture – filled her with a great wave of sadness.

'Don't you like it?' asked Tricia, looking puzzled by her mother's silence. 'Mrs Carter did. She said it was very good, and that I might be a painter one day. And she specially liked the dress, and all the flowers I put on it.'

'She's right, darling.' Ann forced a smile. 'It's very good, especially the dress. They're lovely, those roses.'

She picked up the painting. 'Tell you what, darling, why don't we frame it and put it up in your bedroom? Or even down here in the kitchen where everybody can see it when they come in? I'm sure Daisy would like that, too.'

Tricia beamed.

Suddenly Ann heard the sound of the front door. Relief, Ted was home. Watching her daughter with her doll painting had really depressed her, and right now she really needed his support.

'Hi, guys!' Tricia ran to the hall and was about to leap into her father's arms, but rushed back to fetch the painting from the kitchen table. Ann hoped that he would be more enthusiastic about it than she had been able to be.

'Wow, this is lovely! Well done, honey!'

When Tricia had gone happily to bed, with the painting propped up on her bedside table, Ann was at last able to talk to Ted about the momentous events of her day, while swearing him to absolute secrecy.

CHAPTER SEVEN

Budapest

The pit crew couldn't understand it. The World Champion had announced on his radio link that he was coming into the pits early. And there were only a few precious minutes of Practice time left! The team's sophisticated telemetry monitoring systems indicated nothing technically wrong with the car. But there was no doubt that *something* was wrong. He was a full half a second slower than last year in Hungary, and, with the technical improvements achieved, even slower than he should have been, three quarters of a second – a lifetime in the normal thousandths of a second margins in Formula One racing.

He was still the fastest in practice, because, strangely, everyone else also seemed to be going mysteriously slowly.

The car pulled into the pits. The crew crowded round expectantly. Engine? Tyres?

The World Champion, the richest earner in sport, took off his helmet, removed the wheel and stared at his team manager.

'I'm sorry. I can't do this any more. I quit.'

London

'You mean he just stopped?'

The Sports Editor of *The Times* stared at his motor racing correspondent, just flown back from Hungary.

'Yes, and as you saw, so did three other drivers, once they realised they could stop, like the World Champion, and without shame. The race was miserably slow, and two more drivers quit afterwards.

And the FIA reported that the spectator numbers were right down. I noticed myself that the *Tifosi*, those Ferrari fanatics, weren't there either. If this goes on, the advertisers and the sponsors will start pulling out. I think that Bernie's whole expensive sport may just go.'

'Sure,' said the Sports Editor. 'And it's not the only one. Nobody seems to want to box any more, or watch boxing or rugby either. Half the soccer players seem to have lost their bottle.

And it's not just the braver sports, so to speak. A lot of the male track and field athletes seem to have lost their edge. And the swimmers, too. And even the tennis players are serving more slowly. Testosterone must have been more of a factor than we imagined. Think what it will do to the Tour de France. I suppose we'll end up with a bit of golf and snooker – and the women providing most of the competitive sports.

I wonder how long we'll have jobs?"

Nashville, Tennessee

The group of middle-aged men sat sipping beer in the Nashville recording studio. Even that didn't taste good. Ricky Williams, after three decades a star of Country music, had never heard such depressing news. Not just his own sales, but those of all his Opry colleagues were tanking.

Country music was really very little to do with 'the country', let alone 'Western'. For years it had become, of course, all about 'lurve', romance and sexual tension. And apart from some people apparently buying for nostalgia, the sales figures were now catastrophic. Not quite as bad as the teenage pop music industry which had collapsed in weeks, but terrible nevertheless. The Country radio stations were packing up, too.

'Might as well go back to singing about lonesome whistles, boxcars and goddam train crashes,' Ricky growled miserably.

Atlantic Ocean

High over the Atlantic, the flight deck of the Air France Airbus was a depressing place. The pilot had just been told the news. This was going to be the very last Air France flight from Bogota to Paris. The reason was nothing to do with the passenger numbers. They were holding up quite well, considering. No, it was the flower industry that was collapsing. What had made these flights profitable were those big containers of fresh flowers in the hold. With Colombia one of the world's three largest flower-growing countries, flowers were not only flown daily to the Miami Flower Market, but also to Europe, via Paris and Amsterdam.

But with the collapse of romance came the collapse of flowers, so no more flights.

Jean-Jacques Bertrand, the Captain, broke the silence. 'God knows what'll happen to Colombia. Perhaps they'll have to rely even more on their second biggest export – les drogues.'

Pennsylvania

Marilu was thrilled. She'd just seen – watching the news with her parents – that most people in the world weren't going to be able to have children any more. But she would, unlike her eight brothers and sisters. They might not be as lucky. She would be the apple of her parents' eyes.

It hadn't been any fun, sex with Rob. A quick screw behind the shed at school. Suddenly, a trickle down her thigh before she felt anything at all. And then the horror of a positive result after a pregnancy test. For what? The whole thing had been an absolute con, and now she was three months gone. But now at last she could tell her parents, and they'd be relieved, in fact thrilled. At least one of the family would be able to have children, and it would be her. God's chosen. Her mother was always telling her 'God moves in mysterious ways.' Too right, thought Marilu And this was the perfect proof.

Nine children, and no grandchildren. That would break their hearts. And in any other circumstances,

it would also break their hearts to know than an unmarried daughter would fall pregnant. But not now. She was the chosen one. The one to take her family into the next generation, and probably their only hope of that. The elation and sheer relief were flooding her.

All her siblings were out in the garden. Should she tell them *now*, or wait until after the TV news? Perhaps after, so there was more time for it to sink in.

At last her father switched off the TV.

'Mum, Dad, there's something I need to tell you.'

She had the perfect excuse for them not to be angry. Thank God for that. They'd see it as a miracle, not the result of some tacky fumbling behind a shed with a boy she barely knew.

Manchester, England

Johnny had given up swimming. At fifteen, he didn't want anyone to see him in swimming trunks, or even say hello to the Manager with his high squeaky voice. Too embarrassing. And he was afraid of the girls. And very, very afraid of his future. Could he explain to the Manager, and perhaps have a swim alone before the club opened? No, they'd have to pay the Swimming Pool Attendant extra, and they wouldn't do that for one person. And there weren't many other boys of his age swimming in public any more.

Maybe they'd make pools for boys only – boys like him – in the future. Meanwhile, he couldn't face it. No muscles. No need to shave. None of the strength he should have had by this age. Even the famous, albeit slightly-built diver, Tom Daley looked like Goliath compared with him. It was so unfair. He had even thought of drowning himself, if that were possible. But he had to think of Mum and Dad. They loved him, even though he was a freak, as all the boys of his age were. Puny, childlike, afraid of girls, afraid of even saying 'Good morning' in a high falsetto.

He sat disconsolately at his computer. Once he had loved war games. Not any more. Often he had looked up pornography. Not any more. And he couldn't even wank any more to pass the time. And school was hell. Girls teasing him, because he was so puny. And even asking him what it felt like to be like that. Why didn't the teachers give lessons on what it felt like never to mature? It was all so bloody unfair.

Johnny trawled the net for ways on how to commit suicide and was horrified by how easy they were to find. Would he actually do it? Would he ever dare to? He hadn't even got the strength for that. He hated himself, and he hated the world. Not for the first time, he wished he'd never been born.

These days, the girls at school even called him 'Squeaky'. Not a name he could live with. Not a life he could live with any longer. But how to end it?

New York City

Barnes & Noble – the famous American bookstore – was having a nightmare sorting out its stock and layout, in common with book stores all over the world. Pregnancy and baby-care books, normally such a popular section, would have to go. Ditto, a lot of sex guides and romantic fiction. Poetry, always a difficult section, would have to be sorted out, with romantic poetry strictly edited. Lots of modern fiction would now seem dated – as would many books in the psychology section, with absolutely no mention of the greatest psychological trauma the world had ever faced. And, of course, the children's book section was doomed, or would be before too long. Almost nothing was safe, except for ancient history. And even that was a risk as it might remind people that the human race was headed that way too.

Jim Riley, the middle-aged Manager was exhausted, and the store was fast losing money as his team painstakingly sifted through the stock. Even the popular greetings card section would need a complete re-think. And what to do with the vast piles of rejected books piling up at the door? 'Some day we'll want to read them all again,' his wife had told him, and he'd agreed. But the store simply couldn't hold on to books that probably wouldn't be read again for decades, if ever. About the only safe sections of the store were cookery and gardening, and even the upbeat tone of their authors suddenly seemed out of date, as did titles like 'Romantic Cooking for Two' or 'Cooking with Toddlers'.

The book trade had been struggling for years, fighting the onslaught of on-line book-buying. And now this.

Jim decided to do one more week sorting out and returning unwanted books to disappointed publishers. He knew how much publishers hated returns – as did authors – but there was nothing else he could do in this nightmare scenario. Never had so many books been wanted by so few, he thought grimly.

Then he would re-stock and tidy up as best he could, and wait to see the outcome. And then if things didn't improve after three months – as he doubted they would – he'd pack it in and go for early retirement.

Wearily he took out the check list in his pocket for tomorrow's sorting.

1   Sex Advice books
2   Modern Romance
3   Sci-fi
4   Joke books
5   Monster books
6   Horror
7   Zoology
8   Pregnancy Advice

What on earth time would he be home tonight, let alone the next six nights? But it had to be done. He couldn't just walk away from it all, not after twenty years there, and not after such an unimaginable disaster – far worse than anything he had ever read about in the sci-fi section.

Chicago

'Hi, this is my sister Sue.'

No reaction from the man she was looking at. Nothing. Just a smile.

Sue knew she was beautiful. One of the top models at Elite Models. But this man was looking at her as if she were a piece of furniture.

'Hi.' No interest, not a flicker. She may as well have been another guy.

It was her adrenaline, the ways guys looked at her. She could almost see their pupils dilating. All gone. And probably her job too. What was the point of looking great if men didn't care what you looked like any longer? Except guys who were well past it. Or gay women, and she wasn't into that. At least, not yet. She'd actually thought about it for the first time.

Sales of women's magazines were plummeting, and her salary almost certainly would. All those endless pages of beauty product ads. What point now? And what point fashion shows, and jewellery ads, and perfume ads, unless you were the sort of woman who did things only for your own esteem, past caring what anyone else thought of you. Or men, at least.

She looked at her brother's friend. Handsome.

Really handsome. But a friendly smile, nothing more.

Her world was shattered.

Hastings, England

Veronica Johnson was thrilled. Normally, she would have sold a top pedigree Labrador puppy for around £700. Now, because there probably wouldn't be any more Labrador puppies – or indeed any more puppies of any breed – she had been able to charge double that and get away with it. What's more, her obliging Labrador bitch, Bella, had been kind enough to produce eight gorgeous healthy offspring, the last of which had just gone to a grateful new owner that morning. Veronica worked it out – eight times £1,500. That came to £11,200, and it hadn't even been all that much work. The pregnancy had gone smoothly, there were no extra vet's bills, and the little ad she had put in the local paper had prompted dozens of calls from desperate would-be owners. In fact, thought Veronica, if she could have Bella artificially inseminated for another pregnancy, she could charge even more, although canine sperm was almost certainly running out. Britain was such a nation of dog-lovers, supplies wouldn't last long.

She wondered what to do with the money. A holiday? A bigger kitchen? New clothes? A complete make-over? A facelift? No, little point in that last thought. Her husband probably wouldn't notice it if she had one anyway, or even care if she looked fifteen years younger. And he'd probably say it was a total waste of money. Well, all men would say that these days. After all, none of them had any sex drive, any more than dogs did.

She patted Bella's head. 'Good girl, Bella! You've done me proud.' The still tubby labrador was nodding off in her basket, but wagged her tail appreciatively, no doubt relieved not to have any more boisterous pups to feed or look after. She was exhausted by it all, and glad to see the last one go. Peace at last.

Veronica slipped the last cheque into her purse and put it in her bag, deciding to go to the bank at once. She didn't like the idea of having £11,200 in un-cashed cheques hanging around the house for too long and told herself that she mustn't put her bag on the floor beside her in the front of the car. Too many snatch and grab incidents at traffic lights these days – bags should preferably be locked in the boot – particularly with all those desperate people out of work.

'Back soon, Bella!'

Bella was fast asleep by the tine she slammed the front door, and the ricochet sound throughout the house didn't wake her. She'd certainly earned the rest.

Paris, France

Who would be interested in wearing Louboutin shoes now? Viviane Canonge, the Marketing Director of the famous shoe brand, was seriously worried. Nobody would feel like walking tall in this grim scenario. And no men would care about what shoes you wore, especially as the males gradually became smaller over the next generations. Surely, without any sex hormones men wouldn't reach the same height, and looking down on them might be even construed as an insult. The future of the company, and her future, didn't look good.

And it would be the same for lots of luxury brands that would suddenly start to look ridiculously frivolous in today's grim circumstances.

What on earth would happen to her? Top end luxury and fashion marketing was all she knew about, and she needed good money to stay in her chic Paris apartment, just off the fashionable Champs Elysees.

Already she was getting embarrassed stepping out in those world-famous shoes. And going out in the evening, she'd noticed far fewer women wearing them. It, well, just didn't seem appropriate any more, and it probably wouldn't ever again.

A board meeting had been scheduled for two o'clock that day, and looking at the agenda only heightened her fears. The first item was EXCEPTIONAL CIRCUMSTANCES, obviously a period to discuss the huge implications facing the company. She noticed that two hours had been allotted to this one subject. That didn't bode well.

She might not be walking so tall after the meeting, and who else in the company would? Already she could feel her confidence shrinking fast.

Tel Aviv, Israel

'Mum, I don't want Rafi coming here, or whatever his name is. I'm sure he's very nice, but well, I'm afraid I'm just not interested.'

'But darling, you haven't even seen him. Give the poor lad a chance.'

'Why, if he'll never be interested in me?'

'He might be one day. They may find a solution to all this ghastly mess. And anyway, there's a lot more to life than sex.'

'At your age, probably. You probably wouldn't have said that at eighteen.'

'I was married at eighteen.'

'Precisely.'

'Ruth darling, someone will find out what's happened, and then it'll all be alright again.'

'By which time I'd probably be bored stiff with him, expected to stay at home and be the good wife, and probably him with me. Look Mum, I know we're Hassidic, and I'm happy with that. But I'm simply *not* going to marry a man I won't fancy, and who'd never fancy me, not unless there's an absolute miracle. And look around you, Mum, the world has changed. Look at Arab women.'

'Why? Why ever would I want to look at Arab women?'

'Haven't you heard? Or noticed? Most of them are giving up wearing the hijab, niqab or burka any more because no guys are interested in them anyway. So their men aren't jealous any more and don't force them to cover up. They're safe, they're free, as I want to be, and I don't want a barren man to feel better about himself at my expense. It's just not fair to me.'

Her mother paused 'Alright darling, but look at it another way. What will it be like to remain *unmarried*?'

'Rather more fun, I'd say. Much less hassle. And no having to say you love them if you don't, at least not in the way you'd like to.'

'Ruth! I wonder what the Hasmonean school would say if they heard you talking!'

'They have! We've had all sorts of debates about it. None of the sixth form wants to get married. Or wear wigs. Or sit at home all day. At least not just for some chap who can't even get it up and expects them to wait on them hand and foot like Dad does.'

'Ruth, I think you ought to watch your tongue. And you'll have to talk to your father about that. He's spent a long time finding Rafi, and he's a good boy.'

'Why should I talk to Dad? He's just like the rest of them. Look, Mum, women don't need men any more, not in the way they used to, and if Dad wants me to get married to get rid of the financial burden, I'm quite happy to get a job for myself, and probably a much better one than any husband could offer. Men are such idiots these days, and even in the classroom. And haven't you noticed that three quarters of the Cabinet are now women? These days, it's women who have the balls. Not men.'

'Ruth, *please*!'

'I'm sorry, Mum, but please wake up. And tell Rafi's Dad that tonight's off. I am absolutely *not* going to marry a man who's bee neutered, a man who'll never be able to father kids, and who'll bore me to tears with his psychological problems, and on top of all that will expect me to stay at home for the rest of my life. *And* wear a bloody wig when he wants me to. Forget it!'

Her mother sighed. 'I'm glad your father hasn't had to hear all this.'

'He will, if you ask Rafi round here. I suggest you phone him right now. Or his Dad. I am absolutely *not* going to be a human sacrifice.'

'All Hassidic women are, my darling. At least, up to a point.'

'Well, count me out.'

'Ruth, you'll break Dad's heart.'

'I'm sorry about that, but there's no point breaking Rafi's. And mine too.'

London

'Look, I'm sorry to tell you this, but I didn't ask you all round to have a girlie chat. The fact is, Marilyn and Joyce and Sandie and me, well, all of us are going through exactly the same thing, and we wondered what more we could do about it.'

'Fuck all' said Marilyn, tossing back her mane of red hair. She had always been blunt, even more than an axe that hadn't been sharpened in a hundred years.

'I've done all I can' she laughed. 'And I can tell you what, girls, there's nothing that works. Except dildos.'

'Marilyn, this is supposed to be a serious meeting about a serious subject. We can't just sit back and look at the news and Twitter and do absolutely nothing. There must be *something* we can do. That's what this is all about. Any ideas on anything, anything at all.'

'I *am* serious' said Marilyn, 'there's fuck all we can do. Or, rather, fuck nothing. And I'll be even more serious with a drink inside me. I'm sure we all would. Has this suddenly become a dry house? Life's tough enough without discussing our hopeless men sober. They'll be alright in the end. It's sure to be something in the water or the air that they haven't found yet. Spores floating about. Chemicals we've chucked into the sea. Satellites exploding. They'll find out eventually. It's happened to fish stocks, all sort of things. And it's not the end of the world. At least for me. Frankly, I was a bit fed up with George before all this, so it doesn't matter that much to me. And I've got Albert.'

'Albert? Whoever's he?'

'My dildo, darling. I'm sure you don't want to meet him.'

'Marilyn, you're disgusting.'

'Yep, but practical. No point moping if the guys have lost it. They'll get it back again. And in the meantime, we could start a gay club if we're all that desperate, although I have to say I don't fancy any of you. Couldn't afford you, for one thing. At least I've got a job.'

Marilyn got to her feet, all six feet three of her in her new Louboutins. 'Right, where's the plonk? If the world's coming to an end, we may as well get pissed while it does. And please, someone, get off your arse and bring the glasses. I can't manage them in these new shoes.'

'Oh' she added, at the door to the kitchen, 'I wouldn't mind having a skinny dip if you're all going to bang on about men. None of those builders on the roof are going to be remotely interested. Rather a mercy if you ask me.'

Her Louboutins cluttered on the tiles all the way to the kitchen, leaving a profound silence behind.

The hostess gave a sigh of relief. 'Well, has anyone got any ideas?'

No-one had.

Manila, Philippines

It was the greatest sudden job loss in history. Millions of women worldwide had lost their jobs virtually overnight – in the 'oldest profession in the world', prostitution. Twenty-five year old Carmen was just one of them, now terrified of how she was going to support her two young children and pay the rent for her small but comfortable flat in Manila's Makati District.

She had come a long way from the dreaded Tondo area of the city with its river slum population of over 400,000 people, but not far enough in terms of education to get any other kind of job that would support her in the same way.

Nothing else would be as lucrative, at least nothing she could think of, or was qualified to do. Literacy levels, she knew had risen to an amazing 97% among the young, but too late for her lost generation from the slums, often forced to leave school early to help sick or desperately poor parents before there was any kind of radical social welfare. And now she had only a few thousand pesos left in the bank.

Yes, she could join the vast army of lowly paid workers in the city, perhaps in a supermarket or shop or laundry. But now there would be thousands more women like her going after those jobs – which would force the salaries even lower. But being scarcely able to read and write, what else could she possibly do?

At 'Juanita's' where she worked, the punters of any nationality had just suddenly stopped arriving. Realising her own financial plight, the 'Madame', Juanita herself, had said a tearful goodbye to all the girls the evening before, giving each of them 5,000 pesos 'to tide you through.' It was a nice gesture of goodwill, but only worth about 100 US dollars and would tide her through no more than a week.

Work in a massage parlour? Who would be interested in going to them any more? Perhaps a few old decrepit men. The thought was abhorrent.

If only she could read or write properly in English. But like so many children of Manila's slum population, four million of them, she had never learned, and had barely been to school at all with parents sick and needy. And then she'd become a mother so young. At only sixteen.

Her looks were her only asset, and she had used them. On a good day, up until yesterday, she could get up to 4,000 Philippine Pesos a trick, and as many times a day as she wanted to. In fact, she could afford not to work at all on some days, and never at weekends, particularly if foreign tourists had been generous as they often were, especially the Americans. The Americans, she knew, had once controlled the Philippines and she sometimes reminded them of that, milking their innate guilt and sometimes earning a bit extra –enough to give up work during the kids' school holidays.

Bar work? Waitressing? Factory work? She was barely qualified for anything else, and though she knew she was still pretty, there would be thousands of younger, prettier girls in competition – and anyway, with all that was happening in the news, male bosses probably wouldn't be interested in female charms at all any more. They'd look after their own. Men usually did.

The Philippines were such a Catholic country. Was this divine judgement? Whatever it was, it was now an unholy mess.

Carmen reached for the Fundador brandy bottle, gathering dust in the back of the kitchen cupboard. She hadn't had a drink in years but she was certainly going to have one now. The neat brandy scorched her throat. She'd forgotten that sensation, and now, remembering it, she wondered how long the bottle would last.

No, she checked herself. She had to keep strong for the children and for Angelo. She turned to the photograph of her beloved husband, dead for the last seven years, smiling up at her. What would he have told her to do?

And as so often, an answer came.

Angelo had died in a freak accident on the construction site of the Shangri La Hotel, one of the city's most stylish hotels. Now that so many thousands of women would be out of work, many would apply for jobs in such hotels, and competition to get even the lowliest jobs would be fierce.

But what if she were to go to the Shangri La and explain that her husband had died during its construction, bringing along the newspapers that would prove her story? Might they take pity on her? After all, the compensation money for his death had been paltry, and someone there might remember that.

And perhaps she should take along the photograph she was looking at right now? That, too, was worth a try. The smiling face of her darling husband taken on his twenty first birthday just before he was killed. Surely that might tug at someone's heartstrings.

She picked up the photograph and hugged it to her heart, deciding to visit the hotel tomorrow.

Brooklyn, New York

Sandy and Chuck were in bed in their apartment in Brooklyn. Once again Sandy had been wide awake since the early hours, staring at the ceiling and irritated by her husband's ability to sleep so soundly. He'd hardly missed a wink since that shattering news, and nor had he since returning from their recent honeymoon in Hawaii. Had she slept at all since then? If she had, it didn't feel like it.

It was all so bloody unfair. She and Chuck only really had one thing in common, and now even that had been snatched away. Chuck had his flying – he'd be alright. She knew she came second to that passion, but she had never minded about that, and hated flying in small planes anyway. But now, without any sex, what kind of life could she possibly have? She had never before experienced the pleasure that she had in bed with him, in fact never really experienced satisfying sex before that, and if she were being honest – as she was being now – she might never have married him but for that.

Now, while on one of his numerous flying assignments, there would be no rush of pleasure – or to be more accurate, lust – at the thought of his return.

Suddenly, he stirred in bed beside her. Only days ago she would have woken him up. But what was the point now? And what an appalling waste of money that Hawaiian wedding was. Practically all their savings had been wiped out, and it had only been after massive persuasion that she'd agreed to fly to Hawaii in his private plane to save the cost of a commercial airfare because all the rest of it had cost such a fortune.   The ceremony on the beach, the bridesmaids' dresses, the all night dancing and BBQ, the ridiculous flower garlands, the sleek seaside hotel, the endless and expensive cocktails at the bar, the steel band, the wedding photography and so on. Sandy groaned.

Well, no point in staying in bed she thought, glancing at the illuminated clock on the bedside table. Only 5am. And another pointless day ahead in the baby clothes shop where she was Under Manager – another part of her life that would disappear before the year was ended.

'What a fucking mess,' she whispered under her breath, cross she'd even thought of that now redundant 'F' word.

Georgetown, Antigua

Zeitiah Massiah looked at one-day-old Zak in the cot beside her with his beautiful dark olive skin and shock of black hair, trying not to wish he'd been born a girl. Life would be hard enough in the future for both sexes, but at least girls wouldn't be stunted in their growth and appearance, like her son would be, never able to mature or reproduce or lead a normal life, not unless there was an absolute miracle.

Alton, her husband, was due to see her, and like her he would try not to think of the future, simply relieved that the delivery had gone well, even if it were into a nightmare world.

Zeitiah knew that mothers who had just given birth often tended to be weepy with all that mass of hormones, but that wasn't the only reason she was weepy now. She reached for a tissue. Alton mustn't be allowed to see her like that. It wasn't fair on him, and there would be plenty enough reason for tears in the future. But where was Alton? He was already twenty minutes late.

It must be the extra security, she thought. Zeitiah knew that maternity wards in all developed countries were now on special alert for baby snatchers, with security guards outside the maternity ward and more of them at the hospital entrances. No fathers or family members could ever enter a ward like hers without strict ID clearance, and no mothers could bear their infants to be out of their sight or away from them in the creche, even if their mothers needed the bed rest after complicated and difficult deliveries, or if their infants needed special attention and monitoring.

What should have been a joyful and relaxed family experience was now becoming a nightmare of high vigilance surveillance, even with the mothers wondering if the doctors and nurses could be trusted. After all, many of them would be doomed never to have children of their own, which would make work in obstetrics all the harder to cope with.

At least she and her child had come though the birthing process safely she thought, knowing only too well that many births were now becoming much more complex and dangerous.

She had read that pregnant women were increasingly comfort eating, worried sick about infertile, stunted sons, and secretly and guiltily hoping for girls, like she had. And gross overweight did not bode well for a problem-free delivery Zeitiah had told herself, often while reading articles in the few surviving women's magazines, or looking at the posters in her doctor's surgery.

'Hi!' Alton was there at last. He gave her a kiss and looked at his sleeping son. 'Is it okay if I wake him up?'

'Sure,' smiled Zeitiah, struggling to put on a cheerful fave. 'It's time I fed him anyway.'

San Francisco

There was a long row of expensive cars in tree-lined Walnut Street in San Francisco – Lincolns, Cadillacs, a Lexus, two Porsches and even a Ferrari. Outside number 302, there was a noisy line of smartly-dressed women, some with their husbands, trying to get into the fertility clinic, often frequented by California's celebrities. The receptionist, who had been trying to control the impatient and hysterical crowd, was suddenly surprised to see two women dressed in black in front of her desk. Two men, burly and hard-faced, stood with them. Not the usual type of client at all. They flashed Federal badges at her.

Twenty minutes later, after a heated exchange behind closed doors with the owner and chief physician, the clinic was closed down, ostensibly due to lack of sperm, although the real reason was very different: no more babies could be *seen* to be born. The aliens had to be allowed to think they had achieved their objective. The line of women, some in tears, had gone home.

The Federal car did not leave, and a little while later another car pulled into the curb. Anne Hearst and a man got out and went into the clinic. The Chief Physician was initially in no mood to talk to anyone, but was eventually persuaded to come to reception to find out, exactly, what was going on. Ann's pleasant smile and demeanour calmed him down and he agreed to talk to them privately in his office.

'Doctor Najardi, what if you could rely on a steady supply of sperm, rather than see it run out as you would have done here?

'For the moment, we do have a supply of sperm, albeit frozen. That's because we can use a technique called ICSI. That stands for Intra-Cytoplasmic Sperm Injection.'

'Goodness, what's that?' Ann asked.

'It's a micro manipulative technique that was only developed in the early part of this century, perfected in about 2010. It's when we inject just one sperm into one egg, using a special needle. The crucial ability of the sperm to penetrate the egg is no longer important, as the penetration is achieved by ICSI.'

'So it would have a high success rate?'

'Yes, even with frozen sperm which tends to be less fertile. The other point is that it cuts out the tremendous wastage. One ejaculation during normal intercourse can contain half a billion spermatozoa – or more. And only *one* of those is going to win the swimming race to the egg. The rest are then completely redundant. An appalling waste. But, if you could keep those sperm, you could use them for making many more women pregnant successfully.'

'Is it a difficult technique?'

'Yes, it certainly is. It's highly skilled work. There are only a few dozen clinics in the world that can charge enough, I'm afraid to say, to make it worthwhile. The technique could be taught, of course.'

'Doctor Najadi, if we made it attractive enough for you, would you and your key staff be prepared to re-locate?'

CHAPTER EIGHT

Alexandria, Virginia

'Mummy, why is everyone so unhappy?'

Ann looked at her six-year-old daughter, concerned. Was the grim general mood getting to children so young? And if it were, what on earth could she say?

'They aren't, darling. And we can't be happy all of the time. Here, come and have a cuddle.'

'I don't want one. And now you're going away, so I'm unhappy too.'

'But Daddy will be here with you, and I won't be away for long. Only three nights. And if you're a good girl, I'll bring you a present when I get back.'

'I don't want a present.'

Suddenly, her daughter started to cry, and it was as much as Ann could do not to cry herself. For weeks it had been tough enough coping with her husband. She knew how badly he had wanted another child, and a boy – although he'd never said that. And even worse, she knew how he felt about himself.

Ann lifted her daughter and wrapped her arms around her, wishing she didn't have to go.

What a nightmare.

London

For Ann, the flight from Dulles Airport seemed to last for ages. The President could have taken one of those new supersonic airliners, but had opted instead for the old Boeing Dreamliners of Air Force One and Two. He needed to take quite a few people, and there was no huge hurry. It had taken some time to convene the conference anyway. Enough time for Ann to fly out to San Francisco and brief herself on the ways that modern artificial insemination might be used, and to formulate a radical idea.

In London there was certainly a very different welcome from last year's State Visit. No welcoming King Charles and Camilla, no Wills and Kate, no scarlet uniforms of guardsmen lining the Mall. It was now armoured limousines escorted by hundreds of heavily armed men in flak jackets as they drove in from Heathrow.

London itself seemed sad and subdued. Hardly surprising. The stock market had plummeted, and those ridiculously over-priced central London flats and houses were now mostly for sale. Their speculating absentee Chinese, Russian and Middle Eastern owners would be desperate for cash to prop up their own precarious financial and political positions at home.

The British had had done well in their urgent efforts to house and guard the thirty heads of government. The American delegation had taken over the whole of Claridge's Hotel.

Ann decided to go to bed for a while. She had worked all the way through the flight, naturally enough very nervous about her presentation to the most powerful men and women in the world.

She knew she would be on the stage after lunch tomorrow, because the morning would be devoted to a review by the International Monetary Fund of the catastrophic economic state of the world.

*   *   *

The conference took place in a huge business centre near the House of Commons and Parliament Square. Delegates arrived in their armoured cars, moving slowly past sullen crowds held back by armed troops and police. There were a few waving placards saying SAVE OUR WORLD and GIVE US KIDS! But generally there was little spirit, noise or animation. Ann was able to ride with her father, which made her feel safer. Jim Morrow seemed very tense, so much so that he once leaned forward and distractedly held her hand.

*   *   *

The head of the IMF was Edith Verhaeghe, a Belgian woman of cool Flemish competence and intellect. Her presentation started on a brutally frank note.

'We think the current situation may turn out to be even worse than the Great Depression of the 1930s. The same lack of hope for the future will lead to the same vicious circle – loss of confidence, loss of demand, loss of production, loss of jobs, and back to more loss of demand.

Worse, as you know, there are specific industries and sources of employment that are already victims of the special and unique situation. Maternity hospitals, baby clothes and baby product makers, midwives. But the lack of *any* hope in the future, the *perceived* steady reduction of demand is going to affect every part of the globe. Some countries represented here are already suffering more than others.'

She then began methodically looking at the problems of many of the countries present. China's stalled growth meant tens of millions were out of work, most of them trapped by mortgages and credit. And China's reduced demand for raw materials was already impacting the oil producers and mining countries like Australia and Africa. Russia was in deep trouble, still much too reliant on oil and gas, whose prices had plummeted.

London and New York, as financial centres, were suffering because stock markets and futures markets were trained to look to the future. 'And they don't like what they see. They can tell at a glance that whole sectors are very soon just not going to exist, or be vastly reduced. The fashion and beauty industries, sports and health clubs, teenage products and music, many forms of tourism, and of course, the advertising industries and media that promote them. All those jobs will be going, and nobody will invest in those industries. Would you? And as companies fail, or cannot pay dividends, all pensions will be reduced.

And not much else will escape. In a world with fewer people, we'll need fewer houses and apartments, less fuel to heat them, less cars, less gasoline, less appliances and less equipment.

The service industries will suffer too – less work for lawyers, accountants, surveyors, landlords.

And with livestock depleting within a decade, we'll have less meat products, less hamburgers. And we'll all be vegetarians until artificial insemination brings back some meat at great cost in *some* countries.'

Her gloomy predications then detailed the countries that thought they were secure in their wealth, or at least in their survival, and some that faced almost immediate disaster.

Finally, she warned that it might get even more abnormal and chaotic. The value of everything might disappear, including money. The world might be reduced to a primitive bartering system.

It was a very subdued and worried gathering that broke for lunch.

*　　*　　*

At two in the afternoon the meeting was now strictly confined to Heads of Government. Nobody else was allowed in the room, except, of course, the simultaneous translators behind their glass screens. The only exceptions were David Hudson, the US Secretary of State, Colonel Charles Koenig and Ann, who filed on to the stage. And a figure in a Russian uniform, sitting quietly at the back.

James Morrow, the President of the United States stood at the lectern.

'Your Majesties, Excellencies, Ladies and Gentlemen, I make no excuse for introducing a member of my family to this gathering. Because it was my daughter, Ann Hearst, who first analysed our situation, and has perhaps come up with a radical solution. Ann over to you.'

Ann switched on the projector. She started by running through the inevitable declining population figures for the next forty years, refined since she had shown them to the President's group. Then she explained what could conceivably happen if artificial insemination of humans was introduced and carefully protected.

Then the US Secretary of State revealed the startling evidence of alien involvement in the 'meteorite' shower and the subsequent poisoning of the world's males. He also came out with the news of the US space station's encounter five weeks ago with a strange craft. This brought gasps of astonishment from his audience, with several delegates shaking their heads and muttering with disbelief.

They were soon to be stunned into fascinated silence by Colonel Charles Koenig's infra-red revelation of the 300 drone-like craft hovering in space.

Koenig then added something even more dramatic – information that he had gathered since the Presidential group meeting. 'We have now looked at all the visual evidence of the so-called meteorites. Remember, we had no radar tracking. Some of the meteor trails were obscured by cloud over the target, but we've also been able to track each trail by infra-red as it burned up – or partially burned up.'

Tracking them back, they were fired at earth on nine successive nights and from exactly the same position in space, not very far away. The drones may also have been launched in batches over the same period, but would have taken much longer to get here and then to position themselves.'

Koenig noted the powerful reaction his words were having.

'Whatever launched all this – presumably a big ship – was never detected, and may have withdrawn to wherever it came from. That means, of course, that it, or they, could return at any time in the future, and with equal lack of warning.' He scanned the audience, noting once again the resonance of his words before gathering his notes and sitting down.

Ann came next, with a very receptive audience. She drew a deep breath and laid out her proposition.

'I had thought, at first, that we could get all the available sperm together and share it out round the world. But our enemy up there would detect that we're still reproducing – we couldn't hide it. And there simply won't be enough to go round – leading to social unrest, even much, much worse. So in my view, and deeply regrettably, we have no alternative but to be highly selective and secretive – however unfair that is. It's a vast moral dilemma, but one we just *have* to face.' She looked around the audience and began to speak more slowly.

'This, therefore, would be my advice.'

She began to speak more slowly.

'We should create in each country one, or more, hidden places – let's call them

Havens. They would have to be secret and disguised, but capable of containing several thousand people. In them, women could become pregnant using whatever sperm we have. Nowadays there are advanced techniques that mean we would not have to waste any of that sperm. We'd have to re-locate the specialist fertility clinics to the Havens, of course.

After eighteen years, if things went to plan, we'd have many new women and men of military age, and with top security, and I mean top security, hopefully any aliens up there wouldn't know about them. And if the aliens *did* attack before that, we'd still have our existing military forces, if a little older than normal. On the other hand, if they were to attack later, we'd have been getting secretly stronger all the time. That is, assuming we can keep things secret. Of course, a highly ambitious assumption.'

The President of India put up her hand. 'Are you absolutely *certain* that we can't make these techniques available to everyone? It seems very wrong to favour the chosen few. I'm sure I'm not the only one here who's deeply concerned about selective breeding. And its moral implications.'

'Very sadly, Madam President, I am convinced it's the only possible answer. The specialists themselves are too few, and as I'm sure you realise, there would be immense social unrest if it were known that only a few women had been chosen. Plus, if there was any visible evidence of the presence of more children – prams, playgrounds, schools and so on –' Ann pointed upwards – '*they* may realise that we have out-witted them and thus attack early. No, I'm totally convinced it has to be kept secret. Hidden Havens, I feel, are the only viable answer.

However, if Havens do go ahead, I leave any moral arguments about who is to get AI, and in which country, to others. Thank you.' Ann sat down.

'But how exactly, *can* we keep it all secret?' asked the Prime Minister of Canada.

The Russian President intervened.

'Not easily, but we've brought someone who I think may be very useful. May he address us?'

President Jim Morrow nodded his approval, and the grey-haired man in uniform who had been sitting in the back walked up to the podium to address the audience – a tall, imposing figure with a hard, lined face and the usual Russian massive array of medals on his chest.

'Good afternoon. I am General Ivan Baranov. My President has suggested that I tell you how we use what we call *maskirovka*. Some of you will know what I mean by that. I think the Americans among you call it 'denial and deception'. But since 1380, we Russians have made it into much, much, more than that, indeed an art form. Our army even used to have a Maskirovka School. And some of our greatest battles were certainly won because of its use – Stalingrad, Kursk and Bagration.'

He paused to smile, not altogether pleasantly. 'And, more recently, we didn't do too badly with it in the Crimea and the Ukraine.'

Several of the European leaders frowned, remembering Putin's activities in those regions with extreme distaste. Nevertheless, they now listened carefully to their simultaneous translation headphones.

'As I see it, we need to use maskirovka against two groups: alien enemy forces up there in space, and I'm afraid, most of the people on earth down here. We'll have to use all the elements: concealment, imitation, simulation, denial, misinformation and deception. It will not be easy.

But let's start with what may, strangely, be the easiest part.

Assume we have some kind of alien force up there, one probably more advanced than us. It has already shown that it can bombard earth with some type of missile containing some form of poison, or at least a catalyst agent that has created a poison. These missiles, for some unexplained reason, were not detected on radar.

We now also know it has stationed about 300 craft up there – probably surveillance vehicles or drones, only one of which has been seen, and even then by lucky chance. Their technology is extremely good – but thankfully not perfect. One of their drones went out of control and one missile just missed water. However, most of us would be proud to have such a low failure rate.' He suddenly laughed, incongruously.

'There may be good physical reasons why they need to wait for us to weaken so much. They may not be able to attack us in what we would consider conventional ways – guns, explosives, lasers. They may be more passive – slow-moving like plants or molluscs. We're going to have to guess what life-forms they are and plan for everything.'

'Our objective, in the meantime, must be to make them think that their strategy is working. That we are, indeed, now a dying, ageing planet, which will soon be unable to defend itself. We must use maskirovka everywhere to help us. Masking what we are doing in order to survive.

But we have a second huge problem. Our people. Billions of people of different races, different religions and different political systems cannot be expected or trusted to keep a secret. Especially if that secret includes some of them being discriminated against. Either because there is insufficient sperm to go round, or that they don't want it on principle, or that they can't be trusted with it.

And life is not like the good old days,' he added with an incongruous grin, 'it's not as if we can dominate the media any more and stifle the news. After all, we've now got Twitter and Facebook and all the other social networks. Pretty well everyone is now their own medium. We can't control everything, and even if we *were* to close down the networks, we might still arouse suspicions up there.

No, we have no alternative but to use *dezinformatsiia* or disinformation. We have to tell the world at large that the sperm has definitely run out. That there is nothing to be done. Brutal, yes. But also logical.

Then our rebirth programmes, both human and animal will have to proceed not only out of sight of alien eyes, but also of the vast majority of human ones. An unprecedented world challenge, but one that would, incidentally, make it much more realistic.' He scanned the shocked faces in front of him and sat down, grim-faced.

President Jim Morrow, for one, was not sure that he liked this General Baranov much, but he quickly began to realise that they might need him when the Russian President proposed that Baranov be appointed the head of security. And after some considerable debate about the extent of his powers, the delegates agreed.

Jim Morrow then asked Baranov to stand up and speak again, elaborating on his possible plans.

'First I want to confirm that I totally agree with what Ann Hearst proposed to us a few minutes ago. Probably the only way that this will work is for selected families to be chosen and then persuaded to locate to special places, Havens as she called them, which will have to be urgently built, expanded or modified. These families, together with single women should, indeed must, be given special privileges – in addition to being able to have children. After all, they will have to abandon family and friends. And the families left behind will also have to be given privileges – to keep *them* quiet. It'll be another huge challenge, keeping their silence.'

A buzzer sounded, and the screens showed the face and name of Tomasz Kaminski, the kindly- looking and popular President of Poland.

'General Baranov, I'm sure that I am not the only one at this gathering who feels extremely disturbed and uncomfortable with all this, every word that I'm hearing. The morality, or rather immorality, of favouring certain people against others is, to say the least, deeply unsettling and shocking, and takes us back to a much darker time in our history, particularly, if I may say so, that of my country, Poland. And, like many others must be here, I am extremely alarmed by any methods you may propose in order to keep the general population silent.

If people suddenly disappeared to what you call Havens, news about their disappearances would rapidly become widespread. That is human nature. There would be a clamour for news of their whereabouts, questions in the media and posters of missing people. Your plan, in my view, would be totally unsustainable – not only unrealistic, but furthermore, in humane.

Such a project could not be kept silent, not without drastic methods that don't bear thinking about. I, for one, could not support such methods, and I strongly suspect that there are many others here who would agree.'

Baranov paused to compose himself, knowing that his response would be crucial.

'President Kaminski, you may indeed be speaking for many in this room, but you are unfortunately *not* speaking for the survival of our world. If we publicise what I shall call 'selection', there will be unimaginable consequences, indeed widespread chaos, which will take the world even faster to its doom.'

He scanned the tense faces of the audience.

'If that is what you, and other delegates here, then all we can do is wait for doomsday, quite simply for the end of the human race. That is not, I am sure, what any of us want.

And may I say, Mister President, it seems to me you do not fully understand the powers of 'maskirovka' – there *would* be no news of missing people, no posters, no publicity, no widespread knowledge of what is happening. In fact, every possible effort should be made to keep things as normal as they can be.'

Baranov paused to sip at his glass of water.

'What you, Mister President, will be voting for now, as you all will, is quite literally a future – whatever it takes to secure the very continuation of the human race.'

Listening to Baranov, Jim Morrow suddenly remembered the word gulags. It would up to him to persuade the assembly that Havens would be exactly the opposite of that if he were to secure their agreement. He now intervened.

'I think it is unfair for us to turn on General Baranov and question him about the morality of this project. He, after all, will only be our method of keeping it secret, a difficult enough task.

Let us now vote on whether we are prepared to create these Havens and then to keep them secret, from both our enemies and our friends. It has to be unanimous. I strongly urge you to vote yes. Let's take a break so you can talk among yourselves and come to a decision.

Another buzzer sounded. The face of the Prime Minister of Sweden appeared on the screens.

'Before we make this momentous decision, do we have the absolute and totally reliable assurances that the medical situation is not reversible, and may not in time correct itself?

I, and others here, have of course heard and read numerous reports, notably from the World Health Organisation, that unfortunately viable semen among our male populations cannot and will not suddenly return as if by magic. But I am sure that this assembly would like confirmation of this before we can vote on such a crucial issue.

President Morrow had anticipated a question like this, and reaffirmed that the world's leading health organisations had indeed unanimously agreed that viable semen would not return, finally reading out the latest statement from the W.H.O, which he fervently hoped would sway their votes.

Four hours later, the world decided.

The decision made, once again Baranov was asked to address them.

'The staff in these Havens, plus the construction workers, the recruiting staff and the suppliers, all must be part of the programme. Otherwise they'd have no incentive not to talk.

The men in the submarines, which have sensibly been kept at sea, will have to go to our special locations, together with their families. And the space crews, of course. It is extremely fortunate that they're all used to strict service discipline.

And all Haven locations must be carefully hidden from the air. Our *maskirovka* officers used to fly over our own tanks, artillery and troops to check out their camouflage during the Great Patriotic War. We should do the same, except now of course, we should also use satellites.

And there must be no evidence of new children. Absolutely none. That is vital. No open playgrounds. No visible sporting or recreational areas. It's not going to be easy at all. We'd have to use ruthless methods to enforce this. It's too important for the survival of the world – indeed nothing less than a life and death matter.'

Baranov suddenly noticed the female Prime Minister of Estonia shaking her head, either in disbelief, denial or disagreement. He stared at her coldly, thinking to himself that the Baltic States, of all people, should take a Russian seriously – particularly one like him.

'I mean it. Every word, I say. And for any of it to work, any of it, no word must get out from this meeting. Not to wives, husbands, partners, friends, anyone.'

He stared round the room and then up at the men and women in the translation booths.

'No word at all.'

He paused, taking in the hush.

'Finally, talking about disinformation, I suggest we send out a communiqué at the end of this conference. It should, of course, make no mention of the outside threat. It should say that *some* sperm is available for animals, but for humans, sadly, it has run out or become ineffective. The world should be urged to settle down and make the best of things – as far as that is possible.'

Baranov's plans were voted on. He then asked for, and received, commitment from the countries to provide special personnel and equipment 'for security.' Even so, Jim Morrow and many others doubted that such a huge, diverse and ambitious programme could be kept a secret. It would be a Herculean task.

The watchers above were, as Baranov had said, the easy bit. It was the huge, talkative world below that was going to be the problem.

CHAPTER NINE

Buckingham Palace, London

Prime Minister Peter Wilkins had asked for a special audience with the King, and was waiting in an ante-room in Buckingham Place. King William and his wife Katherine, better known as Kate, were immensely popular. She was still very beautiful, and in the early years of their marriage had even eclipsed William's mother, Princess Diana, as the most photographed woman in the world.

Young Prince George was also very popular, not only for his good looks, but for his adventurous lifestyle. There didn't seem to be any dangerous sport that he would not try, from mountain climbing to downhill ski racing – and the public, and especially his parents, were extremely worried about the risks.

A uniformed official arrived.

'His Majesty will see you now, Prime Minister.'

In the audience room, the King was sitting with the Queen. Peter Wilkins carefully told them of the recent world leaders' meeting convened by the Americans, of the threat that probably faced the world and of the secret decision to create the Havens. By the time he had finished, the Queen looked pale with shock, but the King asked a great number of questions.

'So our people,' he concluded gravely, 'are going to need our example and help more than ever.'

He took his wife's hand. 'That will be our task in the coming years.' Katherine nodded in agreement.

'We'll also have to make sure our children set an example. Unless circumstances change, we'll carry on, and never acknowledge the existence of the Havens. The best of luck, Prime Minister, with all your efforts.'

Peter Wilkins noticed tears in the Queen's eyes.

Rome, Italy

His Holiness the Pope had been surprised. Not by the request for a meeting, but for the insistence that only one English-speaking Cardinal be present. But at a time of such international emergency, he felt that he could not refuse the terms of the Secretary of State. David Hudson was, after all, probably the second most powerful figure in the US administration.

And he was coming with the British Foreign Secretary, so whatever they wanted to discuss must have an international dimension related to that recent big conference in London.

In the event, David Hudson did not ask for formal approval from the Pope. Only that if, in the next weeks and months, he received questions from the Roman Catholic hierarchy around the world, that he should say that the Vatican had withdrawn its opposition to artificial insemination 'in exceptional circumstances.' In the meantime, but with great moral difficultyhe also agreed to a policy of absolute secrecy about the Havens.

Amsterdam, The Netherlands

Like the Pope, Monica and Martin van der Eb had also been surprised by unexpected visitors, in this case a man and a woman. As a Captain in the Royal Dutch Air Force, Martin was used to taking orders, but this seemed more of a friendly request.

'Would you like to be one of the few couples in Holland to be able to have children?'

Of course, the answer had to be yes. But there were strange terms attached to the offer. For some reason, yet to be explained, they would have to move – probably to a special place near Groningen in the north east – something to do with a natural gas complex. Their families would be granted many generous benefits. And they would have to pledge that any male children, and maybe even girls, would be available for military service if required later on.

Martin had no objection to this. His father had been in the navy, and his grandfather had been one of the few Dutch pilots flying for the RAF in the Battle of Britain in 1940.

He certainly had a few qualms about Monica being given the sperm of another man, but was reassured that it would be Dutch sperm and the donor would have been carefully monitored. And in any case, Monica was so very insistent that they take part.

Above all they were sworn to absolute secrecy.

London, England

Susan Jones had always been a bit talkative. It was probably the affable Spanish side of her. Her mother had been born in Seville, where most people were chatty and easygoing.

She liked her job as a simultaneous translator – and that recent conference had certainly been exciting. She had been translating for both the Spanish and South Americans, although she had been surprised that some of the countries in that region seemed not to have been invited. She had discussed that puzzle later in the crowded pub with her boyfriend.

The doorbell rang at about seven next morning, before she had even started on her make-up. There were three men at the door, two probably British and one a foreigner. She couldn't place his accent. They all seemed to be policemen or something.

They asked her about her work and about the recent conference, and whether she had discussed it with anybody. She admitted she had, but only with her boyfriend who was also a translator. Surely that silly Russian General could not have really meant all of that stuff about secrecy?

'You *were* warned,' muttered one of the British men as they escorted her out of the house.

Faslane, Scotland

The members of the crew of HMS *Vigilant* were none too happy as they marched down the dock through a cold drizzle driven by the wind off the Clyde. They had been kept at sea, underwater, for five months, not the usual three. And with no explanation. On a nuclear missile submarine, to keep its submerged location secret, it was normal for the crew not to be able to communicate with home, but to receive messages once a week. And their families were used to it. But even the messages from home had been cut off – which was very worrying for the men. And with the sub apparently overdue, their loved ones on shore had become very anxious, despite being given regular reassurances by the Ministry of Defence.

The marching men were halted outside a big building on the dockside, which seemed, rather strangely, to be guarded by armed Royal Navy Police. They filed in and sat down. On the stage was *Vigilant's* Captain, Commander Hannaford, together with a Rear-Admiral and a Captain. Commander Hannaford stood up.

'I'm very sorry that we've been kept at sea for so long. And kept in the dark about what's going on, too. You must all have been very worried. The fact is that it was for our own good – and protection. Rear-Admiral Leakey, Commander Operations, will now explain the very serious situation.'

The Admiral then stood up and explained in measured tones the disaster that had happened to the world while they had been submerged, and that they, 150 of them, were some of the very lucky few who would now have a normal sex drive and the ability to father children.

He explained that of the four British Vanguard-class subs, *Vigilant* was the only one that had been fortunate enough to be submerged at sea at the time, as were two Ohio-class US subs, the French *Triomphant*, two Russian Deltas and a Typhoon and one Chinese Jin-class. So they shared this piece of luck with only about 800 other submariners, plus a handful of men who happened to be in space.

There was a hubbub of shocked speculation among the men.

The Admiral then told them that they would now be moved to a secret location, with the good news was that their families and partners were already being moved there too. At least *they* might have a normal future, even if the rest of the world was doomed.

'And all of this is totally, one hundred per cent secret. I cannot stress that enough. I see some of you have been trying to use mobile phones. This building blocks all calls, and you will hand in all phones to the Royal Navy Police before you get on the buses.'

He handed back to their Captain.

Commander Hannaford said, and with considerable emotion, 'I have been proud to serve with you. You were, you are, a great crew. The very best of luck. *Vigilant* is now de-commissioned.'

Tancheng, China

It had been an exhausting and dangerous week. Every day there had been riots and Sergeant Xu Chin had donned his bulky riot gear and joined the lines of his fellow policemen trying to control a deteriorating situation.

China's economy had imploded, dependent as it was on exports to countries that no longer wanted, or could afford, her goods. The Shanghai Stock Market had collapsed, taking down with it the savings of millions of ordinary Chinese – always too ready, as born gamblers, to take a bet on anything they thought was a sure thing. But many of them were now slaves to mortgages and credit, and now millions were out of work as factories closed and ports fell silent. And the poor financial position of companies meant that dividends were down as well. With failed companies, there would be no dividends. So pensions, other than the state ones, would all be reduced. Things were getting desperate.

Tancheng had been particularly hard hit, because it was one of a line of new cities of China's much-vaunted Silk Road. Now, with construction halted, the half-built skyscrapers stood empty like bleak skeletons, with the skyline full of silent cranes, the highways empty and the high-speed trains in their sidings. In some cities it was much worse, with deaths among both the rioters and the forces of law and order. As China's leaders wrestled with how to keep the vast country going, and with the multiple outbreaks of serious civil unrest, only the jobs of policemen and soldiers seemed safe.

As Chin Xu was trying to wash the tear-gas out of his hair, his wife called from the front door. They had visitors. A man and a woman in civilian clothes, but with party badges, were standing in the living room.

The man said, 'Sergeant Xu, we have a proposition for you.'

Chapter Ten

London

General Baranov had moved to the secret Task Force Headquarters in London. For the usual time zone reasons, Britain had been judged to be the best location to co-ordinate the programme and its security.

Baranov had bought several of his own men and women from the old days, but he had been surprised how quickly the other nationalities had adapted to the ruthless, even cruel necessities of making it all work. Even the British were at last getting over their gentlemanly soft-heartedness – although they had complained strongly, albeit politely, about some of the forceful actions he had ordered.

It was a British voice on the telephone; their Foreign Secretary, Michael Selway.

'General, we have a problem, a big problem. I don't want to discuss it on the phone. Can I come over?'

The Foreign Office was only 200 metres down Whitehall, and Michael Selway arrived in minutes.

'I had a visit from that creep of a dictator, Alphonse Principe from the Sudan Republic. He's somehow found out about the programme and is threatening to blow the story. We are not yet sure what he wants. He's still in town.'

Baranov, frowning, thought for a moment.

'I suggest you get him round to the Foreign Office and I'll disguise myself as one of your officials. Let's see what he knows and what he wants.'

The next day, the self-styled 'Colonel' Alphonse Principe sat smoking, against all the rules, a big cigar in the Foreign Secretary's conference room. He had actually been a Sergeant in his country's little rag-tag army, but that experience had given him just enough military knowledge to overthrow, and indeed kill the democratically-elected President. The country, with some oil and diamonds, had then become a byword for corruption and incompetence.

Principe was now enormously fat, bulging out of a ridiculous military uniform, that he had designed himself. His greedy little eyes glinted behind tinted glasses as he waved his pudgy hand.

'Ah know's what you's doing. You'se got some sperm and yo'r keeping it to yourselves somewhere – mostly for whites and Asians. You didn't, ah notice, offer it to us. If ah tell de world, you know hell will break loose.'

Foreign Secretary Mike Selway tried to smile pleasantly, and to disguise his absolute contempt for this very unpleasant man. Without arguing about any past actions or trying to defend them, he cut straight to the crucial question.

'Well, your Excellency, may I ask what you want? Some of the sperm for your people? African sperm?'

Principe gave a great belly laugh.

'No, no, no! Forget de sperm. Dey don't deserve it. Ah'd like five billion dollars, thank you. De cost of mah silence'

Selway could hardly disguise his disgusted astonishment. The 'General' appeared not to notice.

'An' here's de details of my bank account in Switzerland.' Principe slid a sheet of paper across the table. 'That arrives okay, an' you won't have to hear from me again on dis subject. I'm flying back tomorrow, an' I'd like it to be there before I go.'

Selway appeared to agree. He did not shake Principe's hand when he left. Ivan Baranov, in his civil servant's dark suit, began to make his plans.

*　　*　　*

The Rolls-Royce picked up the corpulent dictator from Claridge's and drove to London City Airport, and straight to the steps of the aircraft.

He was well pleased with himself, as he settled into his specially enlarged and strengthened seat in his Learjet. He began to dream about how he was going to spend his money. Five billion! Even he would find difficulty finding enough to spend it on. 'Time for champagne!' he said to his only other passenger, his brother, the sinister Minister of the Interior.

Then he shouted towards the cockpit.

'Okay, mister pilot, let's go.'

Atlantic Ocean

The Dassault Rafale had been loitering off the coast of Spain. Its French pilot's Cyrano radar now told him the target was about eight kilometres away, flying south at 32,000 feet through the darkness. The young man at the controls knew it was necessary to wait, as ordered, until it was over deeper water.

Another ten minutes, perhaps.

The fighter had been refuelled in the air high above Cadiz by a veteran Boeing

C-135 tanker from the Fuerza Aérea Espanola out of Barajas. So there was no fuel issue, no hurry. But the pilot was still somewhat tense. He had never fired a missile at a real target, just many times in a simulator.

It was time. He flipped two switches to arm the two MICA missiles, then one more to launch them. They flamed off into the gloom at 4,600 kilometres an hour.

Six and a half seconds later his radar told him the Learjet had disappeared. He muttered 'Parfait', and then banked the fighter and headed for home.

Zurich, Switzerland

Despite the air-conditioning, the manager sat sweating at his desk in his large office on the west corner of the bank's building overlooking Zurich's Paradeplatz.

The two unsmiling men sitting opposite were from the *Finanzpolizei*, the Swiss financial police, and they were not even trying to be polite to him. The days of really secret Swiss bank accounts were well and truly over in these fraught and extraordinary times. They didn't like this type of bank manager much.

'You will return the money at once to the source it came from. We will wait while you do it.'

The banker nodded.

'By the way, your client, Alphonse Principe, has had an accident.'

CHAPTER ELEVEN

London

Audrey picked up the phone

'Hi, Audrey. Fancy joining us for lunch at the 'Coat and Badge'?'

Audrey flinched. 'Sorry, can't face it. All those prams. It was bad enough before, but now – well, I just can't do it.'

'Come on Audie, it would do you good. You haven't surfaced for ages.'

'And nor would you, if you were in my position. I never really wanted a job like you do. All I ever wanted was kids, and now that's gone, I just can't face it. Looking at all those mothers with prams. And no doubt feeling smug, or looking it. Sorry, but count me out.'

'Audie, you can't go on like this. What's happened, happened.' A pause. 'And there's always AI.'

'And massive queues. Haven't you seen the news? They're even closing loads of clinics down. And anyway, I'm not sure I want another man's child. Someone I know fuck all about.'

'You *would* know. Guys have to give all sorts of records about what they're like. Health, interests, education; all that sort of thing.'

'Not for me. I married Geoff because I pretty well knew the sort of children we'd have.'

'We never do – look at mine.'

'Lucky you. At least you've got kids.'

'Oh, come on, Audie, give yourself a break. You can't stay home all day, moping about it.'

'I can do just what I like. And I don't want lectures.'

Another pause.

'Well, Jill and I will be there anyway. And we really want you to come.'

'Well, have a nice time.'

Pattie switched off her mobile, depressed, and hoping Audrey hadn't heard her kids playing behind her in the kitchen. She would have left them behind with the au pair for the sake of Audrey, but now there was no point.

It was almost as if her kids were forging a wedge between her and her oldest friend. Well, if they were, it wasn't her fault.

'Come on, you lot!'

London

Monica was bored out of her mind. For three days nobody had been into the beauty salon or even stopped to look in the window, and today there was only one booking from a regular customer – a woman in her seventies who came in every two or three months to have facial hair removed. How boring was that?

Didn't women want to look nice, even if men weren't interested in bedding them any longer? Where was their pride? Or was it that they needed time to come to terms with it, and simply didn't feel like treating themselves for the time being? Or maybe they just couldn't afford it any more. So many people were losing their jobs. But if things went on like this she would have to shut up shop. The rental was still exorbitant in Barnes – a chic area of South West London – and she couldn't afford another month like this – let alone pay Sonia, her manicurist.

If the half price introductory offer for new clients wasn't working, what on earth would? And how long could she just sit there day after day? And worse, sit there doing nothing? If someone looked through the window, the last thing she could be seen doing was reading magazines to pass the time. That would only make matters worse.

And the magazines themselves were noticeably more boring. Hundreds of advertisers seemed to have pulled out lately, as if they'd noticed that women weren't caring so much about themselves. Less perfume ads. Less make-up ads. Less and less pages every month. Where would it all end?

Suddenly an attractive woman was at the window, reading her half price offer. Monica smiled at her, but the woman looked embarrassed and moved on.

Dejectedly, she decided to close early, only to become more depressed walking down the High Street. The baby clothes shop three doors along had a closing down notice, and there was no-one in the hair salon, and, come to that, hardly anyone out shopping in the High Street.

She decided to cheer herself up with a drink at the Bull pub, a bit further down the street. But that made her even more depressed. At this time of day the pub garden would normally be crowded with proud new Mums and prams. A bit irritating once, but now the lack of them was sad. Where would it all end?

66

Yorkshire, England

Bill Braithwaite, the popular manager of the 'Stag and Hounds' pub in a little village in Yorkshire,

was briefing his new twenty-one year old Polish assistant, Dariusz, on all the changes that needed to be made as a matter of urgency. There were so many things that his customers might now find offensive or upsetting. Overnight, he would have to overhaul the place – as would other publicans if they were to survive the crisis. Certainly people would want to go out for a drink to cheer themselves up, he conjectured, but not if they were constantly reminded of a cruelly changed world. City pubs might be able to survive, but not a country pub like his, even if it was famous for its excellent local ales.

'Here' – he passed Dariusz a long list of cocktails with all kinds of racy names that had once seemed amusing, but were now completely out of order. 'Pop my Cherry', Creamy Pussy', 'Bend over Shirley', 'Deep Throat', Sit on my face'. and even 'Blowjob', only now fully realizing just how vulgar many of them were.

'You'll have to go right through this and knock off everything that even begins to remind people what they're missing. And the sooner the better. Oh, and get someone to take the condom dispenser out of the gent's loo and then repair the wall. Depressing for our male customers. The last thing they'll want to see.. Takings are down already without making them worse. And I think we'll have to get rid of all those happy couples photos near the door, certainly ones of people snogging or showing a bit too much flesh.'

He glanced outside through the open door. 'I'm also a bit worried about the garden. A lot of people won't want to see prams out there, it might upset our younger lady customers. Although I can hardly stop mothers coming here. Perhaps we could hedge off a special area for mums with kids, so as not to upset people who'll never have them. I wouldn't mind your thoughts on that. Oh, and the baby changing area needs taking out of the ladies' loo, or moving somewhere else.'

Dariusz was overwhelmed. And was his English good enough to go through that cocktail list for all those potentially offensive names? Almost certainly not. And who could he ask? Certainly not his Polish flatmates. They wouldn't know either. He was lucky enough to have got to England, but would he get through all this?

'Anything else?' he asked his boss nervously.

'Yup, I'm afraid there is. Some of the pictures will have to come down. Especially that one with lovers on a beach near the door. That should have gone already. Anything that smacks remotely of sex I want out – and fast. Preferably by the time we open tonight.'

Bill suddenly remembered to his annoyance that it was a singles evening that he had forgotten to cancel. 'Damn!' he whispered, punching his hand on the bar. So many things to think about, and others that had completely escaped his mind until now.

Dariusz was becoming more and more worried.

'Is my job safe, boss?'

'It is for now, Dariusz, but we'll have to see how it goes. And we may even have to change our name. A real shame after three hundred years, but it might upset people to have a name like The Stag and Hounds when soon there won't be any more stags and hounds. And any more hunting either without any foxes.'

Another source of income up the spout he thought bleakly, remembering all the hard-drinking hunt followers.

He patted Dariusz kindly on the shoulder. 'Right, better get going, lad. There's a hell of a lot to do.'

London

The Choirmaster at Westminster Cathedral, London, couldn't help but feel elated. All these glorious voices

around him that would never break, never have to stop singing in those heart-lifting high notes that no adults could attain. All these boys who could never have children themselves, but who would be able to sing like angels for the rest of their lives. At least there was one upside to this whole ghastly business. But they were so young. Who was going to tell them? And could they take it in? He would have to talk to the Matron of the Choir School. And to all the parents. And to bring in counsellors. What an appallingly messy business.

But just for now, he revelled in the miracle. The soaring notes that these boys, in just a few years, would never have been able to manage without this human catastrophe. The sheer wonder of the human voice at such an age, but what a tragedy to follow for the rest of their lives. What could he tell them? What could the Matron tell them? What could the parents tell them? For now, it was enough to listen to the magic of them singing, and not think about that. Eternal youth in a human voice. For a few precious moments, that was enough to take in.

Toronto

Janie knew it wouldn't be her boyfriend, or rather her ex-boyfriend, calling on the mobile. She hadn't seen him for weeks. He was probably too embarrassed by everything.

'Hi, it's me.'

'Oh, hi Jane.'

'Look, I wondered if you'd like to come to a party?'

Janie sighed. 'What's the point?'

'Well, it's better than sitting at home all night. Just a girlie evening, with a bit of music.'

'Music all about sex and love. Don't think I can face it. And don't tell me to look on the bright side. I couldn't face that either.'

'Well, what are we supposed to do? What's happened has happened. And if all of us are going to go on moping all over the place, it's gonna get a whole lot worse.'

'Don't preach. Can't face it. I just can't see the point of getting all dolled up and pretending to be happy, happy.'

Marty interrupted. 'Then don't doll up. Just come, and we can cheer ourselves up.'

'And how, I ask?'

'I dunno. Have a spliff. Talk about things. Plan a holiday. Anything to make us forget the news.'

A pause.

'Okay. But no guys.'

'No guys, promise. Couldn't face that either.'

'And neither could they. I do feel sorry for them.'

'So do I. Must be ghastly to feel, well, suddenly neutered. But there's no point feeling sorry for yourself as well.'

'Guess not.'

'Right. See you here at eight tomorrow?'

'Okay. Not much else to do. May as well get trashed. Nobody to care about what we look like, if we do.'

'Except us. Got to have some pride. If that goes, everything does.'

'Don't preach. Not in the mood for it.'

'Okay then, this place at eight.'

'Okay, and no boys, promise.'

'Promise.'

'See you then.'

London

'What are you going to wear?
Nobody there to care.'

The song had been at the top of the charts for six weeks and was making seventeen year Lizzie Kendall an international superstar. Everywhere anyone went, people were singing it, especially people who'd been invited to parties – though there weren't many parties on anyone's agenda. It always got back to the same subject until someone very vociferously banned it.

It wasn't a song much loved by the fashion industry, already in dire straits all over the world. Someone had already daubed the couplet over several fashion shops in London's exclusive West End, a story reported on all the news channels which meant even more fame for Lizzie and more grief for anyone remotely involved in clothing.

Advertisers were desperately trying to get across the notion that you wore things for your own self esteem rather than try and attract a partner, with slogans like 'I DRESS FOR ME', but they plainly weren't working. And anything remotely risqué was seen as something of a switch off. What was the point of slashed cleavages and baring flesh at all, let alone wearing high heels? It was almost like rubbing salt in the wound.

Fashion store after fashion store was closing down, although the cosmetic industry was somehow holding its own. 'Put on a brave face' seemed to be the motto, at least for the moment. And buying a lipstick was cheaper than buying a dress.

Another phenomenon was sweeping the Western world. There were suddenly noticeably less blondes. Partly because so many people had lost their jobs they simply couldn't afford to colour their hair, but also because, if nobody much cared about your hair, what was the point of colouring it in the first place?

It was a duller world in many ways than one, and it spread well beyond the bedroom. 'What's the point?' was not on everyone's lips, but it was always there inside them. Every time people got up, got dressed, made up (if they bothered) and generally went about their daily lives.

The only people who were relieved in any way at all were people who ran the world's schools. In fact many of them were now discussing the possibility of mixed dormitories at boarding schools while discussing the problems of boys who might be bullied for their high voices which would now never break, and their lack of any signs of puberty. Would girls become bullies? Quite possibly.

Every corner of the world was now a duller place. And there was no duller place than the bedroom. 'Just because *you* don't want sex, it doesn't mean that *I* don't' was a common mantra. And divorce lawyers and counsellors were having an absolute field day.

'What are you going to wear?
Nobody there to care.

Nobody there to see.
Nobody there for me.
No kids, no family.
That ain't a life for me.'

The video showed Lizzie clad only in knickers and bra, chucking a dress on a bed, then sitting down and singing her heart out. No mother could bear to watch it.

Chicago

The Sappho Club was packed. Membership had soared in the past twelve months, and from no doorman at all, two were now posted outside every night and had their work cut out to keep the crowds back seven nights a week.

Business was roaring for reasons that were all too obvious. If men weren't interested in women, other women certainly were, and Sappho was the clearest evidence. All the staff were female except for the two doormen, similarly the nightly cabaret which poked merciless fun at men – which kept them firmly out of the place, though legally allowed to come in. Few would have wanted to.

In the very same street, two more nightclubs had just closed down, formerly packed by straight couples. Sappho was now thinking about buying both of them and turning itself into the biggest club empire in the world. On top of that it was considering a fashion label. Its own Sappho T-shirts were already hugely popular. Why not Sappho bras and knickers and sexy nightwear? And come to that, why not Sappho sex aids?

Life was good, and it could only get better. A shame that none of its members would ever have children unless they were lucky enough to get AI. But that was the least of its worries.

And with the Gay Pride march coming up – and with no men likely to attend – their new Sappho T-shirts would bring in even more business.

One day, thought Sappho, the Manager, (real name Isabelle), the club would rule the world. Sappho fashion. Sappho holidays. Sappho healthcare. Sappho books. Sappho records. Sappho insurance. Sappho villages. Sappho anything.

Sappho went to the bar and ordered a glass of her best champagne. Life was good, and it could only get better.

London

The BBC News at Ten had just come up on the screen.

'In the High Court this morning, Nicolae Grosa, an unemployed 18 year old Romanian from Enfield was found guilty of conspiracy to defraud, for selling fake sperm on the internet. Grosa had advertised that he had sperm that was still effective, and for £500 a time, was sending women thermal phials of a substance which turned out not even to be semen at all. Any woman who received samples from Grosa can, however, be assured that the substance was not of a harmful nature. Laboratory analysis has confirmed that it was no more than a mixture of water, milk and washing up liquid.' On the screen came a picture of a phial.

'The Court was unable to confirm how many women had been duped by Grosa, but his bank account turned out to contain nearly £150,000.'

A shiny red car was then shown being hauled on to a low loader.

'Furthermore, he had just purchased a new Ferrari, which was found parked outside the flat he shared with three other unemployed Romanians.

The prosecuting counsel had pointed out that Grosa's only mitigation – that he was planning to send the money to his penniless, sickly mother – was plainly untrue, as his mother had died five years ago.

Grosa will be sentenced later this week, and the judge indicated that he would receive a custodial sentence before being deported. He pointed out that this could be considered lenient, and that in China three men had just been executed for the same offence.'

Kelly and her girlfriend Janet stared at the television, frozen with shock. How could they ever forget that face? The nice-looking boy on the website from whom she and Janet had bought not one but two samples of 'sperm' over the past three months, throwing away £1,000 they could ill afford with their meagre salaries as nurses in the local hospital. Grosa had given them so much hope, the last hope they had.

It was scant comfort to know that they were not alone. Obviously, with all that money in the bank, scores of women had been similarly duped by his story – that miraculously, he was still able to ejaculate and produce sperm and, after much soul-searching, had decided to help childless women, having been brought up in a large and loving family himself. He had sounded – and looked – so compassionate and caring on the screen. Not the callous little crook he really was.

Hoping that she had become pregnant after the second attempt nearly a month ago, Kelly had not had a drop of alcohol since. Now she switched off the television and went to the kitchen to take out the unopened bottle of Lambrusco in the fridge. They had been keeping it for a celebration. Now they may as well use it to drown their sorrows. What fools they both were.

Brussels, Belgium

Emile was wondering if he should even open on Valentine's Day. Normally, his restaurant would have been packed, although he never enjoyed February 14th in spite of the hike in income. Embarrassed men, almost certainly not wanting a three course meal if they were expected to perform later, uncomfortable with all the roses and the spectacle of dewy-eyed partners probably waiting for a proposal, and certainly not welcoming the hike in prices.

This year, he probably wouldn't get any diners at all. Everybody would know it was a bit of a sham, not being able to get it up in a few hours, in fact not being able to get it up at all. It would be a public display of uselessness. And why, unless they were very much older, would people even bother with Valentine cards? He'd noticed there were hardly any on sale in the Grande Place and the surrounding streets.

Perhaps he should open, he decided. Older married couples might want to come. And people needed cheering up, himself included. Thank God he already had two kids, a boy and a girl. But it wouldn't be easy telling his son he would never be able to have children, or come to that, his daughter if AI ran out. Seven and eight now, so that conversation could wait for now. But not for ever.

He'd heard that there was to be a world leaders' crisis conference over in London. What good would that do?

London

Liz normally wore pink or blue suits to the Motherworld meetings in the advertising agency. She felt the clients liked it, and especially her main contact, Norma – a little subtle nod to their line of business. But today she wore a black one with a crisp white shirt. It was not a time for celebration with all births stopping in a few months. She'd heard that they'd even closed down the AI centres because of the lack of sperm. So her client would only have a few months of baby clothes and products, then some for toddlers and then that would be it, unless their desperate drive into clothes for older children paid off. But that was already a crowded market, flooded by cheap foreign imports. And if it didn't work, what then? No Motherworld and no advertising account, and not much time to plan. And very probably no job for her.

Lots of other agencies had already gone because their clients had gone – sexy underwear like 'Victoria's Secret, sex shops like Anne Summers, Club Med – even manufacturers of double beds.

On top of all that, there was a very nasty new trend emerging. There had been three baby abduction cases in the last month alone. How soon before any mother would even dare to go to work like her and leave their charges in the care of often foreign *au pair* girls who simply didn't have the knowledge or the language skills to get help as soon as possible? Liz herself was terrified about leaving her baby daughter at home, but with a husband out of work, what was she supposed to do? She knew he adored his daughter, but he liked drink even more since he had lost his job as a primary school teacher, and she simply couldn't trust him to look after their only child. But how good would Agnieska be in an emergency? Good English, but not perfect. A Pole who was grateful for being in Britain, but childless herself, and probably not tuned in to all the dangers a mother would be aware of. And with only one salary coming in, they simply couldn't afford a top class nanny.

Was there time to go outside for a moment and have a quick cigarette before the meeting? No. And these days she couldn't afford to smoke either. She tried to calm herself. In fact she had thought of a new idea that Motherworld could sponsor – 'WATCH YOUR CHILD!' – a poster with somebody snatching a baby out of a pram, but with so few babies being born at all, the client probably couldn't afford it, and wouldn't want to scare the public more than it was already.

The phone suddenly interrupted her thoughts.

'Liz, it's Norma Clarke on line one,' Her client was probably gong to tell her she was running late.

'Liz, it's Norma. I won't be coming, I'm afraid.'

Liz was shocked to realise that her normally composed and business-like client was crying.

'Norma, what's up?'

'You'll see it in the news. The shares have been so hammered and the banks so panicky that we've gone bust. We were all told a few minutes ago. I'm out of a job.'

'Oh my God, I'm so sorry.'

Liz was stunned.

'Look Liz,' said her client 'I can't talk now. But let's try and meet for a drink. I have to go. Got to sort out my redundancy package. Bye.'

Liz clicked off, frozen with shock. And her concerns for her friend were followed, to her guilt, with more worries about her own situation. Motherworld was her big account, and she knew the agency was losing clients hand over fist. Not to other agencies, but with the clients just not advertising or going bust.

And it wasn't just the advertisers, it was the media they wee advertising in that were disappearing too. Many women's magazines had gone, radio and TV stations were folding, and even the much-rated new 'social media' like Twitter and Facebook were now critically dependent on advertising which was not forthcoming.

Perhaps they could sell 'WATCH YOUR CHILD!' to the Government as a public service message? No, they had enough problems of their own. The tiny ray of hope vanished.

Liz grabbed her bag. She was going outside for that cigarette right now.

*   *   *

Agnieska had a pretty good routine going with fifteen months old Katy. Most days she would wheel her buggy along the towpath by the River Thames, but now she had been frightened by the awful stories in the news. Three babies snatched – and in London alone. And it would be easy to snatch a child on the towpath with not many people there in the daytime. Sometimes she didn't pass anyone at all. And perhaps she shouldn't take Katy to the pub garden either. She loved meeting her Polish friends at the nearest pub – The Coat and Badge – because it had a big garden which was always full of children, and though her English was pretty good, it was sometimes a relief to speak in her own language. But she was beginning to worry about that location, too. What if she went to the loo, and someone snatched Katy when she wasn't looking? Yes, her friends would be there looking after her, but she would still never forgive herself if anything happened. From now on, if she ever went to the pub at all, she'd have to take Katy to the loo with her. She simply couldn't let the child out of her sight for one moment.

And it was less fun these days wheeling her up and down the High Street. She was a beautiful child, with unusually green eyes and a mop of gorgeous blonde hair. Other women often stopped to admire her, but who was safe now? It was women, surely, who'd be abducting these babies. She was starting to get depressed, and extremely worried about the responsibilities of her job, which suddenly seemed much greater than they were before. But if she couldn't go out without feeling threatened, what kind of a job was it?

And she hardly could hardly ask Liz for more money for the greater responsibility with her husband out of work – and from what she could see recently, drinking through what little money was left.

Perhaps she should apply for a job at The Platt Centre down the road, a care home for old people? She knew Liz would be devastated to lose her, especially as Katy loved her, but she also had to think of herself

before the unimaginable happened.

Denver, Colorado

All the television channels were up to their eyes re-scheduling programmes, and desperately trying to find something to replace the huge and growing amount of cancelled orders.

Who would want to see films like 'Love Story' any more, or any film with anything to do with sex, which accounted for most of them? And who would want sci-fi in the current climate? Anything coming from outer space was out, an instant switch-off, as viewing figures had quickly confirmed.

Even the normally popular animal and veterinary shows were risky. Most pets were mammals after all. Dogs, cats, horses, rabbits, Guinea pigs – all unable to reproduce just like their owners. And horse racing was a risk – AI had never been used for race horses. Few people would want to watch the last remnants of a dying sport.

Dating shows, a no-no. Make-over shows, the same. If the opposite sex wasn't interested, what was the point of them? Pride in personal appearance just wasn't enough – those programmes needed a sexual element. And even car shows were way down in the ratings, probably because so many cars were bought to impress the opposite sex, even if people didn't admit it.

What else was left? News shows, of course, but thoroughly depressing ones, although the stations had a duty to put them on. The ever-popular chat shows might still survive, but only if they were heavily edited. People were now immensely sensitive about what could or couldn't be said. So they would soon all have to be pre-recorded, in case hosts and participants might offend the public. More problems.

Even crime, normally a bedrock of television planning, was dipping badly, and not turning out to be the escapism it traditionally was. And, of course, any crime series remotely involved with sex was now in bad taste, which would even make repeats of favourite series impossible.

And history, archaeology and culture were dipping too, because people didn't want to be reminded of a glorious past or a vanishing world. And if humans were doomed, all of that would die along with them. So what was the point of watching programmes like that?

Even holiday programmes were flopping badly. Beach holiday ones had been a particular disaster, probably because women didn't want to see footage of sun-seekers in bikinis when no men would be remotely interested. And popular trips like safaris wouldn't even exist in a few years with all the animals doomed – lions, zebras, cheetahs, elephants, rhinos, buffalo, wildebeest – the lot.

What *hadn't* been affected?

Even comedy shows looked somehow too flippant, out of kilter with the times, even though people badly needed cheering up. It was hard to laugh with all that happening out there, and just as hard for comedians to find anything funny to say about it.

What the hell was left ?

Not much thought Jim Morrow, the Chief Programme Controller at Delta TV

– and probably not even his job, because advertising revenue had run down to a trickle, which meant that a commercial TV channel might no longer be viable.

Jim hadn't had a drink in years. The handsome walnut drinks cabinet in his office was purely there for clients, or for show. Now, rummaging through his desk for the keys, he didn't feel in the least bit guilty.

Sussex, England

The members of the Board of Just Men Ltd, the once giant men's clothing company, were holed up in an hotel in West Sussex, England waiting for the day-long conference which would start at nine tomorrow. None of them would dare to be seen in the bar; their jobs were precarious enough already without the Chairman spotting anyone who might have had one too many, considering the seriousness of the day ahead. There had been a huge downturn in the fortunes of men's clothing, and in all departments – high-end fashion and sportswear, contemporary or avant garde styles, leisure clothing, everything. Didn't men care any longer about what they looked like, just because they didn't fancy women? Or rather, because women didn't fancy them? What had happened to their pride? It had certainly stopped in its tracks before stepping into Just Men, and the company had just reported record losses, even worse than had initially been forecast.

None of the staff could afford not to be on top form tomorrow, and all the speakers would need to be checking and re-checking their proposals for turning round the company.

And that, as all of them knew, might be impossible.

A few themes would clearly emerge tomorrow. Smaller clothes – young men weren't going to attain the height they used to be. A positive and open policy about employing more 'chilmen' – those men who would never have children and would be generally shorter in stature. Brighter colours, amidst all the gloom on the news. But would any of it work?

The Chairman, Aaron Rosenthal, was far from optimistic. Depressed, he fetched a mini bottle of Irish whiskey from the fridge in his suite, and drank it neat, without even bothering to fetch a glass of water from the bathroom. He wondered how many of his staff were doing the same thing. Probably most, and he couldn't blame them.

The phone interrupted his thoughts. Probably his wife, Ruth. He felt a flash of irritation. Why did she ever think she might have come? 'To have a lovely day at the seaside?' Did she have no idea of the trouble the company was in? Or ever read the newspapers? Or even listen to him? He picked it up, in irritation.

'Aaron, I'm afraid I've got bad news. It was his Avi, his advertising manager, 'Seth has just been found dead in a corridor, a suspected heart attack.'

Aaron reeled. Seth, his best friend.

'We're outside room 484 on the fourth floor, you may want to come – and phone his wife.' Click.

Seth, his rock, his mentor, supporter, advisor – dead in a miserable hotel corridor. They'd founded Just Men together twenty years ago, and Seth had been a brilliant Financial Manager. But not brilliant enough to get out of it before the company tripped up. Twenty years of working – and laughing about how lucky they were, recalling their tough times in London's East End clothing markets. Twenty years of daily news, jokes and mutual support. All over.

Aaron Rosenthal slugged the last of the whisky and took the lift down to the fourth floor. He almost envied his closest mate.

Midlands, England

Kenneth Little was travelling by train to a seminary for priests in Murfield, and had booked in early, knowing that it would be extremely well attended and numbers might have to be limited.

Never before had priests had to cope with the challenges they were facing now. Couples questioning the whole concept of marriage, and often cancelling wedding services at the last moment. No christenings, of course, not for years now. Increasingly, same sex marriages which Ken still couldn't come to terms with – and had so far been able to avoid in his job, although with considerable and increasing difficulty.

There were plenty of funerals of course, but sadly, too many of younger people who had taken their own lives, unable to see a future in a nightmare world, or of young boys bullied beyond their endurance.

These days it was best to avoid prayers and hymns that mentioned children, and even the very birth of Jesus at Christmas was a difficult issue with all those childless couples in the congregation. Just the sight of a crib in the church would be too much for some childless couples. It was becoming increasingly difficult to talk to congregations who could not reconcile a God with what was happening any more than he could. It was hardly surprising that many, many priests had given up the battle.

Ken fervently hoped that Father Anselm, who was running the seminary and was a dear old friend, would do far, far more than offer words and prayers of comfort. What was needed was concrete advice on how to comfort congregations, and not with the platitudes that he and others in the priesthood were dishing out now.

Looking at the programme for the first day of the itinerary he was not optimistic. It seemed little different from the itineraries of many years before, and hardly seemed to reflect today's catastrophic circumstances. And what was the point of time set aside for 'Silent Contemplations'?

Ken left the programme on the table and went to the buffet car for a sandwich and a drink – the first drink he'd had in months, since he last officiated at one of the ever rarer weddings.

Suddenly, he felt the weight of the world on his shoulders. If a Bloody Mary helped, so be it. And if the bar staff frowned at someone in a dog collar ordering one at only 11 o'clock, he was not in the mood to care.

For the first time, and like many others dressed in dog collars in the train, he wondered how long he could keep going in the priesthood if there was no down-to-earth practical and truly concrete advice to be had at his destination.

Brighton, England

How were they going to tackle the issue of sex education in schools? That was the key issue at this year's Schools Annual Conference, and it would probably take as much time as all the other issues on the agenda put together.

It was appalling to have to teach boys about sexual organs that could never be used, and hugely embarrassing for them in mixed schools. And it was just as difficult to teach girls about sex when there was no such thing as human reproduction any more. It was like teaching kids history, about the past, not the present – not fair to either sex, or the school staff.

But if all, or even part of the teaching on sex were stopped, it would be like an admission of total defeat.

What was best for both the children and the staff? And come to that, the parents?

Separate classes for girls and boys would probably be the kindest way forward and the most likely outcome. And if pregnancy were impossible, sexual pleasure was still possible for both sexes. There was still pleasure to be had through touch, if not through intercourse.

Sitting at the back of the packed audience was Gloria Hutchinson, the Head Mistress of the Eleanor Hollis Girls School in London.

She was firmly on the side of continuing sex education, when, and if, it came to a vote. At least it would seem optimistic, as if something might change things in the future. But would she be thinking that if she were head of a boys' school? Probably not, she thought.

And what about divinity lessons? That, too, was becoming increasingly hard to teach. If God could allow such a catastrophe to happen, what kind of God was he? She was already having problems with that in divinity lessons at her own school, and was convinced that it was happening pretty well everywhere. And on top of that, history classes were becoming increasingly difficult and depressing, almost seeming irrelevant when the world itself was about to become ancient history. There was hardly a single subject that wasn't affected, or a lesson that didn't have to be radically adapted to the vastly changed circumstances and the 'Who cares?' attitude prevalent among pupils.

'Ladies and gentlemen, welcome to the 2042 Annual Schools Conference. I will make my introduction short, to allow more time for the hugely serious problems facing us. Without further ado, I wish to welcome Professor John Langton, the Headmaster of Westminster to the stand.'

Poor man, thought Gloria as Langton walked to the podium, bowed as if wearing the weight of the world on his shoulders – as indeed he partly was. 'Rather him than me,' she reflected.

CHAPTER TWELVE

Montana

From the air, the complex looked like what it was – or had been – a huge mining complex in the foothills of the Rocky Mountains, in the wilds of Montana, just south of the Canadian border.

The Hoysteds stared out at it from the helicopter, and Chris held Sabine's hand as they landed. When they reached the bottom of the ramp, a pleasant grey-haired woman in overalls approached them and shook their hands.

'Hi Sabine, Hi Chris. I'm Major Jessica Whittaker. Let me show you to your quarters. I know this place doesn't look much from the air – it's not supposed to. But I think you'll like what we've done inside.

It's amazing what you can do in a few months if the situation is urgent enough and everyone pulls together. And it helps if everyone's part of the programme.'

They walked towards a big, dusty, grey old building, streaked with rust and with STAMP MILL 4 written on it in faded lettering. Once through a small door, Chris and Sabine were amazed. Although it was still under construction, it was already like a huge shopping mall or a hotel, brightly lit and with two restaurants in the middle, crowded with young couples, many in uniform. There were rows of doors leading away from it and Major Whittaker showed them to one that was marked 65. She opened the door to an apartment, which, though not luxurious, was large and tasteful. Their luggage was already neatly stacked in the corner.

'These buildings are all connected by underground passages for pedestrians and electric vehicles, so none of us can be seen from the air. We've got bars and restaurants, shops, two gyms, a disco, a cinema, beauty shops, a theatre and a pool. And there's a special area where you can sit in the sunshine and get fresh air, but without being detected from above.'

'How on earth do you keep this place secret?' wondered Chris aloud. 'There must be thousands of people here.' Major Whittaker provided the answer.

'Well, the nearest small town is about 15 miles away and we've told everyone there that anthrax broke out in the few remaining cattle. We even had an ambulance drive through town, siren blaring, which announced it was carrying a corpse. That keeps them away. And we've made sure that any traffic comes through a secondary road from the north, from the mountains. It seems to be working so far. There are other places like this, but you don't need to know where they are.'

She looked down at a tablet. 'There's a briefing by my colleague Alice at five for all new arrivals, and then tomorrow at ten you both need to go to the fertility department at the health centre.' Her voice hardened a little. 'If you've got any form of contraception, by the way, get rid of it now. Also, get rid of any cellphones. They won't work, but you might try, and we absolutely mustn't have any signals emitted from here.'

Then she smiled again. 'Here's a welcome pack to fill you in about anything else, with rules and maps and so on.

Grab some lunch. Everything's free. And welcome aboard!'

'Hope Haven', Montana

'Welcome, everyone!'

Many women in the audience thought they recognised the attractive female speaker, but couldn't quite place her. Blonde, well presented, about forty, with a comfortable figure and a really engaging smile, and a distinctive voice they'd heard somewhere before. Had she been a TV presenter, maybe on a children's programme? Anyway, she seemed warm and welcoming, and they would find out more about her later, just as they would find out more about this place and all the other women in the audience. There would be plenty of time to do so, though no-one attending wanted to think how long that might be.

'Good morning. I'm Alice Gaynor, and I'm extremely pleased to welcome you all here, and must congratulate each one of you on your brave decision to join us. We know that all of you have had to leave a great deal behind you. Your extended families, parents, relations, neighbours and friends, people you loved and colleagues you worked with, probably good jobs and promotion prospects, and good schools for your children. It's a loy to give up. – the list goes on.

Here, at what we've called 'Hope Haven', we cannot fill all those gaps, but we can certainly – and *will* certainly – fill as many as possible.'

Alice paused to sip at her glass of water.

'All of you are from military families, or are in the military yourselves. And all of you have passed our strict vetting procedures and should be extremely proud to have done so, just as the people here are proud of you. They are not easy, and it is not easy to leave a life behind, not knowing what the future will bring. But what it *will* bring, here in Hope Haven, is the only chance we have to bring more children into the world, and to envisage any kind of future for our precious planet.'

Alice looked up and smiled at the audience.

'The education for your children, existing and future, will be excellent here. We have many teacher volunteers in our community, covering all the core subjects your kids have learned up until now. This includes physical education, with coaches for football, tennis, swimming and other sports.

And we would be more than interested if your qualifications could come in useful at Hope Haven. We do have certain details of your professional backgrounds, but will certainly want to know more, for example of any backgrounds in nursing, engineering, teaching, counselling, social care, legal work, retail experience, beauty or hair care, sports management – absolutely anything that would help us and add to community life. Nothing, and no talents are here to be wasted. The project is simply too important. It is, quite simply, vital to our human survival.'

Alice paused, knowing it was a lot to take in.

'This afternoon I will give you all a guided tour of the complex, and I think you will be surprised by the extent of the facilities we have been able to provide, even in an impossibly short time frame. And with your help, there will soon be more.

You will see shops, a gym, an art room, a music area, hairdressers, a hall we use for hobby and reading clubs, a garden, a library, a cinema, a DVD store, restaurants and bars – though there are strict limits on alcohol intake. Health – and healthy newborns – are an absolute priority, as I'm sure you all will be the first to understand.

Once again, Alice purposely fell silent for a moment.

'By the way, you will notice that the many people who arrived with you in uniform are not with us at this meeting. They are at a separate briefing, because we want them to carry on with their military skills. You will not be surprised that the other facilities will soon include a barrack square, a firing range and motor pool and weapons workshops. All to protect us, and the planet as a whole.'

Another sip of water.

'You will all be given a monthly allowance on the first day of each month, and there's a bank here in which your savings have already been safely deposited. As you know, none of the old credit cards are permitted here because details of your transactions could easily spread to the outside world. But we do have our own highly secure credit card system, and our own Hope Haven card. You'll be given free cell phones, but they only work within the Hope Haven complex, for obvious reasons. It's vital that our location never gets revealed. You'll find more information in your welcome packs handed out to you when you arrived. And I must ask you to read it as soon as possible. And if you have any questions, as I'm sure you will, we have a help desk in the information centre manned twelve hours a day. Or please ask to see me.'

Alice paused to look around the room, knowing what these remarkable women had given up.

'All of you have made a very brave decision, but it could be one, at times, that may seriously worry you. On moral or religious grounds. Or grounds of guilt perhaps, if you have needy parents back at home, or grandparents who are ill or with not much longer to live. Or even – and we often hear this – if you've had to leave behind much-loved family pets. For that reason, we have an excellent team of counsellors and psychiatrists. We would welcome your details, by the way, if any of you are also in the counselling professions. And those of you with daughters may one day be able to enjoy grandchildren too, although there will be absolutely no pressure on them – ever – to join the scheme. For young girls in particular, ours is an extremely protective environment, in many ways much safer and less pressurised than the outside world.

Alice looked up from her notes, and around the packed audience. She knew her timing and delivery were vital.

'Not one of us could ever have conceived a world where none of us women can ever conceive ourselves, not without the help we can offer here. Those of you without children will now be able to have families, and each new birth will be a cause of great celebration. And those of you with children already will be able to have more if you wish to, your only opportunity to extend your family in a safe, loving and protective environment. And your existing sons will be able to thrive here, supported by people who understand their predicament, with none of the bullying that would surely face them back home in the outside world.

I cannot pretend that life will be easy, but Hope Haven offers our only chance of human life continuing. You, all of you, are nothing less than the future of the human planet. There is no way that I, or anyone here at Hope Haven can thank you enough for the many sacrifices you've made to come here.

Now, I think it's time to take a pause and have some tea and coffee, and get to know each other a bit. If we move next door we can have a twenty minute break, and then I'd be happy to answer any of your questions back here. And after that, a special welcome lunch will be laid on for us in one of our dining rooms, and then a tour of the complex.

On a last and very serious note, it is my duty to remind you all of one thing. And it's something I will repeat to you time and time again. It's essential for the future of our world that the existence of this place, this Haven, and the many others like it, is never to be revealed. You cannot just decide that, after all, you

84

don't like it here. You cannot just up sticks and go back, as if this was a holiday camp. You all signed forms to agree to that. The privilege of being here entails obligations. I am sure you understand.'

Alice looked out over the audience, and was silent for a full minute. There was no sound from the room, as she knew there wouldn't be. She had learned the vital importance of these last sixty seconds of her introduction. These women, and all those before them, needed every one of them to let things sink in.

The audience did not get to its feet in a hurry. Nor did anyone speak. Most were engrossed in their own thoughts, their brains whirling about the life that lay ahead. But gradually, the women rose to their feet, gathered their paperwork and handbags and went next door, to be greeted by Alice Gaynor as they entered – and each by their first name – as she read the badges pinned to their clothing. That small gesture, she knew, did something to allay the fears of new arrivals at Hope Haven. And anything, however tiny, could make a great difference to these brave new creators and saviours of the human race.

'YOU ARE THE FUTURE' said the banner above the door to the adjoining room. Alice, and everyone passing beneath it, fervently hoped it was true.

London

General Baranov had called a meeting of his people responsible for what he proudly called 'maskirovka', convinced that a review was needed urgently to tighten up procedures.

Brigadier-General Koenig asked if he could speak first with some interesting information.

'Before we start on the subject of concealment, we may have detected something relevant. We've been looking more closely at those recon drones, and feel that in their reconnaissance role they may have some real limitations. They're really pretty small, only three to four metres across and with a similar length. They may have to be on station for months, or even years.

Part of the rear of each ship appears to be some form of solar panel, presumably to generate electricity. It's certainly nothing like the big arrays of solar panels that we use to power our satellites or space stations. The drones, we assume, have to operate their detection devices like cameras and radio receivers, and they then have to re-transmit the data they've collected to someone, or something, to analyse. All using power.

What we *don't* think is that they have enough power for infra-red cameras, or at least powerful enough ones to see details from that height in the dark or through clouds and bad weather.

And the reason we think *that* is because, at least here on earth, we have to cool infra-red detectors so they don't blind themselves with their own heat, so to speak. We'd use things like a Stirling Cryoengine or a Pettier solid-state refrigerator. We don't think their drones have enough power to do all these tasks. So infra-red may be their weak link.

And that, of course, may make all the difference, potentially. Means we can move things at night.'

There was a buzz of speculation round the room, but General Baranov appeared sceptical.

'We must hope for the best, General Koenig, but prepare for the worst. For instance, suppose they turn off their visual sensors at night to divert power to infra-red? Or if their technology is so superior that they can cool infra-red cameras with minimal power? Or if their tiny solar panels provide much more power than we think they do?'

Baranov looked around the group.

'I personally wouldn't bet the world – and I *mean* the world – on your assumptions.'

Koenig had to nod his agreement. He still didn't like Baranov much, but had to go along with his cautious attitude.

'However,' continued Baranov, 'I have a question to ask. Do you think that up there they could detect, by infra-red, the difference between something three and a half metres wide and two and a half metres wide?

Koenig looked puzzled. It was a strange question.

'No, almost certainly not.'

'Good. I have a particular reason to ask that. To explain, we have lots of tanks that we may need. But, for our purposes, they're in the wrong places. We need the bulk of them near Havens, ready for use, and a small number actually *in* the Havens for training. Your Abrams,' he looked at Koenig, 'are twelve feet or 3.65 metres wide, and our Armatas are not much narrower, nor the British Challenger or the German Leopard. We might want to disguise them in regular containers, which are, unfortunately, only eight feet wide, or two and a half metres.

These days, in our political climate of co-operation, a lot of our tanks are half redundant, and if they haven't ben scrapped, they're parked out in the open air. If we assume that our enemies know what they are, we mustn't get detected, or caught moving them near the Havens in case doing so draws attention to the existence of the Havens themselves. However, if we built *over-sized* containers, install the tanks and move them on trucks, and only at night, with weak or imprecise infra-red detection, they'd look like ordinary container loads.

However,' Baranov gave one of his rare smiles to Koenig, 'we can probably assume those bastards can count, so it's no good emptying that desert of yours near Reno. We'll have to replace them with cheap, light replicas – just as we did in World War II. I'm sure you remember the pictures of rubber Shermans and T-34s being carried about by four men.

So, from space, your 2,000 Abrams and my 3,000 Armatas will look as if they're still out there.' He paused to look round the room.

'The same would work for aircraft, providing we folded the wings. And similar methods could be applied – that is, when construction picks up, for the materials the Havens need, like steel and concrete. If we make sure the loads look normal and not too over-sized, we might just be able to get away with it.'

He paused, looking round the room.

'Do we all agree?' Everyone nodded.

'Right, then let's turn to the concealment and deception about the Havens themselves. I suggest we go round the table.'

The delegates from most countries reported that they had opted to base Havens on existing bulky structures. Old mines had been favoured by several, a silver mine in Montana, several salt mines in Siberia, and an iron ore one abandoned by BHP in north west Australia. All were rather remote, and whereas people on earth might know that they were abandoned, up in space they wouldn't. Some traffic to them would be normal.

The Dutch had opted for the huge old gas complex at Groningen, as had other countries with similar former industrial sites. All such places, they explained, were already supplied with electricity and gas, and with roads and sometimes railways leading to them.

Considered equally effective by the delegates were old ports with major buildings on the waterfront, created to service an industry that had died – whaling for instance – or an old offshore oil industry servicing port. The huge facility on the coast near Houston to export natural gas, no longer needed, had proved perfect for one of the American Havens. And the historic naval base of Scapa Flow had been a natural choice for one of the British Havens, with its Flotta liquefied natural gas terminal having conveniently fallen into disuse.

Other countries had opted for huge existing natural cave complexes, like the French in the Massif Central, as had others in Spain, Italy and the Balkans.

And China's half-built boom towns, now derelict, could look from above as if they were starting up again in a small way.

All agreed that the locations must *not* be in places where unusual activity would stand out. Real remoteness could be a flaw.

Through the rather long presentations, Ivan Baranov nodded and occasionally scribbled a note with an old-fashioned gold pen. He also smoked a cigarette – now tolerated in public meetings since the political world had decided that second-hand tobacco smoke, or even first-hand smoke, was the least of its worries. After a break for coffee he called the meeting to order.

'Remember, ladies and gentlemen, what I told your countries' leaders at the outset. Tricking *them*,' he pointed upwards at the sky, 'is less than half the battle. Keeping the secret of the Havens, their purpose and the continuing presence of sperm for selected people, is absolutely critical. And for that we must use all the maskirovka techniques, not just concealment of the Havens and simulation using dummy tanks and aircraft.

Can we now please review what you've all been doing, perhaps starting with our American friends.'

Colonel Tasker , Charles Koenig's Deputy, stood up.

'Well, we've done one obvious thing. New arrivals always come by night and down disused roads. And that must go on even in sparsely inhabited areas – maybe *especially* in such areas – where we are not going to be able to hide the fact that *some* activity has started or increased. In Montana, that anthrax story was never going to work for very long.

So, as disinformation,' Tasker noted Baranov nodding approvingly, 'we've used the story that mining has started up again, but for secret, special government stuff. We've used that in other mining sites, too. All with special security, of course.

In Florida, we've masked our activities by appearing to start up an old shrimp fishing factory, and in Alaska a fishing station. As we mentioned before, for the vast natural gas terminal near Houston, we've cited the need for a new strategic US oil reserve, essential after the whole Saudi royal family quit and the Saudi oil industry collapsed.'

Delegates then explained that, in some countries, difficult political situations or the physical problems finding locations meant that they'd placed their Havens off- shore, outside their territorial waters or even in another country. Perhaps the strangest example of these was the one in the Falklands donated by the British to their old rival Argentina.

They all agreed that this type of imaginative lateral thinking was crucial when building or concealing Havens, and that Copsa Mica was a perfect example – probably the world's most polluted town. In reality, the Romanian delegate reported, the wrecked town was now clean, but it had been easy for the regional authority to say that new pollution had been discovered and to create an exclusion zone. The activity and transport used to install the Haven could then be attributed to a huge 'pollution clean-up'. The Chinese delegate reported that China had even sent observers to Copsa Mica to learn how to apply the same techniques to the Havens they intended to build up in their old industrial complexes and ghost towns.

General Baranov now emphasised two further helpful factors in hiding the Havens, the first one being that they could start small. The inhabitants, he reiterated, could arrive in small, inconspicuous batches. He paused and gave another of his rare smiles to the British Colonel at the end of the table.

'After all, I believe that your first little group of code-breakers to arrive at Bletchley Park was called 'Captain Ridley's shooting party' and *they* grew to ten thousand.

Secondly,' he pointed out, 'while some of the facilities are needed very quickly – hospitals and maternity clinics – others can come much later, like the drill halls, motor pools and firing ranges. So the Havens can be built up carefully and fairly slowly, much better for hiding them from space and from people a few miles away.'

Baranov wound up the meeting by urging everyone to maintain absolute vigilance.

'We must never, *ever* drop our guard.'

CHAPTER THIRTEEN

Birmingham, England

The suicide rate was increasingly alarming among 'chilmen' – as males who would never mature soon came to be known – despite tremendous Government pressure to ban the word. And why so many of these unfortunates decided to end their lives was no mystery to anyone. With their high voices, lack of facial hair, undeveloped muscles, shorter stature, and of course, no sexual development, theirs was a cruel life, so much so that many schools, universities and colleges had become 'chilmen only' establishments, although the actual word 'chilmen' was strictly banned in the media. But in private, and especially among girls, the word was rife.

The only people who had anything to celebrate about this were psychiatrists and counsellors, many of whom were now specialising in this burgeoning and hugely lucrative arm of their profession. Hardly a boy grew up to be psychologically balanced. Many were afraid to speak because of their high female voices. A great many more had become reclusive, sitting at their computers all day, or drinking themselves into oblivion. Or, at worst, even planning suicide and checking out the best ways to do it.

By now there were thousands of self-help websites for the boys who would never mature, but far too many that gave them the final way out of it, and so common were teenage suicides becoming that they were no longer in the news.

And suicides among their parents were far from uncommon, especially among fathers, although the burden of mental support mostly fell to mothers, many of whom could no longer work outside the home for fear of what might happen in their absence.

If there was any silver lining to this desperate situation it was the vast amount of 'CHILL OUT' clubs which were now worldwide, along with 'CHILL OUT' holidays, 'CHILL OUT' clothing, 'CHILL OUT' TV programmes and the weekly 'CHILL OUT' magazine – now translated into eighty languages and the biggest magazine in the world. And nobody could ever go down a High Street without seeing a 'CHILL OUT' T-shirt.

Mark Ronson, the founder of CHILL OUT was now, at only 21, one of the richest people in the world.

California

Veronica was getting fed up. More than fed up. The queues to get into California's Disneyland were enormous, and her six-year-old twin daughters were getting more and more irritable – the last thing she wanted on their joint birthday. She should have booked this ages ago, but with Derek losing his job at the sports club she'd had so much else to think about lately. What was he going to do? Well, that would have to wait until she'd got today over. And so would the subject of the cost of coming here. She and her daughters needed to have some fun in life, even if their father didn't.

Phew! She looked up at the scorching sun. Thank God she'd remembered the sun hats. In fact, she'd forgotten them until a hundred yards after she'd parked the car, but the blast of heat on her head had quickly reminded her it was worth going back.

'I'm bored' said Trixie. 'So am I' said Belle. There was not much that Veronica could say, not with at least a hundred people yet to go in the queue ahead. It would be another half an hour at least before they got to the front of the line.

'Well, it'll all be worth it when we get in' she eventually mustered. You'll see all your favourite people. Mickey and Cinderella and the Seven Dwarfs and ...'

'I don't like the Seven Dwarfs' interrupted Belle.' I don't want to see them. And I'm *boiling.*'

'And I'm thirsty' said her sister, angrily kicking up a bit of dust with her toe of her sandal.

'Damn' thought Veronica, suddenly remembering she'd left the Coke in the car, along with the sandwiches she'd made for a picnic. Now there would be even more queuing to get anything to eat and drink, when, and even if they ever got through to the other side.

The girls had been so excited when she first mentioned the idea. Mickey Mouse had always been a favourite of the twins, and their bedroom was almost a sanctuary for their hero. Mickey wallpaper. Mickey posters. And even more Mickey in the wardrobe, with Mickey dressing gowns, Mickey T-shirts, Mickey slippers, and Mickey party frocks. But this was beginning to be a nightmare.

At last they were at the kiosk, and the girls were now excited, both giving little hops of glee, and twirling around in their skirts. Mickey skirts of course, to match their Mickey sun hats.

And then Veronica saw it. A huge board behind the smiling cashier with faces of children. Missing children, presumably abducted in the vast theme park, now only ten steps away. HAVE YOU SEEN THEM? was written in huge letters above their smiling faces. Had they been abducted here? If not, why would they have the face board at all? Veronica's mind whirled. She couldn't take the risk. One child would be enough to take care of, but two boisterous children who were prone to run off would be too much. It was far too big a risk. And if anything happened, well, it was unthinkable.

And she'd never ever forgive herself.

She smiled at the cashier, 'Look, I'm really sorry, but I don't think we can come in. One of my daughters suddenly isn't feeling that well.'

'Who?' frowned Trixie.' I'm fine.' 'And so am I' said Belle.

'Well, actually it's *me* who's not feeling well. Look you two, I'm really dreadfully sorry, but we'll have to get back to the car and probably do this another day.'

The children were dumbfounded. And just as suddenly, extremely angry.

'Fuck, fuck, fuck!' screamed Trixie, stamping her foot.

Veronica was horrified. She never thought they knew that word. And horribly embarrassed in front of the cashier. What must the woman think of the way she brought up her children?

Sydney, Australia

'Why can't you have any more babies?' asked Posy, interrupting the bedtime story her mother was reading to her – about Bambi and his mother. Her mother paused. 'Well, because people can't have them any more. I've told you already. Lots of times.'

'But why can't mummies have them any more?' Her daughter had lost all interest in the book. Janice closed it gently and looked at Posy? 'Well, something just happened, in the air or somewhere, and suddenly mummies just couldn't have kids.'

'So why don't daddies have them, if mummies can't?'

'Because daddies aren't made to have kids, darling. They don't have the tummies like we do.'

'That's sad' said Posy. 'So now I'll never have someone to play with.'

'Of course you will!' said her mother. 'Think of all your friends at school. My goodness me, you had at least twenty at your birthday last week!'

'But it's not the same as having someone else here' said Posy.

'No, it's not the same' said her mother, deciding to change the subject. 'Now, do you want a few more pages about Bambi?' She suddenly remembered that

Bambi's mother would be shot in the next few pages, and couldn't bear to witness her daughter's tears again. Why had she ever picked up this wretched book?

'Look' she said, stroking her daughter's long hair. 'Right now, mummies can't have babies. But someone will find out why, and then we'll all start to have them again. And one day, you will have a baby too. I promise.' A stab of guilt. She knew she couldn't promise that at all.

Her daughter's eyes were beginning to close. Her mother gently wrapped the duvet around her shoulders and kissed her goodnight. She hoped that she had told her daughter the truth – that somewhere, somehow, they would find out why testosterone and sperm had suddenly vanished, though there was never anything on the news that suggested that anyone was near the answer. Perhaps they were, but were keeping it quiet.

To be plunged in ignorance was bad enough, and to be plunged in official silence was even worse. Normally she'd have said a little prayer with her daughter after reading to her at night. This time, she prayed alone for herself and the planet, asking for an answer, if not from man, from God.

New York City

Joe Stein couldn't believe how much his business had grown. His once tiny massage parlour in a grubby street in the Bronx in New York had long since blossomed into a booming business in Manhattan in the chic upper West side district, and waiting lists for new appointments were getting longer every day. He would soon have to hire even more masseurs. Why was he doing so well he wondered, when so many other businesses were floundering? Time and again he came back to the same conclusion. People were desperate for touch, for human contact, even if it were only from the hands of a masseur, and women especially. He knew only too well that there were many masseurs who would go further than he did for frustrated female customers, but that wasn't Joe's line of business although he knew it was lucrative.

His customer base was spread pretty equally between men and women of pretty well all ages up to the mid-sixties or so, and though about half of them talked during sessions, the other half preferred to keep silent, and nobody ever mentioned their desire for human contact of course, or about the circumstances that had, in his view, led them to his massage parlour.

It was notable that hardly any of them came in for sports injuries or bad backs, but purely, it seemed to him, for comfort, relaxation – and touch. Well, if he was giving a public service and an escape in these appalling times, he was proud of it. And so was his wife Danni, with their smart duplex apartment looking over the city's Central Park, and her brand new Lincoln car to park beside his in the underground parking lot. No children, of course, but looking at the miserable faces of so many kids in the street, that didn't weigh too much on his heart. Or that of Danni's. He was thankful for that, although he sometimes wondered who they would give the business to in their will. Well, he was only forty. Plenty of time to think about that.

There was another reason for his happy marriage. He suspected that he was one of the few men who bothered to keep his wife satisfied in bed, despite his total lack of desire. Danni had known what she was getting into right from the start, and maybe that had helped. And she was no doubt grateful for his lack of selfishness, particularly as, according to Danni, so many people were divorcing because men only thought of themselves.

He wondered what she would be wearing for dinner tonight, and hoped it would be the Valentino dress he'd just bought her for her birthday. He and Danni would be dining out with his chief financial backers at the Waldorf Towers, now lavishly redecorated by its new Chinese owners. It would be worth the expense. He was thinking of branching out in Boston and Atlantic City, and pretty confident they would back him.

Life was good. At least, as good as it could be in this troubled world.

Kampala, Uganda

'Lexi. I've got wonderful news for you. You're going to have a lovely new Mummy and Daddy. That's if you'd like that.'

The little Albino girl in front of her looked confused, and her pale blue eyes widened.

'Not my *real* Mummy and Daddy.'

'No, darling. Not your real Mummy and Daddy, but an even better Mummy and Daddy.'

Like so many Albino children in this remote part of Uganda, Lexi had been confined within a sprawling wired compound for years, dumped outside the locked gate at only days old. This was an area where locals still believed that Albino body parts would cure a host of illnesses. Many Albino children had been found murdered or mutilated. And many more of them had simply disappeared.

Lexi had not been out of the compound since her arrival, and only knew about the outside world from the few books the organisation could afford. And she had never owned her own clothes or any toys of her own.

'You remember the nice couple who came to see you the other day?'

The child's pale blue eyes widened again.

'The people who gave me Tammi?' The little girl looked at the doll she was carrying. It had hardly been out of her arms since their visit.

'Yes, the nice people who gave you Tammi. They want to be your new Mummy and Daddy. And if you'd like that, well, they're waiting downstairs.'

The child frowned, looking down at the floor. 'But where will I go?'

'To a lovely country called Spain. And a beautiful house with a garden where it will be quite safe to play. You'll even have your own playroom with your own toys.'

'And can I take Tammi?' The child looked lovingly at her doll.

'Yes, you can take Tammi. And when you get to Spain, Tammi will have more friends too. Perhaps a new sister doll. Or maybe a nice cuddly teddy bear.'

The child paused. 'But can I ever come back and see you? And my friends?'

'Yes, Lexi. You're very lucky. Your new Mummy and Daddy have enough money to bring you back once a year. And they've given us a lot of money to keep us going. They're very, very kind people. And they really want you. Otherwise, I wouldn't have let you go.'

Sister Mary looked at the child. So vulnerable. So fearful. But at last she smiled.

'Shall we go and see them?' The Matron held out her hand.

To her vast relief the little girl took it. She would miss Lexi terribly, but she would be going to a better life. With no children being born, at last there was a chance for these Albino infants. Ten of her charges had been adopted already. Hopefully all of them would find new parents. There was still some good going on in this troubled world.

Although she often feared that the Albino children in Uganda *not* being protected would now be in greater danger than ever. Now there would almost certainly be *more* people who thought Albino body parts would cure infertility. The thought made her shudder.

Verona, Italy

Twenty-eight year old Sofia Merino was sitting in the back pew of the crowded Duomo cathedral in Verona, with her husband of eight years, Angelo, but with anything but devout religious thoughts in her head, instead wondering why they had bothered to come at all. Force of habit, she supposed. And when she was younger she had plenty of reasons for which to thank God, not least her looks which had made her the city's Beauty Queen and shortly after catch the eye of Angelo.

So many years had now passed praying for the human race, but there had been no answer from a supposedly loving God. To her own shock, she was now even reflecting on how ironic it was that Our Lady Maria had been granted a virgin birth, but no-one else on the planet had been allowed that blessing in today's dire circumstances. And if God had granted Maria a virgin birth, didn't that somehow suggest that the Almighty did not approve of sex? And was *that* why he was still turning a blind eye to everything that was happening to the fast-diminishing human race? At least there was some kind of logic in that, she thought.

And what about all those miracles in the Bible? Raising Lazarus from the dead. Turning water into wine at a wedding. Walking on water. Feeding the five thousand with five loaves and two fishes. Surely if all that could happen, it wouldn't be beyond the Almighty to make some sperm fertile again? And what about the Resurrection too? Wasn't it high time the Almighty saw the irony in all that? Why couldn't he resurrect the human race?

She looked dismally around at all the many images of Maria cradling her baby, a joy that had been denied to her and Angelo since their marriage, and one that they had yearned for. Today's celebration suddenly seemed totally inappropriate with a packed congregation devoid of children, and she had barely bothered to listen to Pope Stefano's new opening prayer for human salvation which had been introduced into churches right across Italy and the Catholic world in time for Christmas.

There was little enough to celebrate or even smile about, but looking around the beautiful twelfth century Romanesque interior and at the carved angels, smile she suddenly did, remembering how, as a little girl, she had always wondered how the angels and Archangels had managed to get their flowing robes around their huge wings, long before zippers had been invented. It was somehow a comfort to see the funny side of things, on the rare times you could.

She and Angelo were now alone in their pew as everyone else went up the aisle to take Holy Communion. Neither of them felt able to partake of the bread and wine. It simply didn't fit with the concept of a loving, divine presence, not these days – whatever the Cardinal said, whatever anyone said. And, as if he could read her thoughts, Angelo took her hand in his. Such a good man. And such a good husband. But one who had longed for a son, as she had longed for a daughter, although neither of them had mentioned that in years. It would only make things more painful.

'God moves in a mysterious way, his wonders to perform' – the choice of the last hymn was certainly appropriate thought Sofia, and she sang along with the rest of the congregation, but still in fury with a God who could leave the world – and her and Angelo – in such frustration and despair.

At last the Cardinal ended the service with one of the most intense passages in the Mass. 'Agnus Dei

Qui Tollet Peccata Mundi Miserere Nobis' – Lamb of God who taketh away the sins of the world, have mercy on us'.

About time he did, thought Sofia.

Abu Dhabi, United Arab Emirates

The two men in their immaculate white robes greeted each other with a traditional embrace, and sat down in the vast and lavish lobby of the Emirates Palace Hotel.

They had been meeting up for years in the same place, and always found something to talk – and laugh about. It would be no different today.

Cousins, both the same age, handsome, rich, and until recently living with several wives , not unusual in this part of the world. So much in common.

They sat down and ordered coffee.

'So, how are you, Omar?'

'Fine, thanks. And you?'

'Not too bad,' smiled Ahmed, 'at least life's less expensive with only one wife, although it cost a bomb to pay off the others.'

'Don't tell me,' smiled his friend. 'And less exhausting too. All that pestering for perfume and jewellery and fancy underwear from London and Paris. It was all getting a bit much.'

He looked around to make sure nobody was listening, and leaned forward.

'And quite frankly, I didn't much like the thought of them playing with each other either.'

'Nor me,' said Ahmed. 'Do you think they did?'

'Probably. Couldn't really blame them. Human nature, I suppose.'

'Guess so.'

'And anyway, with all that out of the way, I can concentrate on ArabOil. Things are tough enough already with prices plummeting.'

'Same at AraBank. Losing money hand over fist.'

Omar's thoughts drifted back to his ex-wives.

'Would you believe, Ahmed, their perfume bill was running at about 20,000 US dollars a month?'

Ahmed laughed. 'Yes, you don't surprise me at all. Lys Bleu, I suppose.'

'Yup, shipped out from Harrods in England.'

'Ditto. Began to hate the smell of it.'

'Me, too.'

Both men sipped their coffee.

'But don't you miss the old days?'

'Well, the sex, yes. But not the other wives. And Alimah was always the best.'

'My first wife, too. You know, Barika. And I have to say, I don't miss all the petty jealousies. So tedious.'

'I guess they both needed a bit of a break. Who'd be a woman?'

Omar laughed, sardonically. 'Who'd be a man either these days?'

'At least we'll marry for richer, rather than poorer. That's if we bother to marry at all.'

'Guess so,' smiled Ahmed. 'And on the subject of money, we're thinking of down-sizing here. No point in all those bedrooms and bathrooms any more, or maids to clean them. All wasted space and wasted money. But as you know, I've just got rid of my place in London at a huge loss.'

'Same with us. Our house is far too large now. In fact, almost everyone I know is thinking of selling. But goodness knows what we'll lose if nobody wants big places any more. Millions. Doesn't bear thinking about. And I've heard it's even worse down in Dubai.'

'Time for more coffee?' asked Ahmed.

Omar glanced at his latest Rolex watch.

'Sure. I've got time for one more, as long as we stop talking about money. I'd far rather hear about your new Ferrari. Have you got any pictures on your phone?'

Cambridge, England

Millions of university students all over the world were reconsidering their degree courses, and if in their final year, their preferred career choices. Psychiatry? Yes, but not child psychiatry, with no new children and no paediatrics. Primary school teaching? No, another dead profession. Veterinary science? With no more mammals being born, except those by AI, that was just another dead end or a dying one. Architecture? Fewer people would mean fewer buildings, and vastly increased competition for jobs. Banking? Whole sectors of it would be crashing or under threat, with sector after sector going under. Advertising? Millions of products would soon be disappearing, and with them, thousands of jobs. The law? Yes, there would always be room for that. And divorce law might become a boom sector. Take sex out of a marriage and millions of partnerships wouldn't survive. Some hope there, but in a miserably bleak scenario. The retail industry? Possibly. People would still need food and clothing. And the general gloom might perk up certain markets – alcoholic drinks in particular.

But huge sectors would be under threat. The toy market. The baby clothes market. The cosmetics and beauty industry. The list of non-starters, or rather, imminent finishers was endless.

Journalism? A possibility. So many areas of life would be affected, and the human stories amidst the changes would be legion. But magazines and newspapers would need advertising revenue to survive, and if the advertising industry collapsed, so would the publishing industry, particularly in the female sector.

With markedly less interest in female products, few women's magazines would survive.

Jenny sat bleakly in her digs at Cambridge University in England, wondering what she was going to do. As long as she could remember, she had wanted to be a primary school teacher. Now, with no more babies being born, she would be lucky to have a job more than a few depressing years, every day being reminded that her profession was at a dead end.

And her boyfriend Ben, sitting in his room at Manchester University was similarly gloomy. With a predicted first class honours degree in one of the hardest courses of all – Politics, Philosophy and Economics – he should have been set for a glittering career in almost any profession.

But what?

Day after day, the papers were full of stories about business sectors in trouble, or on the point of collapse. And what was called 'the milk round' – the day when potential employers came to the campus to meet and hopefully recruit future graduates – was depressingly badly attended. No more than a few stalls this year.

What would he and all his friends and Jenny do? And after all their hard work and three years getting into a pile of debt with student loans?

It was all so unfair.

And if he and Jenny got married, they wouldn't even have a normal sex life or the comfort of children.

She was coming up to see him at the weekend. Perhaps he shouldn't propose after all.

London

'THERE'S MORE TO LIFE THAN SEX! proclaimed the huge advertising poster in London's Canary Wharf district, with a bottle of Coors underneath it. Coming out of the tube station on her way to work and looking up at it, Delia Rogers wasn't offended, as she knew a lot of people would be – and evidently were. Only last night she had seen a group of commuters complaining about it on the television late night news.

Maybe it was going a bit far for the public mood, but in a way it hit the button. If you couldn't have sex in any normal sense of the word, then you might as well enjoy other things to drown your sorrows, and Delia rather admired the courage of the advertising agency behind it. However had it managed to sell that ad to the client? It can't have been easy. Perhaps both the agency and the Coors people knew it would kick up a storm, but one that could actually *increase*, not decrease sales. Suddenly she remembered the old adage that 'any publicity is better than no publicity.' Well, the ad was certainly becoming word of mouth. She smiled as she walked past it. Good for them.

It would probably spawn a whole lot more ads like that, she thought, as people gradually accepted that things weren't going to change, and jokes about lack of sex would probably become the norm rather than the exception the longer things went on. And comedians would probably start thinking about that, if they hadn't already. They had made so many jokes about lousy sex in the past, and it wouldn't be a massive jump to make fun about no sex at all.

On the way home from home that evening, and still curious about the ad, she decided on a sudden impulse to pop in to the pub by the tube station, right beside the huge poster. Probably curiosity was embedded in her nature as a market researcher.

Ordering herself a lemon spritzer at the bar, she asked the publican about it. 'Doesn't that hoarding outside upset your customers?' she said, nodding towards the door.

'What, the Coors one?' The publican laughed. 'Nah, look around you, darling!'

Delia did.

Coors bottles on almost every table she could see, with mostly young men swigging from them. And all, apparently, drowning their sorrows with a good laugh after work. Funny world she thought, even if a lot of people didn't think the poster was.

*   *   *

No more than two weeks later on the tube to work, Delia noticed another ad in the same vein, this time for a bold new range of Rimmel make-up. A teenager's cheeky face smiled down at her from an ad above the seats opposite – a girl about seventeen, all made up in unusually bight colours: purple eye shadow, scarlet lips and lashings of brilliant blue mascara, and to top it all, a shock of brilliant magenta hair. The headline proudly proclaimed 'PUT ON A BRAVE FACE', and at the bottom of the ad was a strapline – RIMMEL, FOR A BRAVE NEW WORLD.

There we go again, thought Delia. So the Coors ad must have worked. Well, it was better than looking on the grim side, certainly. There was more than enough of that about.

Hope Haven, Montana

Josh Jensen couldn't believe his luck, or his ears, as a handsome eighteen-year-old newly recruited

submariner, after just three months on the USS *Michigan*. Now he would be actually *paid* to make women pregnant! Was this a dream? No, it was reality all right, but one he and his shipmates could never have envisaged in a million years.

He sat in the welcome session along with his friends in increasing astonishment, shocked to hear what was happening in the outside world, but equally stunned by his own good luck, and that of all the other young men in the audience – those who would be positively encouraged to ensure a future generation. Who would believe it? And all of them would have their own double bedrooms, not a single shared bunk like the one he was used to on the sub, pretty cramped if you were well over six feet tall like he was.

There would be nightclubs, discos, parties and even bars (although participants would be excluded from the programme if they ruined their health), in fact limitless opportunities to meet girls, and the more sex there was, the better it would be. Indeed, there would be a bonus every time you made someone pregnant.

Who would have thought it?

There were no girls in the session. They were attending another one, where they were presumably being told the same thing: that some unknown force had wiped out all production of male sperm – except frozen stuff and in the case of a tiny number of men who'd been in space, or under water like him. And that the boys they would now meet would be their only chance to have sex – and children – and do their bit to save the planet.

Indeed, they might be actively encouraged into having as much sex as possible, and as many kids as possible. Just like the men they would be told that contraception was strictly forbidden, and pay radically reduced for those unwilling to take part. Would that last part really be the same for women?

For Josh, coming from an extremely stuffy town in America's 'Bible Belt' where it was difficult enough to meet girls at all, let alone have sex with them, this would be amazing. Even the thought of it was beginning to give him an erection.

Only the married women would be off-limits, unless you had written consent from their husbands. But he'd already seen loads of single women – and lots of pretty ones at that.

When would the action start, he wondered. Tomorrow?

*   *   *

'Jensen. This way please.' A Medical Officer, a Lieutenant Commander, was calling him into his office.

'After I've checked your sperm to make sure it's healthy, we'll need you to provide samples twice a week. No normal sex within 48 hours of that.'

Josh was a bit shaken by this request, or order. He had imagined that *his* sex life was going to be a bit more direct, so to speak. And a bit more often. And they hadn't mentioned anything about samples in the session.

'And what if I can't manage that, Sir?'

'Oh, I'll use PESA.'

'What's that, Sir?'

'Percutaneous epidydimal sperm aspiration.'

Josh gaped at him.

'What does that mean, Sir?'

'Well, we stick a needle in your balls and suck the stuff out. Now be a good fellow, Jensen, and take this bottle behind the curtain. I should try and think of something sexy.'

CHAPTER FOURTEEN

Siberia, Russia

They had been pleased to be selected, of course. But apprehensive, too. And it was sad to have to leave all their friends in Moscow without saying goodbye properly. At least the cover story had not sounded too implausible – that Igor, 'as a military man', might suddenly be posted away for a 'special assignment'.

They had not been told the location, but Igor could easily work out that they were going both east and north. And six hours in the air meant at least 3,600 kilometres.

All the people in the twin-engine Ilyushin seemed to be of the same age, twenty-five to thirty years old. Most wore a variety of armed services uniforms, together with some police and paramilitary. They were mostly couples, but there were young single women too.

The engines' note changed, the flaps started extending and the undercarriage lowered. Natalia reached for Igor's hand. The aircraft swept past some snow-covered mountains, down over the flat white plain and touched down. There seemed to be no proper airport buildings visible through the windows. Probably a military landing strip, Igor thought.

Three dark green buses were parked on the snow-swept road. Plus two army trucks, presumably for the heavier luggage.

The staff, men and women, who guided them to the buses were pleasant enough. Some were in civilian clothes, others in uniform, with several of them talking into old-fashioned short-range 'walkie-talkies'. Igor supposed that the ban on mobile phones extended to them too.

It took only forty minutes for the buses to wend their way through the deep, snow-covered forests and grind up into the hills, shrouded in low cloud. There was no talk in the buses; everyone seemed a little on edge.

They arrived at a big wooden gate, guarded by soldiers. Natalia did not like what she saw. She suddenly remembered the old documentaries she had seen about Stalin's gulags, those horrible camps where millions of Russians had worked and died – usually condemned for no good reason.

The worst she remembered were the poor Red Army soldiers surrounded and captured in 1941 in their thousands by the invading Germans, because of Stalin's own military stupidity. After only just surviving the prisoner camps for three horrible years where nearly all their comrades died, they were liberated by the Red Army. Handed weapons, they went straight back into battle, eventually taking Berlin. Then, with the coming of peace at last, instead of returning as they expected to their families, their sealed trains steamed on past Moscow eastwards to the gulags, where they were kept for years – because Stalin considered that 'they had been contaminated by western influence'.

This desolate place looked just like one of those gulags. Had they been tricked into coming
here?

After passing through the gate, where the guards seemed admittedly very friendly, they approached a big wooden structure, apparently the entrance to a mine.

Then everything changed, and Natalia felt a welcome flood of relief.

The inside of the building was huge, like a cathedral. Warm and brightly lit. There were wide galleries leading away from it with electric vehicles passing and people strolling down them. The tracks of a narrow-gauge railway went down the side of one of them. A train full of men and construction material was leaving.

Once they had all gathered in the middle of the chamber, a green electric UAZ Patriot jeep with a tall, older woman standing up in it drew to a stop.

'Welcome, all of you. I hope you had a reasonable journey.

You may wonder where you are. It's an old salt mine, left over from the bad old days. It's colossal, and extends deep into the mountain. But, as you'll soon see, we've spent millions of roubles making it a considerably nicer place than it used to be. It's very much work in progress and will take a long time to even get near completion, but even now it has most things we need.. All the staff and the workmen who created it are part of the programme. They can have children, like you. And, as you can imagine, it will be, if we're careful, a safe place for our great purpose.

You'll be shown to your accommodation and then you're invited to meet some of our other residents and to join in a welcome banquet. We do allow vodka here, but not enough to endanger your health. That's far too precious.

Tomorrow morning, please go in designated groups to the fertility clinic at the times specified in your welcome packs, which are stacked over there on the table.

In the afternoon, there'll be a technical briefing about the next construction phases for the volunteer engineers and architects in your group.

Once again, welcome!'

CHAPTER FIFTEEN

New York City

President Jim Morrow wondered if this was the last crisis meeting he would ever chair. He also had to decide about now if he was going to campaign to get re-elected. It was certainly not enjoyable being in power with the world going to hell, including the United States. And no doubt he would be blamed for pretty well everything, and, he thought rather bitterly, he wouldn't even be able to mention his one great success – the creation of the 'Havens' and their hope for mankind.

He asked the twenty people round the table to report on their areas of expertise. The American Jim Haskins went first, giving an update on the population situation. 'Of course, in just a year, with the last of the pre-meteorite babies being born, the population hasn't actually gone down that much. Maybe by a few million. The economic crisis is being caused by the certain knowledge that inevitably it *will*.'

Gustav Holst, the German economist, reported next.

'As Jim indicated, the *expectation* that the world will shrink and get older is what has caused the economic crisis we face. The world's stock markets and futures markets, together with commodity markets like the Chicago Mercantile Exchange, have looked into the future and everyone has pulled their money out. Some industries will disappear altogether or rapidly reduce. Many have gone already. Finance has dried up and a great deal of trade has collapsed. Even in the more successful countries the unemployment rate is now around 40%, but in other countries it's much worse.

The food situation is dire. As you know, meat temporarily disappeared and then came back, but at huge prices. There have been many food riots, with bloodshed among both the rioters and the police.

We think fish will do very well. Many of their predators will die out, like seals, dolphins and killer whales. We must stop people getting over-confident and greedy and starting to over-fish.'

Jamie Abongo was looking particularly downhearted. 'I regret to say that I'm a bit ashamed of my continent. Africa, you'd have to say, is a total mess. Many of the governments have lost all control. Some have fallen, blamed by the people for the crisis. Out in the bush and among the tribes, witch doctors are more listened to than politicians.

With the meat supply drying up, and with very little livestock artificial insemination, the locals have taken to eating the wildlife – zebras, wildebeest, antelope, impala – everything. Even the elephants and hippos. And, perhaps worse, the very last rhinos. Just for their meat, much of which people cannot carry, so it's just left to rot. Needless to say, any wildlife tourism has long gone.

Grimmer still, the raw material commodities are not wanted now, especially by China, so mines are shutting down all over the place, throwing thousands out of work. It's the same story with Nigerian oil.

Worst of all, Ebola has tragically broken out again in six African countries, and this time we think nobody is going to fly in to help. It may kill millions.' He sighed and shook his head. 'All in all, a very bad picture. Very bad indeed'

The delegates could only nod in sympathy.

Next it was the turn of the oil and gas expert, Mark Campbell.

'With the perceived drop in demand, the price of Brent Crude's down to twenty dollars, West Texas Intermediate about the same. Leaving aside the halt in investment in shale or expensive deep-water rigs, this price slump has had some pretty big political effects, as you know.

The Russian government has fallen, and they're now trying to pull another one together. Venezuela is the same. But the most dramatic move, of course, was last week with the entire Saudi Royal Family, hundreds of them, just leaving, rather than risking the mobs. Most went to the UK and here in the US. May have briefly helped London and New York property prices I suppose, but it's done nothing for stability in the oil market. Saudi production is right down to five million barrels a day with the turmoil there, but now it doesn't matter. There's such a glut, the price has hardly moved.'

The media expert, Sally Jones, was next.

'Once again, it's the *perception* rather than the reality that has wrecked the media scene. For example, in contrast with Europe with its government media like the BBC, America's media was entirely founded on either sponsorship or, more recently, paid advertising, spawning thousands of radio and TV stations. With hundreds of key products disappearing, advertising has shrunk to a trickle. So the media outlets have been going down like ninepins. Women's magazines and baby-related media went first, but local print, radio and TV soon followed.

The biggest shock is in the social media. Twitter and Facebook have folded, as I'm sure you know, with their founders going off to live on their ranches. And the mobile phone networks, which now depend on them so much, may go next. We may go back to using phones just to call people up and talk to them, even ones attached to the wall.'

The meeting turned to another crisis, migrants trying to cross borders to look for work, welfare or even food. The United States had finally sealed the border with Mexico with minefields, barbed-wire and machine-guns. And horrifyingly, Southern European nations were beginning to sink migrants' boats rather than rescue them. And after a shoot-out in Calais, Britain had reluctantly closed and sealed up the Channel Tunnel. Eurostar had quickly gone bust, as had Groupe Eurotunnel SE.

Jim Morrow, listening to speaker after speaker, was beginning to consider whether he had the strength to continue, not just as the Chairman of this monthly meeting, but as President of the United States.

Already his hair was turning prematurely white.

Guiltily, he thought of a relaxed life on his ranch in Idaho, away from all this. But if he decided to go, he would have to make sure the incoming President and his Cabinet would keep the secret about the Havens.

That would be tough, but it would be his lasting legacy – if he could pull it off.

London

General Baranov was in his office thinking to himself. And, as usual, while smoking a cigar. Not generally approved of in public places, of course, but a bit of second-hand smoke was hardly very important when compared with a world that might die out completely in a few years.

People needed to get their priorities right, he thought, and stop worrying about petty little things. Keeping a lid on the Haven story – now that *was* a priority. It was going to be enormously difficult whichever way he looked at it, perhaps impossible unless ruthless methods were adopted.

It was all much easier in the old days, when his father and grandfather were in the service. Nobody questioned the OGPU or the NKVD back then. Or the KGB later. And they certainly didn't ask them to put their cigars out. Mind you, old Vladimir Putin probably would have – with all that fitness stuff.

It was difficult for foreigners to understand quite how tough we're going to have to be, he thought. Some would understand, of course. The Russians, the Chinese and the Germans, with their usual discipline.

But with their talk of liberty, free speech and investigative journalism, the Americans and the British were a different breed altogether. Thank goodness the media were going down like ninepins. And the social media too. It was really great without Twitter, screwed by lack of advertising. Imagine, a few months ago, if a leaked story about the 'privileged' Havens had gone viral.

There was no doubt that they were going to have to jump on people who stepped out of line. But how to avoid the bitching from the softies? Nobody had complained about that awful Alphonse Principe – he was just so obviously unpleasant and greedy that most people would have loved to shoot him down. But there was an awful and unnecessary fuss about that silly, talkative little translation girl and her boyfriend – both totally expendable. Why two deaths counted at all when you were worrying about billions was completely beyond him.

What he really needed was less weakness and argument, and more and tougher agents, more equipment, more phone hacking, more bugs, and the end of that ghastly phrase – 'human rights'.

Suddenly his thoughts were interrupted by a Russian Captain coming in to his room.

'Sir, we've got some trouble in India.'

CHAPTER SIXTEEN

London

Charles Koenig had been forced to make a detour in Clapham to avoid what looked like a food riot. When he pulled into the underground car park, he noticed it was half-empty and that several of the cars were covered in dust, obviously abandoned. Car parks were yet another business *not* to go into, he mused grimly.

He had been promoted to Brigadier-General, mostly for his much-appreciated work on detecting the drones, and was now part of a small committee set up to try to analyse the strengths and weaknesses of the suspected enemy in space.

The team collected coffee and sat down. The Chairman was Professor Max Underwood, a Canadian. And there were several nationalities present, including a Chinese, a Russian and two Indians, all leaders in their fields. Ann Hearst was present as a guest, and as liaison with other committees.

Professor Underwood opened the meeting, 'Charles, what's the status of what we called the drones?'

Charles took a deep breath. 'First, it's worth reiterating that they *are* almost certainly drones – in that they are unmanned vehicles. They have no radar image, but a tiny heat one. Our satellites have sidled up close enough to see them, so to speak.

We found they're quite small, about three to four metres across, and they're shaped a bit like magnets pointing downwards to the surface of the earth. The two downward-facing projections could contain something optical, the equivalent of cameras or eyes. And also something for listening, like microphones or ears, perhaps picking up sounds – or more likely radio, TV and other waves.

Our scientific people question how good their infra-red capability is, but we've opted for caution about moving things at night.'

Charles paused, anxious to get his facts absolutely accurate.

'One other fact that may be significant is that over the last ten months some of them – five to date – have malfunctioned. For some reason, they seem to drift out of orbit, like the one that collided with the space station, and then go lower and burn up when they start hitting the atmosphere. They cannot have any kind of shield, as we do, to deflect the heat. It also shows that their technology is not flawless.'

'Very interesting, Charles. We'll need to keep searching for any chink in their armour, any opportunities, anything.'

'Well, let's now turn to the physical evidence,' the Professor continued. 'We have about two grams
of material from the Black Sea shore site and that curious green smear from the US space station.'

The Russian, Igor Sikorsky, addressed the Chairman. 'We kept some of the Black Sea material and gave the rest to the Americans. Both laboratories agree that when it entered the atmosphere, it was alive – at least in some way. Most got burned off, sacrificed in the entry, but more than enough was left to create the water plumes. There was some white powder residue, a silica fume. So I have a theory that they may be silicone-based, not carbon-based.'

The meeting fell silent for a moment.

'Do you think there's any significance in the fact that nearly all these things hit salt water, rather than fresh water?' asked Dr Sanji.

'We have no scientific reason to say yes to that question yet' replied Charles Koenig. 'However, they didn't seem to miss much, only one out of 130 possible hits. So you would have to guess they don't make many mistakes.'

He looked at his colleagues, considering his words carefully.

'Lake Michigan has a tiny amount of salt, but it's 220 times less salty than the oceans. I suppose the Lake Michigan one might just have been another mistake. So salt might well be a factor. We certainly can't rule it out.'

'The poison that created the male reproduction problems, it may not have been carried here.' ventured Mikhail Gorlov, Sikorsky's colleague. 'It's possible that the material in the vapour plumes was merely a catalyst. It probably combined with something here on earth, something found everywhere, to create some kind of chemical effect or even create a virus. Salt might be it. The trouble is, we can find no trace of it now.'

Underwood frowned. 'If it was designed to combine with something here on earth, that means that they must know this planet quite well, in addition to knowing what it would do to male mammals. That is *really* frightening.'

Doctor Lee Wan joined the debate. 'If the Space Station hadn't happened to see that first drone and then you detected the others, we'd have put the whole thing down to an act of nature and suspected nothing more.'

The meeting fell silent again, with everyone deep in thought, until Professor Underwood spoke again. 'What do we think they, and their ships look like?'

Charles Koenig volunteered an answer.

DONOUGH O'BRIEN & LIZ COWLEY

'Well, the only eye-witness account of a drone came from the Space Station. They were understandably very worried that it was going to crash into them and wreck the integrity of the Station. So they were more concerned with getting strapped in with their suits and helmets on, and didn't look very hard. But I was struck by the way they described it as soft. Like a sponge, one of them said.

As for the creatures themselves, while they might not have a frame like a skeleton, they could have some kind of soft structure that could harden itself when needed, a bit like when a muscle hardens.'

'And by the way,' interjected Lee Wan, 'we mustn't assume they'd all be identical, as they are in sci-fi films like *Independence Day* or *War of the Worlds*. After all, if the creatures on earth had equal intelligence, they could be used for different skills – birds for flying, fish and dolphins for swimming, humans for manual dexterity, and so on.'

'They might also have used other species and races, like the nomadic Mongols used the Chinese they'd captured for their wall-breaking catapult expertise. A real shock for the cities they were about to attack.'

'By the way', added Dr Sanji, 'I would think some of them are small, smaller than us anyway.'

'Why do you say that? 'Koenig frowned.

'Well, if you look at the size of the drones, they're about three to four metres wide, but also about one and a half thick. You have to assume they'd have to get inside them to install or service their drive system and surveillance equipment, so that would make them no larger than four feet tall, 1.2 metres, or smaller.'

Ann intervened.

'I've been thinking. Consider the softness of that drone, and the slime. Suppose some of these things are rather vegetable-like. Remember *The Day of the Triffids*? They might be quite slow-moving, and might not have any more weapons, at least what *we* would call weapons, apart from the meteorites and plumes – which were effective enough.

That might explain the strategy of trying to reduce our population right down and make sure our survivors were old. There could be lots of them, and they could merely occupy the land, which might be what they might want or need. Like a swarm of locusts, or ants. Or a mass of something like slugs, or big versions of slime mould.'

She shuddered slightly at the thought.

Professor Underwood raised his hand.

'If that were the case, we'd have to create weapons specially designed to destroy such soft-bodied creatures. Our modern small high-velocity bullets might be useless. They'd go right through unless they hit something vital, like making a hole in a melon. Even dum-dum rounds might not be enough.

But lasers might work, something like that horrid anti-personnel weapon that can blind people. They got banned by the Geneva Convention, but I don't expect our friends up there have signed up to that.

I'm no expert in all this, but someone should get working on it.'

'Hope Haven', Montana

Eighteen-year-old Naomi Lethbridge had just discovered she was pregnant – and with twins – a source of particular joy at Hope Haven. She did not know who the father was, having opted for artificial insemination, although there were plenty of girls in her intake who didn't.

Coming from a quiet rural background in Washington State, she was not used to the far more confident city girls on the programme, nor the kind of things they talked about. But at least there were plenty of country girls like her, and she was part of a coterie of good friends – most, like her, opting for the AI route. Although there was no moral objection ever voiced in Hope Haven about pregnancies achieved in other more normal circumstances, or indeed pressure to get pregnant at all, although it was gently encouraged after one's eighteenth birthday; probably why all girls reaching that age were given a very special day of celebrations.

One day, she told herself, she would meet a man and fall in love, if not here in Hope Haven then in the world outside. Surely there would come a time when everything would return to normal. And even if he could not make love or father children, well she would have her twins to keep her happy. Right now, pregnancy was a duty, why she was here, and she had made a contribution – in fact two – to the project, if all went safely. And there was no reason it shouldn't, especially as she was teetotal.

She knew the New York set sometimes swapped their drink allowance tokens to get another – and forbidden – drink at the bar. But alcohol had never meant anything to her, not since seeing a load of drunken lumberjacks in a bar in Wenatchee, and putting up with their revolting remarks when, at sixteen, she was a part-time cleaner and bar-girl.

Would her babies be boys, girls, or one of each? The ultrasound would tell her, if she wanted to know. But maybe, she didn't. It would be enough to know that they were healthy and that she had done her bit.

And in the meantime she would still continue in her hairdressing course in Hope Haven, until the bump became too big to stand comfortably behind the clients' chairs, or if she could no longer stand on her feet all day.

The only thing that worried her was her mother who had brought her to Hope Haven and was part of the project herself.

What if her Mom became pregnant too, as well she could at just thirty-six years old? Naomi felt uncomfortable about that, and suspected her father did too. It would be weird if she had a child the same age as a grandchild, even if it were to help the human race.

She fervently hoped that now she was pregnant, her mother would opt out of the breeding part of the programme and that her own pregnancy would provide a good excuse for doing so. And go back to weapon-training or whatever she did in the Army. But would her Mom be allowed to opt out? Naomi reminded herself to revisit the familiarisation brochure in her bedside cupboard, not looked at since she first arrived a year or so ago.

Her mother was her mother. She didn't want sisterly chats with a pregnant mom. It wasn't natural. But then, what was natural any more in this God-forsaken world?

Washington, D.C.

'Mommy, why are you going away *again*?' complained Tricia. 'You're never here.'

'That's not true, darling,' said Ann, with a familiar stab of guilt. 'It's just that I have to visit some people. It's very important.'

'But it's Betsy's birthday tomorrow.'

'I know darling, and Dad's going to take you. Don't worry. And we've got her a lovely present.'

'What?' The little girl became suddenly interested.

'That Barbie you said she wanted.'

Tricia smiled and started playing with her own Barbie doll.

Ann caught Ted's eye, indicating they should go into the kitchen.

'Thanks for all this.' She poured them both some wine. 'I'm really sorry I have to go.'

'Don't worry at all, honey, I've been in the Marines half my life and know when things are important. When are you off?'

'Tomorrow, really early. I'm being flown north to visit the first of our Havens. You know I can't tell you where. Wish I could.' He nodded his understanding.

'I need to check how it's getting on. It was one of the first. So if they've learned anything – good or bad – it'll be helpful for the other American ones. And the foreign ones, of course. We seem to have kept them secret. God knows how. But I expect that Baranov guy has been using some pretty scary methods. In fact, that really frightens me, what he might be doing. He sometimes really gives me the creeps, I have to admit. I seriously hope he doesn't find out that I've told you anything. Anyway, I'd better go pack.'

*   *   *

At six the next morning, a black car was waiting outside her house. Ann had snatched a quick coffee and kissed Ted goodbye, but had decided not to wake Tricia. She hoped Betsy's party would quickly take her mind off her absence, but nevertheless there was a pang of familiar guilt.

The driver was in civilian clothes, but from his fit look and short hair she suspected he was Army or Air Force. The traffic was light through the suburbs, not just because of the early hour, but because, sadly, there were now already fewer people needing to get to work.

The car did not take her to the usual Washington airports, National or Dulles, but to an Air Force base the other side of the Potomac. They drew up at a heavily-guarded gate and then straight to the steps of a grey twin-engine transport. Her colleagues were already seated: Brigadier-General Charles Koenig, now quite a friend, just back from Europe, an Army Colonel, a doctor specialising in artificial insemination, a psychiatrist, a paediatrician, a rather grim-faced FBI agent from Baranov's security organisation and a genetics expert from Ann's company.

While the Haven did have its own airfield, carefully designed to look like an ordinary stretch of highway, the team did not fly in there. Rather, they flew into Browning, Montana. There, they picked up the 'Empire Builder', a veteran Amtrak tourist train that was surprisingly still running. After two hours, looking like tourists, they got off at the Glacier Park resort station and were picked up by a nondescript bus. They then drove deep into the Rockies. It had all taken a long time, but it did shield them from any possible prying eyes hundreds of miles above them.

The bus drove straight to the door of a big, dirty old building marked STAMP MILL 4.

*   *   *

Even though she, of all people, knew all about the Havens, Ann was amazed by what they found. The place was already huge, and obviously getting bigger. They were met by Major Jessica Whittaker and Alice Gaynor, who escorted them to a conference room, with a glass wall overlooking the main concourse. There they were introduced to all the specialist heads of departments.

They sat down and were offered coffee and croissants. 'They're from our own bakery,' said Alice Gaynor, rather proudly. 'Our patissier trained in France. It's amazing, the skills we've got her.' She then started the meeting, and the Haven's head paediatrician took over.

'You'll be pleased to hear that the first babies have been born, all successfully. About one quarter are natural, the rest from artificial insemination. All the male babies have turned out to have normal testosterone, which is brilliant news, of course. Another thing, about thirty per cent were multiple births. So it looks as if things are going fine as far as our procreation plans are concerned.' He sat down.

'Other than the babies, how's the general health situation? asked Ann. The Chief Medical Officer spoke up.

'It's excellent. No problems of disease. Everyone was pretty fit when they came here, of course. We do have some mental problems, though. Some of our people are really missing their families, even though they know that they're being looked after okay. They miss being able to talk to them.

We let them watch CNN, but only in the theatre. Actually fewer and fewer of them are going there. I think they can't be bothered. Perhaps a good sign. The ones with children and new babies are fine and the others will, I think, slowly get back their morale.'

The Quartermaster reported that the food situation was fine, with supplies from

AI-induced livestock getting more plentiful by the day. Vegetables, he explained, came from carefully disguised gardens open to the sun. In winter, special lights would go on propagating them.

The FBI man leaned forward. 'Has anybody tried to leave?'

'Only very limited cases,' said the Head of Security, 'regrettable though they are. Only one way in or out, guarded all the time. There are frequent checks and informal roll calls all the time, and nobody's currently missing. I think people know how important this is and that they're privileged to be here.'

'Well, I'd like to check all that out myself,' said the agent, 'that's if you don't mind.' It was perfectly obvious that he didn't care if the security man minded at all. Baranov's high-handed attitudes were spreading to even his American representatives. And this cold attitude was spoiling the optimistic atmosphere of the meeting.

'How are you doing on the military side?' asked Koenig, a lot more kindly.

'We've moved quite a bit of equipment into the Haven, Sir,' replied a US Army Colonel, the Haven's senior officer for the moment. 'We need just enough to keep up the training of our existing military personnel, and then to work with the kids when they're old enough. The rest is being stored all over the country, kept ready for use. We'll have to develop our own secret arms development industry, because some of this stuff is going to get old or out of date. Not that we really know what we may be up against.

But we have to keep it all hidden. It's easy enough with the small arms, the Bradleys

and the Abrams tanks. But aircraft are another matter. Helicopters can be disguised as civilian ones, but the fighters have just been parked and kept serviced. We've got simulators, of course, to keep up the training. We can show it all to you when we go round.'

At that point Alice Gaynor judged that it was time to start the inspection, and they all went down and climbed into four electric trucks. Deep in the mountain they discovered the maternity block, the medical centre, the sports area with its pool and track, the farm with its cattle, pigs, sheep and chickens, and then the barracks. Here they saw drilling, lectures, and weapons training and testing.

Everywhere the people seemed relatively happy, positive and enthusiastic, all in sad contrast, thought Ann, with the already declining 'outside world'. But she was desperate to hear on the way back what their team's psychiatrist had *really* discovered. The Haven was a bit like an island you could never leave. Worse, it did not really have access to normal fresh air and sunlight. She could well imagine that there might be serious morale problems. If there weren't, it would be a miracle.

Faced by the realities of seeing the Haven in operation, she also started thinking about their potential enemies above. How much could the aliens see? *Really* see? Would they recognise suspicious traffic, different types of aircraft? Possibly. Had this all been a ridiculous dream?

As she settled into bed, she became convinced that they had to prepare for the worst and never let their guard down.

Probably that damn Baranov, with his *maskirovka* and his nasty methods, was right, although she dreaded to think how many people might have been eliminated to make the Haven programme work.

How much blood did *she* already have on her hands? It didn't bear thinking about, but the thought of those who couldn't cope with such confined environments was beginning to haunt her. '*Only very limited cases had been unable to cope*', the Head of security had said. She seriously doubted it.

PART TWO

CHAPTER SEVENTEEN

London

Ann Hearst looked out of the window of her office. London stretched out before her in a slight autumn mist.

So much had happened in eighteen years, since the momentous first arrival of the 'meteorites' and the plumes, and their devastating effect on mankind and the future population of the world.

She was now nearly fifty, although she prided herself on feeling and looking younger. So many women didn't bother these days. Her husband Ted had retired early at fifty-eight from the US Marines, and now spent most of his time fishing in the lake outside their house deep in the woods of Connecticut, while Ann had to fly all over the world. She made sure she visited him at least twice a month for a long weekend, preferably with Tricia. Ted had been a rock to her, and a big influence on their daughter, encouraging her through school and then into a military career – something which was now far less unusual for girls.

Her father, now 74, was also living alone in the country in Idaho, his wife having passed away. Jim Morrow had reluctantly run again for President in 2032. And he had won, albeit now having to contend with a much less pliant Senate and House and his own failing health. But he had known that it was vital to keep the 'programme' going, to make sure the Havens were up and running and that the deteriorating world outside them did not go completely out of control, a Herculean task which had almost exhausted him. This time round, Ann had played little role in his election campaign, far too involved in her work in running the Haven programme – always hoping for the best, while preparing for the worst.

Jim Morrow had handed over the Presidency in 2036 to Jane Hansen, the former Senator for Minnesota and the first woman to make it to the White House. He had made it his first priority to reveal to her the secret existence of the Havens and their vital purpose. 'It was like Truman being told of the atomic bomb', he had later said to Ann. And fortunately, although from the opposite Party, President Hansen was both intelligent and pragmatic and had promised all the hidden support she could give.

One valuable example of such support, with the increasing shortage of commercial flights, was the provision of a grey US Air Force Boeing C-32 that flew Ann and her team everywhere they needed to go – back to Washington, up to the Havens in the States and Canada and to those in Europe and Asia. They all seemed to be doing well. The birth rate achieved was far higher than expected and some of the children had already spent time in military schools. In the Havens, small versions of military colleges like Westpoint, Sandhurst, Hamburg and St Cyr were already enrolling their first cadets, and the plans for viable military forces were going well.

However, the same could not be said of the 'normal' rest of the world. As Ann had predicted, health care had broken down badly, partly because of the lack of young doctors and nurses, but also due to the lack of morale and motivation. Diseases had begun to run wild, not just Ebola in Africa, but lethal forms of flu and even plague. The resulting death toll had, appallingly, halved the population to four billion and several years ahead of Ann's original calculations.

She had seen the devastating results on her last inspection trips around the world. Empty countryside bereft of people and livestock, half-empty cities with half-finished skyscrapers and shanty-towns full of desperate beggars. The chaos of food riots, badly controlled by ageing cops and troops. And hoboes clinging to the boxcars of the few trains, just as in the 1930s.

Richer parts of the cities and the suburbs had become heavily guarded enclaves. And Ann knew that both Ted and her Dad had armed themselves to the teeth to live in the country. They had no alternative.

She sighed, gathered her papers and prepared herself for the Weapons Development Sub-Committee. It was going to be another long day – and that evening she knew she had to remember to call Tricia who had texted that she had something important to say. She really hoped it was good news; there was far too much depressing stuff about and it was getting increasingly difficult to remain positive.

*   *   *

Down a long corridor in the same Ministry building in Whitehall was a door marked 'Economic Development S/5'. It was actually the home of a small weapons development team specially created to prepare for a future war that seemed inevitable.

'Morning, Ann.' She was greeted by the head of the team, the affable John Browning. Ann knew that he was the great-grandson of the weapons pioneer, John M. Browning, the prolific firearms innovator whose pistol slide was used in every pistol in the world and whose famous 'Fifty Caliber' machine-gun was still in service after 110 years. Despite his calling – lethal weapons – he was a nice, kind guy. The absolute opposite of Baranov, thankfully.

She was introduced to the others – a Brit from BAe called Martin Stevens, a Russian from Kalashnikov – Igor Oumanski, and a German from Krupp, Otto Heinz. Apparently, the Chinese member had been delayed by lack of flights.

Ann realised that they must all be part of the programme, with their wives probably in the Havens and privileged to have babies. It was a miracle, she thought, that nobody had talked. Or maybe they had, and Baranov's bunch had silenced them. Once again, she shuddered at that thought. How many people had 'disappeared'? That thought continually plagued her.

John Browning opened the meeting, forcing her to concentrate on less gruesome things.

'Let's review what we may have to deal with. As others have pointed out, it's entirely possible that our potential enemies may not all be the same. The same species that can build spacecraft may not be able to fly them. Nor the same species who could land on our planet to fight – or to colonise, perhaps even to farm.

So we have to prepare for what we might call both conventional and unconventional enemies.

Let's talk first about the conventional. These things, for instance, *might* be quite like us. Standing up on a skeletal structure, with a blood supply, muscles, binocular vision, and lungs that breathe air. For them, we'd have to use our so-called conventional weapons, rifles and machine-guns firing bullets, guns firing artillery shells, high-explosive bombs, fragmentation grenades, napalm, missiles, lasers, tanks and aircraft.'

Stevens raised his hand. 'I suppose, John, once we know what they are, we *could* use chemical weapons – gases and so on. I don't see atomic weapons being appropriate.' Browning nodded.

'Do we have enough of any of these weapons available?' asked Otto Heinz. He was conscious that his once militaristic Germany had played very little military role in the last few decades, instead conquering the world with Volkswagens, Audis and Mercedes rather than tanks.

'The need for huge secrecy has hampered us, of course,' replied Browning. 'But in the US the tacit support of the President, Jane Hansen, has been crucial. So, for instance, we have been able to quietly re-commission and move some of those 2,000 Abrams tanks parked out in the Nevada Desert and put them in secret depots where we can get at them quickly. Some examples have gone to the Havens for training the kids.'

'We've done the same,' said Ouminski.

'Yes,' said John Browning, 'and it seems to have worked with aircraft too.

We've quietly been 'retiring' them, as no longer needed in today's special circumstances. They're stored, and selected pilots have been moved to the Havens to train new young pilots. Ammunition, vehicles, fuel and stores have been secretly moved and stored, too.

So, all in all, we're reasonably well prepared. As are the former NATO countries with the Chinese, Indians, Australians and Israelis. All the same, and all doing pretty well. The big gap, as usual, is Africa and South America. There we have few Havens – indeed hardly anyone is in on the secret of them. They'll be our weak link, tragically.' He got up to get himself a coffee.

Then Martin Stevens stood up. 'Let's look at the unconventional side now. As you know, John, we've been looking at this in depth. Reading the description of that drone thing that slid into the Space Station leaving a green slime, and also studying the reports into the Black Sea residue, we conclude that some of these things may be like plants or soft animals. Perhaps no skeleton or bones with their structural vulnerability. Altogether softer.

As such, the type of smallish high-velocity rounds we use nowadays may be rather ineffective, going right through without inflicting damage. That would equally apply to the shrapnel pieces from a fragmentation grenade or shell.

So we've concluded we'd have to use a variety of weapons. First, chemical warfare, once we know what they're made of. If they don't have lungs, an inhalant gas like chlorine, phosgene or mustard gas isn't going to work, for instance.

And if we're faced with great numbers of them, and they have penetrated buildings and cellars and so on, we think we'd have to use so-called 'fuel-air' bombs, thermobaric weapons. You had your really big one, John, MOAB, officially 'Massive Ordinance Air Blast', but usually called 'Mother Of All Bombs', and you Russians, Igor, responded with your 'Father Of All Bombs', which was as powerful as a small nuclear device. We may well have to go back to such things, unfortunately.'

He went over to a DVD player.

'Ann, let me show you a video of what we're talking about. Here, watch this. An aircraft drops the bomb on a parachute. A small explosion occurs which disperses the fuel into a vapour cloud, which mixes with oxygen. Then …'

They all watched the screen intently. 'Bang! A second explosion detonates the cloud of fuel, causing a massive explosion.' He switched off the machine.

'We wouldn't need to use monster bombs, but rather, lots of smaller versions. Aircraft could drop the American BLU-72b, and infantry could also use the Russian TGB-7 for rocket-propelled grenades and the GM-34 launcher and so on. There are lots of these weapons. Many countries have them, I was amazed to find. Of course nobody has needed anything like this for years, so we've have to start up production again secretly.'

John Browning took over.

'I think I can arrange for FN, who took over our Browning company way back, to make stuff for us in Belgium.

And Ann, we've looked at another situation too. If you were fighting in a confined space, like a cellar, cave or underground car park, you wouldn't want to use thermobaric weapons because they'd take you out too.

So we've looked at some infantry weapons, especially combat shotguns and grenade launchers. The problem here, as we've said, is that small fast-moving bullets or pieces go into a soft body – either right through, or lodging without doing damage because of the lack of vital organs. Even dum-dum bullets may be useless. We need a small shell that enters the body a few inches and then explodes. Otto has been very helpful on this.'

The German stood up, smiling slightly at the praise.

'The issue is the sensitivity of the fuse. A normal fuse in the nose of the shell requires something hard, like steel, to set its timer as it hits the target, to explode a fraction of a second later. But here we may have something much softer. So we've been experimenting for months at a special facility at Krupp's in Essen. We even imported lots of Jell-O from Kraft in Delaware to make blocks of it to shoot at.

But we eventually made a fuse for the nose of a quite low-velocity shell that's triggered by the surface of the Jell-O and then explodes twenty centimetres further inside.'

He then inserted a DVD and the group watched a series of slow-motion images. The first few showed failures – the shell going right through, or else igniting on the surface. The last three showed the shell and its fuse performing perfectly, with the Jell-O block blown to nothing.

The meeting then turned to the use of lasers and they agreed that they should be free of the 1995 United Nations Protocol on Blinding Weapons, although that nasty Chinese ZM-87 Portable Laser Disturber which had been banned might be only too useful.

John Browning concluded, 'So, Ann, in addition to our conventional weapons being ready, those two will need to be made, and in great quantity and secrecy. If there's nothing else, let's go down for a bite lunch. But, Ann, I'm afraid I can't promise you any Jell-O!' Ann smiled. Even the merest touch of wit was welcome in such depressing circumstances.

*   *   *

Allowing for the five hours time difference, Ann waited until the afternoon to call her daughter.

While Tricia had grown up as quite a tomboy, tall, fit and muscular, she was now a beauty – with blonde hair like hers, but with her father's brown eyes. Ann knew, with some considerable guilt, that she had been forced to neglect her daughter too often because of her frantic work for the programme. Thank goodness that Ted had stepped into the breach and played a major part in her upbringing and shaping her career. But who would ever have thought she would have joined the Marines?

But she had done just that, Quantico basic training and all. The Corps was much reduced in size of course, with half the recruits girls and with Drill Sergeants now in their forties. But Ann had been so proud sitting with Ted in his Colonel's uniform when they had watched Tricia passing out at Officer School. Thank God she'd made the grade.

Trish had even seen combat. Not at a very intense level, but combat all the same. Argentina had given up trying to get back 'Las Malvinas', mostly because the British had stopped looking to pump oil from around the 'Falkland Islands', as they preferred to call them. With the oil price on the floor, the rigs were now rusting in Port Stanley harbour, with the workshops closed and the people gone.

But that had not stopped the Argentinians from going to war. And for one of the usual reasons governments went to war – to cover up their own incompetence, this time in managing their meat industry. Even with artificial insemination, they had ruined everything and had ended up with hardly any cattle. So they'd attacked Uruguay, which had made a rather better job of its meat industry.

The little 'task force' that Tricia had joined as a Marine Lieutenant had been a joint US/British affair. It had amused her that the Brits, whom she really liked, took some satisfaction in teaching the 'Argies' a bit of a lesson. As they travelled south on their assault ship, she had noticed that *their* Marines had plainly never got over being forced to surrender to overwhelming odds after the sneak attack back in 1981.

This time, the shooting didn't last long – a few hours. And after the little 'Battle of Frey Bentos', the Argentinians surrendered in droves, probably to get some nice American food.

'Hi, Mum. How goes it?'

Ann knew better than to discuss military or political matters on an open line, if at all. For all she knew, Baranov's people were probably bugging *her* too. She planned to fill in her daughter fully on her next visit to the States, as far as she could.

'Oh, fine. You?'

'Great. I thought you'd like to know I made Captain.'

Ann was filled with a rush of maternal pride.

'That's great, Trish! I knew you'd do well. You always work so hard.'

'I'm going on some special course after I take some leave. Can we meet in Washington? I need to talk about Dad and other things.'

Ann knew that Tricia was being guarded in her conversation. She probably had more to discuss than Ted's fishing in Connecticut.

'Sure, let's see. I can make lunch on the Wednesday after next.'

'That suits.'

'Usual place, usual time?'

'Sure, see you there. Love you lots. Bye!'

Once again, Ann was filled with a pang of remorse that she hadn't been there for her daughter more often. A hugely demanding job involving loads of travel could be a curse, and at times it hurt Ann deeply that Tricia tended to confide in Ted rather than her, simply because she had so rarely been around. There was a touching tenderness between her and her Dad that was missing in Ann's communications with her daughter, and at Tricia's age, that was very sadly unlikely to change.

She only had herself to blame. But no, she quickly reminded herself, she *also* had the world to blame, and Tricia would hopefully understand that one day. She dearly hoped so, and it would surely help that her daughter was now in a demanding role in the the military. But all of those secrets had been a heavy maternal burden.

Looking at her watch, she suddenly remembered teaching Tricia how to tell the time on the kitchen clock at a remarkably young age, no more than about four. 'When the hour hand gets to here, I can play with you, but not until then.' Tricia had watched the clock so often for the time to play, but even then had sometimes been disappointed. 'Five minutes more?' 'Okay, Mom.' Tricia would go patiently back to what she was doing, until one day she didn't ask Ann to play at all.

London

Sir Timothy Fitch, the chairman of GEO or its private code name 'Populous', was feeling tired, and not tired in the normal way after a hard day's work. This was a different sort of tiredness, which he privately recognised as a lassitude with life; a concept that frightened him at only sixty years old, and one that he had not admitted to anyone, let alone Valerie, his wife of thirty years. He had often pictured her reaction if he had confided in her. 'Oh, for God's sake think of other people, or if you can't do that, think of me.'

Not being able to talk to her about his day-to-day job was enough of a strain without the impossible burden of his special government assignment, which he had been flattered enough to accept, such was its importance: making sure – as far as it was possible – that news about the Havens would never get out into the public domain, at least in Britain.

Of course it would get out – somebody would be bound to talk – even if they'd been impossibly lucky so far, but only thanks to the hundreds of highly trained and expensive operatives keeping their ears to the ground by day and night, and the huge expense of keeping their families silent – who knew that their relations or children were on a secret government assignment. It was running into astronomical and unsustainable figures. He couldn't see it lasting. Every day, sitting in his office in London's Whitehall, he felt like the Greek anti-hero, Sisyphus, wearily rolling a huge stone boulder uphill. It was an image that never left his mind, not even in his dreams at night.

And how long before the newspapers would raise a stink? Many, of course, had closed down due to lack of advertising, as had scores of magazines. But even the ones that were left were being paid an enormous amount for 'omerta' – their silence – money that compensated for the lack of advertising as more and more company sectors collapsed. But it would only take one of the surviving papers – or one truly brave journalist to ask questions and blow the whole fragile edifice apart. Indeed, the fact that none of them had done so already was a total miracle. He dreaded to think what Baranov was doing.

Up to a point he felt he could trust his operatives. After all, they had all been offered the chance to go to a Haven, and were among the strictly chosen few who would be offered that opportunity. No doubt their partners – if they knew – were helping to keep their mouths shut, but it would only take one of them to bring the whole edifice crashing down. And any one of them could make huge money blowing a partner's cover.

At least his operatives had a job, and one that wasn't as dull as most, often deployed to listen in at bars for idle conversation when they weren't hacking phones and websites – their main speciality. And able, of course, to consider the possibility of having children while witnessing the agony of the poor souls who never would.

These days, it was almost as if he could never speak his mind outside the office. Social engagements with his wife had become an absolute nightmare as people enquired about his job, and cracks were beginning to show in his marriage. How long had he had this assignment? Only three years, but it was beginning to feel like thirty, and at forty-five he looked at least ten years older.

Poor Valerie. He felt sorry for her. It was very hard for an established children's author – almost as successful as Enid Blyton had been in her time – to have to put down her pen, or rather computer, after more than thirty years writing, and to know that all her once popular books – at least twenty of them – were doomed to become museum relics unless they were fondly remembered by nostalgic childless parents, reminded of the last vestiges of a happy childhood.

It was even more unfortunate that her other great interest in life was horses. The availability of artificial insemination for breeding horses had long since become scarce, and the stable block at their home in Hampshire had for years been devoid of equine inhabitants, as had the two fields at their extensive but now hopelessly overgrown property.

Even the downstairs cloakroom at their home looked depressingly obsolete, still filled with riding paraphernalia and all the rosettes now gathering dust that Valerie had won at county dressage events.

He looked at the photograph of her on his desk. Valerie, at about 28, holding a baby in a christening robe in one arm – their youngest – Gemma, and holding Nicholas, three years older, with her other hand.

At least the two kids had been able to have kids of their own before the tragedy struck. He had something to be thankful for, at least.

He reached for the phone. It was time for his regular weekly conference call to report to that unpleasant Russian Baranov.

Munich, Germany

Munich had always had a split personality, thought Petra. Bavarians prided themselves on being fun-loving and relaxed, with their great beer festivals of Fasching and Oktoberfest. The city had long boasted of its artistic and liberal attitudes, with its many students, and its bohemian Schwabing district full of writers and artists. So different from those materialistic cities in the north, especially Prussian Berlin.

Yet she was ashamed that Munich had been the birthplace of the Nazis and Hitler's favourite city, where he had first led his followers to failure and then to success. Petra knew he used to wait for Eva Braun to leave the Hoffmann studio where she worked in Schellingstrasse, and had wooed her in the Osteria Bavaria a few metres down the street; the same restaurant where the obsessed young English aristocrat, Unity Mitford, had gone every day until her hero noticed her and allowed her to join his Nazi circle there. She knew, too, that trains had left from the Hauptbahnhof packed with Jews for the East, ignored by the locals. She never went through the station without a sense of shame.

But, in spite of its growth and prosperity after the war, Munich was now a shadow of its former self. The population had halved and seemed to be getting older all the time. Many of the companies like BMW, Allianz, MAN and Siemens had shed thousands of jobs. The vast hostel blocks of the Studentenstadt now stood empty, and the last students had graduated two years ago. It was sometimes difficult not to get depressed, but her job helped.

Petra was forty and unmarried. In a brave decision, she had broken away from *Münchner Mercur* to run her own newspaper out of a big old house in Schwabing, not far from the Englische Garten where Unity had shot but only wounded herself, distraught when war broke out between her beloved countries, England and Germany. The district was going down rapidly, not only half-empty but with many of the lively bars and jazzkellers now shut down for lack of young customers. But Petra was determined to keep cheerful, and loved running her little weekly, *Schwabinger Beobachter* , which had a reputation for being outrageous – no bad thing in these gloomy times. Yes, it only sold about 30,000 copies in Munich and the surrounding area, but many more online. So it was more influential than it appeared. What's more, it was one of the few papers to have survived at all. Others like *Süddeutsche Zeitung* and *Münchner Mercur* had gone under as the advertising had dried up. Luckily Petra's paper could count on the advertising and sponsorship of the big local beer producers like Löwenbrau and Höfbrauhaus who almost supported her on a whim.

And just occasionally, something came along to lift her spirits, and to make her life and job worthwhile. Better still, now Petra thought she might be on to a real scoop. Some woman had called a week ago, completely out of the blue. She didn't give her name, but said she had something really momentous to reveal.

'Momentous?' That was a word people never, or very rarely used. But if it *really* was 'momentous', what a coup that would be for a small paper like hers. She felt a rush of excitement. But frustratingly the woman had rang off suddenly, saying she would call again.

And this morning she had, sounding highly agitated as if she was frightened, and still unwilling to give her name. Then, composing herself, she claimed she knew something so extraordinary that Petra had to take it seriously. There was a secret place, she said, indeed maybe more than one, where thousands of people lived. And, cut off from the rest of Germany, it had lots of young people. What is more, she claimed that somehow babies were still being born there, probably from semen preserved in some way, and that the young seemed to be training for some military role.

Petra was as astonished as she was shocked. *How monstrous*, if the caller's story were true. *Someone has decided to choose just a few people to survive into the future? And they seem to be training as soldiers? Here we go again* – she thought – *racial selection, combined with military training! Would Germans never learn?*

The woman had even told Petra where this place was hidden. It would not be difficult to go there and check out the strange story. Perhaps she could rope in her brother Hans to drive up the autobahn with her over the weekend. They could do a cautious reconnaissance together, and if there really *was* anything there, she could run the story a week later. What a coup!

Suddenly, the bell rang down below, and Eva – the elderly receptionist – buzzed Petra. She had visitors, unexpected visitors.

There were three men, all quite elderly, naturally enough. One was local, and seemed quite friendly, from Polizei München, maybe one of her readers. The other two were from out of town, and anything but friendly. One was dressed in a leather coat like a former Stasi cop. The other had a foreign accent when he spoke.

'Fraulein Gümmer, certain information has come to our attention. We have some advice for you.'

After they had gone, Petra was nearly shaking with fury and frustration. She had *appeared* to agree to their 'advice', or actually demands, knowing they had the power to close her down.

But she resolved to keep going and reveal the story when the time was right.

'Bastard Nazis' she almost shouted.

Birmingham, Alabama

'Hello Chillo!'

Damon flinched. It was bad enough that boys like him were referred to as 'chilmen', though it was against the law. But there was no point reporting it to the police. They couldn't do anything, and it would make his life even worse if he did.

Behind him was the usual gang of girls sitting on the wall by the bus stop. He had to endure them every Saturday on his way to his job in a local car wash, all of them sitting there as if with only one purpose: to taunt him and see him blush if he was stupid enough to turn round. He had often walked the three mile journey to the car wash rather than wait for the bus – and the insults – but that meant getting up an hour earlier. He would have to learn to live with it, as most boys did, and force himself not to blush which always made things worse. He wished he was black like his best friend Tom Meredith – then it wouldn't show.

He told himself to relax and take it on the chin. After all, they hadn't roughed him up as yet, as he knew a lot of boys had been. You only had to look at the news to see that.

'Chilly day, isn't it?' said one of the girls and the whole group exploded into laughter. Damon felt his face flush scarlet again, and even his neck. All of it was prickling with sudden heat.

Thank God the bus was coming, but oh so slowly, stuck behind a long, long line of traffic coming down the hill. Only minutes to go, he told himself, his heart pounding.

'Relax! Chill out!' said another voice behind him. Again, the group burst into gales of laughter.

Next Saturday he would walk, and probably all the Saturdays after that, or he would have to give up the job.

There was no point in hitting out. Not with ten of them, and mostly taller than he was.

At last the bus was there.

He climbed aboard and went upstairs where the girls wouldn't see him, almost crying with relief.

It was like entering heaven.

Fertility Clinic, Hope Haven

A small group of women was gathered in the fertility clinic. Many of them had not really thought much about the role of nutrition in helping them to become pregnant. Their lecturer was a kindly, middle-aged woman in a white coat.

'Good morning, everyone. Thank you for coming. What we are going to talk about today is how diet and nutrition can really help with successful pregnancy. First, the easy bits. I'm sure I don't have to tell you that alcohol is not much of a friend to your baby.'

There was a ripple of laughter round the room.

'No, seriously. If you can keep off it entirely, that would be best. And, if you have to drink, please no more than two units a day.'

Then, smoking. I know how few of you smoke these days. But this might be the opportunity to give it up. If you *really* can't, please, please no more than five a day. And no prescription drugs, unless you get our advice.

And needless to say, what we called street drugs like pot are a big no no. Unfortunately, and despite our best efforts, we occasionally discover these drugs have been brought in, God knows how, or even grown here. Do *not* be tempted.'

It's important that you realise that the nutritional status of *both* partners, if you know the identity of the partner prior to conception, can affect every single aspect of fertility and pre-natal health. A good diet full of the right nutrients is so important, not only to your fertility, but to the pregnancy that follows too. Getting your diet and lifestyle working in harmony with your body, rather than against it, can really make a difference.

But it's often not just a case of eating well generally; the specifics can matter too. Iron, for example – found in foods like dried apricots, vegetables and beans – has been shown to be particularly important for fertility. And meat, of course. Inadequate levels of what we call 'antioxidants' can also impair fertility by resulting in DNA damage to both the egg and the sperm. If your diet contains too many of what we call 'environmental endocrine-disrupting chemicals' – trans-fats, refined sugars or excess additives – or if it's depleted in nutrients, this can significantly affect your fertility too. I'll expand on all that a little bit later.

Each partner's nutritional status can be extremely important to the prospects for conception and pregnancy. Anyone trying to conceive should think about having a three-month nutritional 'preparation' period. This is approximately the time it takes for the follicles to develop and to release an egg at ovulation. Whilst a woman can't make any more eggs, the environment in which the egg develops will be crucial to its quality.

Now, on to the subject of weight. We know that weight problems are a risk for infertility, IVF failure, and miscarriage as well as problems in pregnancy generally. But, being underweight can also affect your health and fertility – just as much as being overweight. Even small changes in body weight may be associated with alterations in the menstrual cycle and with adverse affects on a woman's ability to conceive. The quality of your oestrogen also depends on how much body fat you have. Looking around the room, I think most of you look healthy enough in that department.

And as for the sperm you'll be given, you can be sure that it's been thoroughly checked and will be from the same ethnic group as you. And if you have a preference, say for fair or dark-haired children to look more like you, you may well be accommodated. Most of it's coming, as you know from donors. But, if you *do* have a natural partner, a piece of advice.' She smiled at her audience.

'Tell him to keep his balls cool!'

Massachusetts Haven
Patrick O'Connor and his wife Mary were proud of being Irish. In the old days, they had marched in the Boston 'Saint Patrick's Day' parade and once, unlike so many fervent Irish-Americans, they had actually visited the 'Ould Country'. Both the O'Connors and the O'Neills used to have large families and it had not been difficult for the scout to persuade them to come to the Haven and have children.

That morning Mary had noticed that Pat was looking worried.

'What's up, Pat?'

'Oi've been thinking, ever since we left Boston – and especially when we got to this place.'

'Well, what?'

'Oi'm sort of not happy about you having a baby, you know, without me. With another man's, what's it called, sperm.'

Mary stared at him, suddenly irritated. They had come all this way, made this huge commitment and now Pat was getting cold feet. It was too much. She leaned forward.

'Have we *not* been Catholics all our lives?'

'Yes, sure.'

'And haven't we *talked* about the Blessed Virgin Mary and the baby Jaysus?'

'To be sure.'

'And haven't we *always* been told that Joseph wasn't the father?'

'Oi suppose so.'

'And that somehow God was the Dad? On the word of some angel? Well, *tink* about it. How'd the *hell* did that happen?'

'Oi dunno.'

'There you go. Now, My name's Mary – and *I'm* a virgin. And *Oi'd* like to have a baby, if you don't mind. This is the equivalent.'

Pat nodded glumly, wondering if Michael's bar had at last managed to create some decent Guinness.

Hope Haven, Montana

Jack looked up from his homework while his mother started laying the table for supper.

'Mummy, who's my *real* Daddy?'

It came like a thunderbolt. Monica was shocked. This was a moment she had put off for years.

'Well, Daddy of course! Joe, my husband! He's your ....'

Jack interrupted. 'He's not my *real* Daddy. Someone at school said none of us had real Daddies. He said we all came from a bottle or something.'

Monica had rehearsed this moment for years, but was suddenly stumped for what to say to her seven-year-old son. She knew she should have explained it all a lot earlier, exactly as the clinic had advised her to do, but there was never the right moment. Well, she would have to explain now.

She pulled up a chair beside him, her brain racing, and put her hand on his, desperately thinking how best to explain what artificial insemination was to a sensitive seven-year-old, and why no-one who gave birth at the Havens was allowed to know the identity of the father. What a dreadful thing to have to do.

Ten minutes later, having struggled through some kind of feeble explanation, she was hugely relieved to hear her husband turning the key in the lock and coming into the kitchen.

'Hi, both!'

'Hi,' replied Jack, barely looking up.

Monica noticed with a great wave of sadness that he didn't say 'Hi, Dad!' as he always had before, and didn't jump up as usual and give his father a hug, instantly burying himself in his homework again.

'You okay, son?'

Jack didn't answer.

Mumbai, India

Indra Patel was once again luxuriating in the wonderful pleasure of having a seat on the train going to work.

India's population had dropped by nearly half over the last eighteen years, Mumbai's by more, and millions of jobs had dried up, so the terrifying days of clinging on to the outside of a jam-packed commuter train – or even standing on the roof watching out for bridges – was a thing of the past. A shocking number of people used to be killed, two or three every single day.

What a nightmare it used to be, getting to work and back. Once Mumbai's magnificent main station had been an elegant symbol of the British Raj, serving a few privileged passengers and shipping out precious cotton from the port that used to be Bombay. But by the twenty first century it had become the impossibly crowded Chhatrapati Shivaji Terminus, or 'CST' to the locals. And the hard-pressed management had another expression for the mass of seething morning and evening commuters: 'Super Dense Crush Load', with hundreds of trains crammed with 5,000 people, inside and out. Five and a half million people all trying to get to work at the same time.

'Push or be pushed'– there was nothing else for it, with trains leaving after just thirty seconds. When he had managed to get aboard, Indra remembered being squeezed like a tube of toothpaste by the tightly- packed throngs, in boiling carriages with feeble fans where temperatures often soared to forty degrees. Any fresh air was a precious commodity; that's why so many people hung out of the doors despite the obvious danger. And it was just as bad for pregnant women assigned to the so-called 'Disabled' carriages. There was no extra room there, and sometimes pregnant women, as his wife had told him, vomited in the heat. At least there were no more pregnant women to suffer that daily hell any more.

Now, reading his newspaper and sitting comfortably on his way to Mumbai, he reflected that despite all the horrors, certain blessings had come out of the nightmare.

It was sad that he and Rahanna had never been able to have children, but at least she had stayed with him as many wives hadn't. And, as one of India's army of female doctors, she would never be out of work – even with the reducing population.

He looked back on the time when India's female doctors frequently retired immediately on graduation from medical school to get married and have children, wasting their years of precious training. It had led to furious debate two decades ago as the Indian government considered whether to restrict the amount of places for women in medical training, or make them pay the cost back if they then opted out. It had not come to that, but it had been a very close thing. The newly qualified female doctors had all too plainly been using their enhanced social status just to attract a husband.

But all that was a thing of the past, as was the pitiful sight of child beggars and child sex workers in the street, or crowded into the thousands of wretched shacks and slum buildings that used to line the railway on his way to work. And it was in many ways a blessing that Mumbai's population had been so drastically reduced, down from seventeen million to less than half of that. So many millions in those days had been crammed into illegal slums. Now, no children meant no slum children, no child prostitutes and no infant beggars barely four or five years old roaming the streets every day and sleeping rough at night. At least a tiny bit of good had come out of all this.

There were benefits to be had, even in this world of unimaginable horror, and he and Rahanna had much to be thankful for. Good health. A small, but comfortable apartment. A happy marriage, despite the lack of sex. Parents still alive, who had long since stopped bemoaning the lack of grandchildren as they used to. Enough money. And, of course, the simple pleasure of a seat on the journey to work.

The Times of India that he had bought before boarding the train at Mulund had a leading story about the imminent peace talks with Pakistan. Apparently, both sides now realised that it was no longer worth quarrelling over Kashmir. What a relief, thought Indra. He would have to remember to watch the news with Rahanna tonight. Once again he reflected on the blessings he and Rahanna still had – rather more than a train seat when commuting.

CHAPTER EIGHTEEN

Jacksonville Haven, Florida

It was early evening on a Saturday night at the Haven in Florida. Susan Willis, a middle-aged piano teacher, was sitting alone in the Roman Catholic Church, desperately needing to feel she had a drop of faith in God left. It was increasingly difficult to believe in a divine presence who apparently could condone such a disaster for the human race, and not just for the childless and frightened populations outside the Haven. Being confined for years in what was, in fact, no bigger than a small town of around twenty five thousand people, she, like many of its inhabitants and most of her friends and neighbours, found it a daily struggle to keep positive – however much they reminded themselves that this and other Havens were the last hope for humanity to survive.

Sometimes, indeed, most times now, it was like living through a nightmare from which one would never wake up, even though inhabitants of the Haven were constantly reminded how privileged they were compared with people in the outside world. And It was even worse for the young, she thought, even though none of them had ever seen the outside world, so were far less able to make comparisons. But they still had access to books, films and DVDs that would tell them what they were missing – above all, the almost unimaginable freedoms denied to them on a daily basis in such a confined environment.

More and more of her piano teaching lessons were now taken up by answering endless questions from children – and many teenagers – desperate to know what life was like beyond the strictly guarded perimeter of the Haven, rather than teaching the works of the great composers.

'What was it like to ride a horse?' 'To go camping?' 'To climb a tree?' 'To swim in the sea?' 'To fly in an aeroplane?' 'To go hunting, fishing or shooting?' 'To go to a baseball or football match?' 'What was Miami like?' 'What was Disneyland like?' 'And New York? Were the buildings *really* as tall as that?' 'Do you have any photographs we could see?'

She always had to be careful how she replied, not making the outside world sound too exciting or glamorous, and often pretending that it wasn't – for the

134

most part – that different from life inside the Haven. And she herself often felt as trapped as they did, despite the admirably concerted efforts of those in charge to make daily life as normal and fulfilling as it possibly could be.

She had sometimes even wondered whether it would have been better for the kids in the Haven never to have been born. But she mustn't think that, she scolded herself. That was the whole reason for the Haven's very existence, to spawn future generations, to keep the world population alive, whatever it took to do that. And that's why she was here too, to help that to happen. But what a heavy moral burden that was, or as she sometimes thought, an immoral one. Was it right to bring up children in what was, in effect, captivity? And what kind of adults would that make them? Would God condone this place and her reasons for coming here? She had thought so at first, but now, after all these years, she was increasingly unsure. Perhaps, sitting here in the church, she would find some answers, some comfort.

It was a relief to be by herself sitting in the dim light, inconspicuous. The priest, Father Michael, had asked her if she would like to talk to him or take Confession, but she had politely declined, adding that she might welcome both in the near future. She had often confessed to herself privately that she had deep and growing reservations about the Haven – far, far more than she ever had initially. And it would be better, perhaps, to confess them to God, rather than just to herself. But that could wait.

Now, reflecting on all that had happened over the last eighteen years here, she suddenly thought about the extraordinary and enduring faith of the Holocaust survivors. How would they have gone through so much, yet still held on so strongly to their beliefs? Had they somehow thought that God was divorced from all the horrors around them? Was the need for a divinity so powerful that no suffering could shake their faith? Susan had had several Jewish friends back in Miami, and had made several more in the Haven since, but she had never broached the subject with them, largely because they had never broached the subject themselves. And she somehow didn't want to be the first to bring it up.

Perhaps most humans simply needed a God, she thought. Father Michael had told her that church attendances were surprisingly high in the Havens, and for those in all faiths; probably not that surprising for Catholic, Muslim and Jewish believers she felt, but maybe more so for followers of other beliefs. Perhaps the crisis element of being in a Haven at all helped to explain that. Or was it that more and more people simply wanted to give thanks for a chance to have a family? Certainly the population of children was growing rapidly. The aim of the Haven was clearly being accomplished.

Her thoughts turned to her family back in Miami, as they so often did. And she tried to imagine what they were all up to. It was so hard *not* knowing. That had been the biggest sacrifice since coming here, and perhaps one to which she should have paid far more attention from the start. Were her parents still alive, she wondered? And if they were, would they ever really forgive her for coming, despite the considerable compensation they would have been paid for their silence? She comforted herself with the knowledge that her large and strictly Catholic family would be sure to rally round. But how had *their* silence been guaranteed? And had anyone spoken? And if they had, what had happened to them if they had been discovered? In the end, had she made a terrible mistake? And if so, should she now pray for forgiveness – from them and from God? If only the Almighty could give her some sign, however tiny, that she had made the right moral decision.

Suddenly she recognized the unmistakable opening bars of Handel's Messiah flooding from the church organ. She had not noticed the organist coming in, presumably to practise before the busy Sunday service tomorrow. And nor, certainly, had he noticed her, a tiny and unobtrusive figure huddled in the dim light at the other end of the church. She knew there was another door behind the altar, and he had obviously come in that way, not spotting her, or choosing not to disturb her contemplations.

Was that glorious music somehow a message from God? No. Her faith in the Almighty did not run to that, but it was nevertheless a huge comfort to sit there listening, while pondering – yet again – her reasons for being in the Haven. Not to have children, that had never been her intention, but to bring the comfort of music to a deeply troubled environment, and above all, to bring a sense of purpose to her life.

Two hours later, at last, feeling stronger and more able to cope, she slipped out quietly and back to what she now felt was a less disturbing place – at least for now.

High above the church door was a banner with those all too familiar words; 'YOU ARE THE FUTURE', seen everywhere in the Haven. For the umpteenth time, Susan fervently hoped that it was true.

Hope Haven, Montana

'Well, you were right to ask me to do another survey.'

Professor Bob Lister was a veteran market research analyst. Since leaving Kansas City, he had spent a lifetime telling corporations what the public really thought of them and their products, and the rest of the time telling politicians what the voters thought of them and their policies.

In the 'outside world' not much of that was needed now, but in the Havens it most certainly was. The scouts for the Havens had been able to recruit him to visit them specifically to use his skills in tracking the moods and anxieties among the inhabitants. He was addressing the Board of Management of Hope Haven, about twenty men and women. The results of his work were projected on a screen behind him.

'We interviewed about 2,000 people, nearly eight per cent of the Haven's population. That's a high sample and gives us a pretty accurate take on what is happening.'

He turned to look at the screen.

'As you can see, morale – or the level of general contentedness – has slipped over the year. 80% going down to 65%. But, as before, this picture varies a lot between men and women. 85% of women are reasonably content, but only 45% of men are – disturbing to say the least.'

Allowing his audience a little time to take in the figures, he turned back to face them.

'What we are seeing is logical enough. The women are happier because they feel they're fulfilling themselves – their destiny, so to speak – at least those with children.

By contrast, with men we have a problem. Many of them left well-paid and active jobs back in the outside world to come here and be the partners of the women who are fulfilling their role and ambition of becoming mothers. Some of these men clearly feel that they have been reduced to mere house-husbands. There are only a tiny number of natural fathers here. Nearly all the others are watching their wives or partners bearing and bringing up the child of another man. A difficult situation for anyone. If they themselves have no real work, unsurprisingly they become bored, and more worryingly, bitter about the situation.

Many have joined the construction teams even if not very qualified, just to get out of the house, have something to do and find some comradeship. And there are other deep misgivings.

Let me illustrate them with some audio clips – anonymous, of course.'

'Not enough interesting to do.'

'No proper sunshine.'

'It's too prissy. Nanny state, especially with all that stuff about not drinking much.'

'Like being back at school.'

'Like a prison.'

'No gardens, no real green space.'

'Unnatural, cooped up.'

'Like living through a bad dream.'

'Too many rules.'

'I miss not being able to watch sport.'

'The food's boring. Like the mess-deck on an aircraft-carrier. What about some decent Mexican or Chinese?'

'I don't believe in aliens. I'm beginning to think it may all be something of a trick.'

'We can't ever leave, even if we wanted to. I almost *want* the bastards to invade so we can get out of here.'

'Seemed a good idea at the time, now it's boring.'

He switched off the recorder and looked around at the group.

'All a bit worrying, you have to admit. And I'm sure you can draw some conclusions and take relevant action, although some of the problems are, of course, intractable due to the nature of the situation.

However, I'd like to draw your attention to some possible good news. Many of these interviews were recorded a few weeks ago. Since then something significant has happened. The first intakes of recruits have just been inducted, and are starting to be trained. That means many of our military men have gone back to their old work – in drill instruction, weapon-training and, very soon, tactics. They are notably happier. And so are the radio people and mechanics. Very clearly, Haven people need a sense of purpose, other than furthering the population.

But overall, we'll have to admit that it won't get a lot better until it gets worse. Rather like America after the Crash and during the Depression. It only really got better – if I can use the word 'better', when the Japs attacked at Pearl Harbor and we geared up for war.'

Siberia, Russia

Marina Krupski felt devastated and lost, listening to the fertility nurse.

'We're really, really sorry. I wish I didn't have to tell you this, but I'm afraid you won't ever be able to have children.' She paused. This was always the most difficult part of her job. 'It's complicated to explain, but you have something called 'endometriosis', which the doctors tried as hard as they could to cure through surgery. Sadly, it didn't work.' She paused again, coming to the hardest part. 'And I'm afraid there's absolutely nothing more we can do.'

Marina, only twenty-three years old, started to cry, and for several moments that was the only sound in the room. At last her husband Ivan spoke, 'So does that mean we can leave, you know, to the outside? Well, if my wife isn't going to have children, surely there's no point staying here.'

'I'm afraid not, Sergeant Krupski,' said the nurse, a little less kindly. 'Nobody who has been chosen, who has actually been *privileged* to come here is allowed to leave. You were told that at the start. The risks are far too great if a whisper of our existence gets out.' She paused. 'I can't leave either, by the way. None of us can.'

'But we wouldn't talk,' said Ivan.'

'Perhaps not, but sadly that won't change anything. It would be almost impossible not to tell someone in the outside world. Too much of a burden to carry. A little too much vodka, and it would be out.'

She smiled at them, trying to be kind. 'It's best not to think about it, or even talk about it. I really wish it had been different for you.'

But Marina and Ivan *did* talk about it, and way into the night.

'I just can't face it it,' sobbed Marina. Ivan stroked her hand. 'I really miss St Petersburg, my family, my sister, the kids and all the others. Terribly. And now we can't even have our own children.' She looked at Ivan in the early morning light, tears streaming down her face. 'What's the point of being here now? What shall I do? Look at all the other mothers, as I get older and older?'

She burst into another wave of tears.

Ivan felt utterly helpless. 'Don't worry, I'll think of something.'

*   *   *

Only a few days later he did just that, discovering that their friends, Ludmila and Sergeant Vasily Markov, were in exactly the same situation – with no possibility of children, and now trapped, like they were, into a fruitless existence without even the comfort of their extended families. Perhaps, when volunteering, all of them should have paid far more attention to what their officers had told them, Vasily thought ruefully. But the possibility of being able to have kids had blinded them to any other reservations.

Ivan had suddenly and excitedly revealed to Vasily that he had spotted a hole in the fence, just south of the mine entrance, and, better still, out of line from the CCTV cameras. Obviously, security was not all that it had been cracked up to be. Vasily's brain started racing. 'It's now or never', he thought, with a sudden rush of excitement. It was summer, and the snow had gone. It was reasonably warm, with plenty of vegetation and underbrush to hide in on the steppe stretching away from the old mine.

One night, two weeks later, the four of them packed food and water and some scant belongings into rucksacks, and just after midnight, scrambled through the wire. They set off, part elated, part terrified, wondering where, and if, they could find any transport. Where the hell were they, anyway? And would the Haven tokens work as money? After so many years, so many questions lay unanswered. They trudged on into the early light, heads bowed.

'HALT!'

A loudspeaker suddenly echoed across the plain, stopping the four of them in their tracks. Two hundred metres away, standing up in a green UAZ jeep, was an imposing figure in army uniform. And he was surrounded by armed men. The little group stopped and huddled together. Three vehicles, two jeeps and a truck, then roared up and stopped in a cloud of swirling dust.

'You were warned, all of you, *well* warned, at the very beginning – and many times since – that you could not leave. Did you not understand?' shouted the burly, red-faced officer. For several seconds nobody spoke.

'Yes, but we're desperate to see our families,' cried Marina.

'Maybe.' said the officer. 'But you were warned, not once, but, as I said, many, many times.' He took a deep breath and exhaled. 'I'm sorry.' And then he nodded to his men.

A brief clatter of gunfire echoed across the steppe.

Then down a ramp from the tailgate of the truck trundled a little digger on caterpillar tracks. It made short work of digging a pit in the soft sandy soil.

Colonel Vladimir Petrov lit a cigarette. This was the hardest and most agonising part of his job and he had to steel himself to do it. But, he reminded himself – and not for the first time – that it had to be done. It was the only way of saving the world.

Some of his soldiers were equally appalled and sickened by what they had to do. They had families in the outside world too. No-one spoke.

The plain fell eerily silent again.

Hope Haven, Montana

For Josh Jensen, submarine days seemed two centuries ago, not two decades. So much had happened since those momentous days. And those first few weeks in the Haven.

He remembered *those* quite fondly. Apart from the rather undignified sessions at the Clinic, he did have rather a good time with the girls. But, after a while, it palled. He began to understand the feelings behind that old complaint from women 'You only want me for my body.' But he had been glad to do his duty, although after a few years he had began to look hard at children to see if there was any resemblance.

But then he had met Carmen Sanchez, a dark-eyed beauty whose grandparents had escaped to Florida from Castro's Cuba in the 1970s. He had decided that he wanted her to be his wife and the mother of his children. And not surprisingly, he had not only lost interest in other girls, he had lost interest in fathering anyone else's. As he had been mustered out of the US Navy (there not being much call for a navy in the Haven), he was now a civilian mechanic working on the heating and ventilation of the Haven, and so no longer under naval discipline. The people in the Board of Management were very understanding about his opinions. Indeed, they admitted that they had several of the former submariners feeling the same way.

Now Josh had two children, a boy and a girl. And his son, Juan, was soon to leave his military school and join the Army proper. The boy was nervous about it, but also looking forward to a man's world where he could play the role he had been chosen for. Unlike so many men the Haven, Josh Jensen was glad he had come.

Hampshire, England

Sally-Jane, Susan, Elizabeth and David – all in their forties – had driven to their mother's house in the New Forest, a leafy part of Southern England, three days after attending her funeral. Having sorted out her financial arrangements, she had made a most unusual request in her will made many years ago. There would be a stopwatch on the dining room table, and she wished each of them to go through every room, taking it in turns to choose, and in just one minute, any item of furniture they wanted – and then give all the rest to charity.

But which of them, they were all thinking, wanted any of it? None of them had large homes, as none of them had families. And if they were to be among the last generations on earth, who else would want it after their deaths? All of them were secretly of the opinion that they should get rid of everything right now, but not wishing to say that out loud in deference to their Mum.

It was all so sad; historic furniture that had survived centuries, but soon – like humans – would turn to dust. A Queen Anne desk, a fine Italian credenza, a Steinway piano, beautiful card tables and crystal glass decanters and silverware embossed with the family crest. All of it doomed like they were, out of place in today's circumstances as well as being painful reminders of a glorious past.

At last with all the furniture divided up, they had got to the last items; the piles of boxes from the attic to sort through. But once again, who wanted any of the photos and letters inside them? Black and white photos – many faded with age – of a world gone by, sharply reminding them of the crueller and greyer modern one; romantic shots of holidays on some foreign beach, of dances and parties with other unknown happy couples – and all in romantic poses together. And worst of all, at christenings, holding babes in arms. A world gone by.

Dutifully, David was sorting them into piles of four for each of them to take home, but increasingly aware there was a downbeat feeling hovering over them in the process that somehow went way beyond their grief at their mother's death. It was as if, on top of that, they were now grieving for a world gone by, and a new one in which possessions and mementoes meant so little – nothing more than depressing reminders of happier times.

And all of it was a tiny microcosm of what was in the world's museums and art galleries, all destined to become dust, as if all artistic endeavour through the centuries had become pointless. It was hardly surprising that nobody wanted to visit museums and galleries and great libraries any more; all depressingly redundant. Out of tune with reality.

David suddenly broke the silence. 'Does anybody actually *want* any of this?

With all four of them never married, childless, and with all of them never having experienced the romantic love in those photos, nobody spoke. But each implicitly knew what the others were thinking.

'It might be better to burn them,' said David.

Nobody disagreed.

CHAPTER NINETEEN

Miss Porter's School, Connecticut

Judy was wondering what it was like to have a man. And wondering what it was like to have full sex. Would she ever experience that? There was no good news about the worldwide infertility crisis, nor even a glimmer of a breakthrough. And sex lessons in the school had been temporarily cancelled because it made the girls feel depressed. All she could ever find out about sex was on the internet, and would she and her girlfriends ever know what it was really like?

At least boys weren't the bullies they used to be. It was all to easy to bully them back, and they knew that. These day most of them kept to themselves or moved around in sultry gangs avoiding the girls. She was glad the High School Prom had been cancelled 'because of the world crisis.' What was the point of all that primping and dressing up, for a boy that didn't give a damn for what you looked like? And didn't even feel a flicker of desire?

And what was the point of having boyfriends at all, if, on top of having no testosterone, they weren't remotely interested in you, only themselves and their problems.

She wondered how many other girls in the dormitory had given up. What a world, and one that in spite of all the fantastic science advances, didn't have a clue on what had happened.

Would it ever?

London

Tim Taylor was making the usual weekend run to the waste re-cycling centre. It was amazing the amount of rubbish that could pile up in a week with four children, far more than the refuse men would take away. And things were even more messy while they were excavating in the garden to make a separate underground bedroom for their eldest, John, now sixteen and desperate for more space and privacy from his three younger sisters.

It was so sad for John – now growing into a fine young man, but another one who'd never be able to lead a normal life or father children of his own. And it would be equally sad for his three small girls, now all too young to understand what had happened. He would have to tell them in a few years time, but in the meantime it was hard to see them display the first signs of coquettishness and play with things like dolls and know that they would never be mothers themselves. Not unless they had artificial insemination, and how long would that last? Semen had probably run out already.

He tried not to think too much about the future on the way to the waste centre, although it was almost impossible not to. Too many reminders at every turn. Even the country music he was playing on his car radio was depressing – all about 'lurve' and human relationships. It was suddenly a thing of the past. Redundant, as was most of his Pop and Country DVD collection. Almost all of it had some kind of sex or love theme, and the shelves of them at home were beginning to gather dust.

All along the route to Mortlake, shops were boarded up – even more than he'd noticed last time. Obviously people just didn't want or need certain things any more. 'Tiaras' the bridal shop where his wife Susie had bought her wedding dress eighteen years ago seemed to be the latest victim. Tim wasn't surprised.

Without sex, far fewer men would want to get married, and probably far less women too.

The waste centre, always busy, was even more so than usual, and he quickly realised why. Queues of people were chucking things out that they wouldn't need any longer – anything from cots and baby clothes they'd been keeping for future offspring to piles of magazines including the now redundant *Playboy*. Buggies were everywhere, thrown on the vast heap, along with dozens of double mattresses. Were people even sleeping together any longer? Thank God he and Susie had a close enough relationship to weather all this. Many couples would be less lucky.

He climbed out of the car wearily, parked as close as possible to the massive heap of junk and started to clear the boot, surprised to find a box he had certainly not put in himself. A pretty white circular box, tied with a pink ribbon. Whatever was it? Obviously, something Susie wanted to throw out. Curious, he untied the ribbon and pulled out the christening robe that had been worn by all their four children. He felt a pang of sadness as he stamped on the box to flatten it and tossed it on to the vast pile.

Throwing it up into the mountain of rubbish was almost symbolic. Watching the box soar to the top in a sudden gust of wind was like watching the last remnant of yesterday's world blow away.

Rotherham, England

'Same again, Stan?'

Bill nodded. 'Why change the habit of a lifetime?'

To say that their daily meeting at the ' Jolly Gardeners' pub was a bit of a ritual would be to put it mildly. But the two retired policemen had seen enough unpredictable and violent events in their lives not to be perfectly content with the predictable.

With their beer in front of them, they could put the world to rights – or what was left of it. They were in the garden, so Bill was allowed to smoke.

'Tell you one thing, Stan. At least one good thing's come out of all this.'

'What?'

'Well, none of the crimes that came from sex. Nobody getting raped any more. Nobody grooming under-age girls for sex. No murders related to sex. Less wife beating ...'

'And no paedophiles, either. The Catholic Church hasn't had a scandal in years!'

'Now, now. It wasn't *just* the priests, and you know it.'

'Okay. It was Members of Parliament, peers and other worthy souls.'

Bill laughed and sipped his beer. 'And a good many others.'

'No, seriously, the lack of sex drive has changed all sorts of things. Men hardly ever get into fights any more. And certainly not over women. These days lots of blokes barely talk to them, let alone fight over them. The problem of genital mutilation has gone away. And we've got no honour killings.

And there's no road rage. So little traffic, so nobody gets angry. Come to think of it, Stan, I don't know what the police do these days. No fights, no sex crimes, hardly any traffic accidents, less domestic violence. It must be quite a cushy number.'

'I wonder if we should go back?' Stan joked.

'Nah, don't think they'd have us. Rather elderly Chief Inspectors might have difficulty fitting in. And frankly, with so much less to do, it might be bloody boring.'

'Last one for the road?'

'Don't mind if I do.'

Milwaukee, USA

Seventy-year old Bill looked down at his pride and joy. A superb model 4-6-2 'Pacific' locomotive, 'O' gauge, weighing about five pounds. Made from brass, it had taken him nearly three years to complete, all hand-machined. Now that he had painted it beautifully in old New York Central livery, he thought it was time to take it down to the model railway club and show it to the other members. He knew they would be proud of him, clustering around to admire the little details he had perfected.

He would be the star of the meeting and for some time to come, and it would be nice to be the centre of attention for a while. He missed admirers, especially younger ones.

At least it was a lot safer, he reflected, than his old interest – young girls, and a lot more convenient – being as how he'd lost all interest in sex years ago. And anyway, there were no young girls any more. Thank God there were still old trains, albeit model ones.

He packed the model into a specially padded carrying case, got out his bicycle and peddled off to the Milwaukee Model Railroad Club.

Lourdes, France

While populations around the world were dwindling rapidly, that of Lourdes – an already sprawling city in the foothills of the French Pyrenees – was exploding at a truly remarkable rate. But perhaps it was not that remarkable, with the vast numbers of visitors from all over the world wanting to pray for St. Bernadette's healing powers for a miracle. It used to be only the sick and their families who came here, but now it was everyone, and the city's infrastructure was seriously struggling to cope. As soon as new hotels were finished, more were needed. As soon as a new runway had been added to the airport, another was in the planning stage. The rate of growth was nothing short of a miracle, but how the city's planners were going to be able to cope with even greater numbers could be another one – and one St. Bernadette might not be able to solve.

Sitting in the packed plane to Lourdes, fifty year old Billy Tate was reading the story of Bernadette in a pamphlet the air hostess had handed round to all the passengers. In fact, he already knew the story, but he was finding it interesting to read it again. Apparently, way back in the mid 19th century, young Bernadette had been collecting firewood near a grotto in Lourdes when she saw the first of a series of apparitions of a lady dressed in white, who was to tell her 'Que soy era immaculata conceptiou' – 'I am the immaculate conception.' A bit more of that was certainly needed now, thought Billy to himself.

Reading on, he found out that when news of this spread, the Bishop of Tarbes had set up an enquiry, which in 1862 reported its conclusion. *'We're convinced that the Apparitions are natural and divine, and that, by consequence what Bernadette saw was the Most Blessed Virgin. Our convictions are based on the testimony of Bernadette, but, above all, on the things that have happened here, things that can be nothing other than divine intervention.'*

The Bishop, Billy knew, was referring to the astonishing and apparently miraculous cures that started simultaneously with the teenager's apparitions. People judged to be incurable had been inexplicably healed when they drank the waters from the grotto where Bernadette had first seen her visions. *'Two hundred years later,'* said the leaflet, *'her body can still be seen, in a perfectly preserved state, with only a thin layer of protective wax applied to her face and hands. And people are flocking in greater numbers to see* her, *a figure now long referred to as the sleeping Saint of Navarre.'*

The air hostess stopped beside him with a trolley, interrupting his thoughts, 'Any lunch, sir?' Billy ordered a baguette and a can of lager and went back to the leaflet, thinking that, whatever the truth of the story, there was still no let up in the millions of people – like him – who felt compelled to visit the Good Lady. The sheer weight of numbers, he reflected, might sway Bernadette's heart.

He knew he had been lucky to book a hotel and flights. With the vast amount of would-be visitors, it was getting harder and harder for the airport and the city of Lourdes to accommodate them, and these days everything had to be booked months in advance. His hotel wasn't near her shrine, but close enough if he couldn't get a bus or taxi. And luckily, his arthritis was not playing up. That was something of a miracle in itself – it usually felt worse while flying – but maybe it was more to do with the flight socks that Brenda had begged him to wear.

The next day, having stood in the queue for five hours, he was at last getting near to Bernadette's shrine. As a father of four single sons in their twenties, all unemployed builders, chilmen, and all still living at home, he fervently wanted his prayer answered, albeit, he knew, a selfish one – that his offspring would become fertile, get married and at last move out. It would save his sanity, and that of his wife. Their house back in Lancashire was far too small for the seven of them, and if none of his sons could find a wife and a job and live a normal life, he feared that Brenda and he would go slowly mad.

He knew it was not only Catholics who were turning more and more to religion. His Hindu neighbours had told him they were offering prayers to Shree Krishana. And the mosque down the road was always crowded with Muslim worshippers, all asking Allah for help. One only had to look at the news to see that the same thing was happening all over the world. People flocking in increasingly dangerous numbers to beg their deities for human salvation, sometimes clinging desperately on to their last vestiges of belief. Packed mosques, packed churches, packed synagogues, packed temples, and in India, distressing reports of the death toll on the annual pilgrimage to Varanasi.

At last he was gazing down at the curiously waxen face of Bernadette, praying that it had been worth the journey to see her.

Dublin, Ireland

'Will you marry me?'

Geraldine had dreaded that question for some time, and now it had come she simply couldn't think what to say. She loved Sean. He was such a kind man, in fact a rock, but of course there were problems. And they were likely to get worse. In fact, they were already getting worse although she tried not to talk to him about it, only when she felt she really had to.

It was hard to feel desire that could never be reciprocated, and to live with someone who could never be anything more than a great friend. If she were a lot older it might have been different, she thought. But she was only twenty-two. Of course he tried to please her now, but how long would that last if they were married? Probably not long. And she wouldn't be able to blame him. And nagging would be intolerable for both of them.

'Well?' he said.

She looked into his worried face. Such a youthful face for his age. Two years older than her but looking four years younger, and so impossibly smooth-skinned. She felt a flush of pity, and suddenly knew her answer. Pity was the worst ingredient in a marriage.

But how could she tell him? He would be heart-broken.

'Look, Sean. I need a little more time. Well, it's such a big commitment. And I'm not sure I'm ready to make it.'

'I'm beginning to think you never will,' he said sadly.

Swindon, England

Eighteen years after 'Missile Day', as it was now called, Bill and Anne were watching the ten o'clock news. The government station was called BBC P.O. One, or 'Positive One', in a rather feeble attempt to make people feel jollier. But there was seldom much positive news on it nowadays.

It started with the news that Disneyland had just closed down, due to the lack of children under eighteen. Girl gangs were becoming even more aggressive, and more common worldwide. Walmart had just announced its latest smaller range for 'chilmen', a word that at one time was never supposed to be used in public but was now in common parlance. But it was forbidden in their house, because of their son Nick, born almost nineteen years ago. He was now on his computer upstairs because he found the news so depressing. Or maybe asleep, cuddling his almost furless teddy bear, still his adored comfort companion despite his age.

The news went on to describe the endless out-of-work squatters who had occupied buildings in capital cities. Then it reviewed the number of whales and dolphins being washed up on shore, apparently dead from old age. Surely it couldn't get worse.

In fact, it could. It was Nick's birthday tomorrow, and he hadn't wanted anything. Getting much too old for toys, except for that bear, although he had never shown much interest in them – the model trains, forts and Action Man things his father had bought him when he was younger; utterly uninterested in pop music, and in anything to do with his personal appearance. Money seemed such a boring present, but after much soul-searching, they had decided it was the only thing to do. There was almost nothing you could give to a nineteen year old boy these days that didn't remind him what his life would always be missing.

Bill had nodded off on the sofa, as usual, probably as depressed as she was by the reported string of disasters. After three more news stories – the unemployment rate now 70%, the construction industry in dire straits worldwide, and the fact that three quarters of the Cabinet were now women (a fact that ten years ago she might well have celebrated) Jane decided to go to bed. But not before pouring herself another slug of vodka. She dreaded tomorrow.

Bill had decided to take Nick out to a nearby shooting range with a group of his school friends, but would the boys even be able to hold up the heavy guns? Not all industries had woken up to the fact that everything, almost everything, had to be adapted for this new generation of rather puny boys, constantly embarrassed by what their fathers had once been able to do. If only they'd had a daughter. But she mustn't think that. And from what she'd seen on the news, girls were increasingly showing their ugly sides and it wasn't pleasant to watch. Thank goodness they'd managed to get Nick into an all-boys school. Children, especially girls, could be so cruel these days.

She climbed upstairs and checked on Nick in the bedroom next door. Fast asleep, clutching 'Fatso,' his beloved teddy bear as she expected. Such a child, it wasn't fair. And she couldn't expect any comfort from her husband. He couldn't face the situation any more than she could.

And she was changing, she knew, as much as the world was. Throwing her clothes on to the floor instead of into the laundry basket, she realised that she simply didn't care about certain things any longer. Who cared about a tidy house if the world itself was in such a bloody mess? And who cared if you climbed into a bed without a shower either? Or the day before?

And what did it matter, she thought, as was increasingly happening, if you went to bed alone?

Dallas, Texas

DOGGONE, the now famous American and publicly quoted dog funeral service company, had just reported another record year, and the Chairman, forty-two year old Brewster Cross, was feeling in a really upbeat mood, despite the company's rather grisly line of business, deeply relieved that he had left his stockbroking job in Wall Street six years ago – far too precarious an environment these days. At least his business could only go up for the next decade or so – as long as most dogs lasted, and by then most owners of pedigree dogs bred by AI would no doubt join the clamour for a decent send-off for their pampered pooches. He congratulated himself on having a strict staffing policy, with branches now throughout the U.S. manned by people put through a month of professional grief counselling. His wife Maya had said it was all a crazy idea at the start, but she hardly complained now with a walk-in wardrobe crammed with designer clothes and shoes she would never get around to wearing, not to mention lavish holidays almost anywhere that took her fancy.

He was the first person to understand how much people loved their dogs. After all, his mother had once bred boxers and dachshunds, and even called the females she kept 'her girls' which people always found confusing, thinking she was referring to her three daughters – his sisters, rather than her canine companions.

And why not branch out into cats? Now he was giving that serious thought for the first time. After all, dogs' lives weren't all that long, indeed pathetically short in some cases, like those of high-bred pugs and pekineses and bulldogs. But maybe he would become bored of the business a bit further down the line, and be content to retire comfortably in the country and spend more time with Maya, and the grandchildren they were lucky to have.

Pouring himself a glass of Jack Daniels whiskey, he thought of all his friends who had left the financial sector, many of them now struggling to support themselves – unlike the ones who were now working for him – but not, he suspected that happily. He knew all too well what it was like to admit that you worked for a dog cremation company rather than a high-flying firm in Manhattan. But any job these days was better than no job at all, with so many millions out of work. And he could afford to be generous when it came to salaries.

If only more of them had found a niche like him, he thought, not only giving much-loved pets a dignified ending, but actually arranging a chapel service and cremation with all the frills – a carved wooden coffin, an engraved cross if owners wanted one in the garden outside, and even an urn with the dog's ashes to take home later. It didn't matter that they wouldn't know exactly to which dog those ashes belonged – after all, a number of pets had to be cremated at any one time to make incineration costs worthwhile.

And nor did it matter that the choice of hymns at the services was almost always exactly the same, usually starting with 'All things bright and beautiful, all creatures great and small.' At least he and his staff knew the words of all the favourites off by heart, which meant he didn't have to publish any extra order of service programmes for his people, who looked even more professional into the bargain while singing the words without even glancing at the hymn sheet.

Dogs were becoming rarer, and those disposing of them in the usual way – in the local vets' crematoria after being put down humanely in old age – were becoming rarer too, thanks to DOGGONE. It was as if humans wanted to give their last respects to a dying breed, although many of his customers were able to afford the huge cost of a new pedigree bred by the ever-dwindling supplies of AI. And it was truly amazing what people across the U.S. were now willing to fork out to give a much-loved family pet a decent send-off, in some cases as much as they would have spent on their human loved ones, or shockingly, even more.

Only last week he had attended yet another of his lavish chapel services – as he always tried to if the costs amounted to twenty-five thousand dollars or more – complete with printed order of service programmes for the mourners with a picture of the pooch on the front, more photos dotted around the flower-filled chapel, friends and family recalling fond memories of the pet in the pulpit, and a lavishly festooned coffin – with the dog's lead resting on top. That all cost money, as did the priest, the organist and the funeral cortege of cars to take the mourners there and back.

And training his staff properly didn't come cheap. His professional mourners and coffin bearers had been strictly instructed never to laugh unless dog owners made a funny comment in the pulpit, and to look down at their highly-polished black shoes when listening to any sombre recollections. It was all paying off.

What a mad, mad world Brewster thought to himself. But certainly not a mad line of business these days, and one that could easily go international. And cats were certainly a possibility. He couldn't stand the things himself, but it might keep his wife Maya purring to have even more money pouring in. And, he reflected, most cat owners – exactly like dog owners – could afford to give their pets a decent send-off. After all, meat was getting ever more scarce, and it was extremely expensive feeding a dog or cat at all. Even dry dog and cat food still contained meat ingredients.

In fact, Maya was now dreaming up all sorts of names for a cat funeral sister company, most of them laughably inappropriate, especially 'CATASTROPHE',

'CATAPULT', and even worse, 'CATATONIC'. But now she had suggested 'CATNAP' – and even better, 'PURRFECT SEND OFF.' He could see that last one working.

Not just a pretty face, he thought, even if it cost a bomb to keep it looking twenty years younger.

Nevada Desert, USA

The sun was already up and the desert was already beginning to shimmer in the heat. Sergeant Hank Ledbetter drove his jeep slowly down the line of tanks. There were hundreds of them, parked in neat rows. Except that many of them weren't tanks. They were quite crude rubber and canvas imitations – same size, same colour as a real Abrams, but weighing about 200lb not 68 tons.

Hank's job was to make sure they stayed looking realistic. He had an air pump mounted on his jeep and if one of the replicas was sagging a bit, he would pump it up.

He had no idea why the real tanks were being replaced by these dummies, nor where the real ones were going, usually in batches of ten, twice a week. Who were they hiding this from? The Russians and the Chinese were now reasonably friendly, after all – especially as everyone was in the same awful boat.

He wondered vaguely where the real tanks were going. Probably off to be serviced. There was that huge row back in 2015, when the government wanted to scrap all the tanks 'as surplus to requirements' in the post-Cold War era. But some of the servicing workshops were in places where Senators and Members of Congress needed to show they were keeping jobs. So the tanks were kept and they were serviced and then brought all the way back here. That's real, old-fashioned 'pork-barrel politics' for you, he thought,

Now it was getting hot, so he decided to stop thinking about politics and get back to his base in the shade. A cool hut and a cold beer, that's what he needed.

CHAPTER TWENTY

Falkland Islands, South Atlantic

The Americans think that only the British understand the concept of irony, thought Colonel Jim Smith. And if you wanted to find something ironic, you wouldn't have to go much further than what he was doing right now in the Falkland Islands.

First, there was the big ship. The last time a big ship was there was 1982, with the *Sir Galahad* blazing from the bombs of the Argentine planes. Now they were unloading the *Bristol Swan* on to smaller ships. They were soon going to head for the ports of Rio Grande, Punta Loyola, Mar del Plato and Buenos Aires to deliver desperately needed food and medical supplies, thanks to the generosity of the British Government and British charities.

The British had always quite liked the 'Argies', Jim recalled, and even during the Falklands War. After all, during the century before, Britain was easily the biggest investor in Argentina, even creating a Hurlingham Club and a Harrods store there, as well as a British-built railway system still dotted with English-sounding stations.

Jim Smith certainly counted himself among the British who had forgiven them for their rather hysterical desire to invade 'Las Malvinas' – after all, they *were* half Spanish and half Italian. 'Emotional sort of people', he thought.

In fact, Jim was a real expert on South America, speaking fluent Spanish and adequate Portuguese and married to Juanita, a Peruvian. He had recently travelled all through the continent as part of the Haven programme, under the assumed name of Juan Perez, a Paraguayan businessman. He had been trying to assess the full situation.

It certainly wasn't a pretty picture. Brazil and Venezuela had been devastated by the collapse of the oil price, and Bolivia by that of tin. Argentina had so mismanaged its cattle industry, even when rescued by artificial insemination, that it had seen fit to attack its neighbour Uruguay. It was a war that an Anglo-American force had been obliged to put a stop to. All the countries had falling populations and increasing health problems. The only bright spot, perhaps, was that human encroachment into the vital Amazon rain forest had stopped. There was no point cutting down the forest to create a cattle industry – there was empty land everywhere.

But there was a final, really strange irony that Jim Smith was part of. West Falklands was now a 'Haven' – and one for South Americans – organised by the British!

The problem had started with the Catholic religion. In spite of the Pope's intervention, the South American Cardinals were sufficiently set against artificial insemination to cause a real problem. Because of the secrecy around their locations, even Jim did not know if any Havens had finally been set up in South America, but he suspected that Brazil might have one or more, and maybe some others in the north of the continent.

But he had been part of the planning group that had decided to set up a Haven on West Falkland. Virtually uninhabited and part of a military zone, the island had proved perfect. Even the termination of oil drilling had been a help in keeping the secret.

Then the frequent flights to deliver aid had provided the cover for bringing back families from southern Chile, Argentina, Paraguay and Uruguay. Enough 'Hispanic' sperm from Los Angeles had completed the picture. And, as was often the case, families from a military background had been preferred and Jim had been struck by another irony. He and the team had deliberately chosen the granddaughters of the courageous Argentine pilots who had sunk ships like *Sheffield, Coventry, Ardent* and the *Atlantic Conveyor*. You couldn't get braver stock than that, they had figured.

While the problem of secrecy from the rest of the world might have been solved, there remained the reconnaissance drones above. An old, large whaling station had provided the beginning of the visible buildings, and for extra deception they had parked a disused oil rig nearby off the shore. A massive amount of work had been needed, but the good thing about Havens, he reflected, was that you could start quite small and steadily build them up. The maternity wards were needed first, then the creches, then the kindergartens. Only now were they beginning to need the drill halls and the firing ranges.

Africa

Joe wondered if they would even make it to the airport.

The taxi had turned up on time. But then, just 300 yards from his apartment in a crowded high street, it had run out of petrol. The driver leapt out muttering something to himself, leaving a furious Joe being stared at by a none-too-friendly crowd. Five minutes later the driver struggled back through the throng precariously carrying an old one-gallon peach tin full of petrol, some of which he had sloshed over his clothes. They made it to a filling station, the car reeking of petrol and Joe had then had to give the driver money for fuel, the last straw. Thank goodness he had learned to leave a huge amount of time when catching any flights in Africa.

Joe Ovinga was the local representative of AfricAid, one of the few surviving charities still trying to help the beleaguered continent. And he was on his way to a crucial AfricAid conference in Johannesburg. Looking out of the window and trying to ignore the chattering of his driver, let alone the petrol smell, he was not heartened by what he saw. The road out of town was littered with vehicles – cars, vans and trucks – abandoned either because of lack of fuel, or perhaps because their owners saw no point in driving them any more.

There was little enough money around. Food exports from Africa had stopped because of lack of demand from Europe, the hotels were empty with most of them closed down and the last wildlife safari had been two years ago. Almost all of the interesting animals were dying out.

They passed a food queue in the suburbs. Probably one of our AfricAid ones, Joe thought. The grassy plain outside town was dotted with skeletons – either cattle or maybe zebra and wildebeest. Not a sight to raise the spirits, and nor was it a cheering sound when his driver turned up the radio to the sound of the country's boy band, all eighteen years old, and defiantly calling themselves 'The Chilmen,' reflecting what they were – the last children to be born there and who would never reach puberty. The hit they were singing was, ironically, 'It'll be all right'. No, it won't, thought Joe.

The airport was almost empty, and his flight was only half full. Joe felt it was a miracle that the pilot didn't have to go off to borrow some fuel.

Yet again he was asking himself a key question. He knew *his* country had a 'Haven', hidden deep in the bush. But how many of the other African countries had one? He would probably never know.

Johannesburg, South Africa

The AfricAid conference started at nine in the morning. Most of the delegates were, like Joe, their country's representative of the charity, managing the distribution of the food and medicines on the ground. There were white faces too, from London and New York, the main sources of the money that kept the charity going.

The Chairman was British, Sir Michael Bevan, a man who had devoted himself for decades to the charity, and generally to the cause of Africa. He himself tackled the first item – income.

'Ladies and gentlemen, welcome. Let me first brief you about our funds. I'm afraid to tell you that fundraising has been slower than we had hoped. In spite of our excellent and evocative advertising, which you have all seen, there is no doubt that people in the north are suffering from 'appeal fatigue'. To be blunt, they're beginning to think that they have enough problems of their own without helping a continent that has given them plenty of problems.

And, I have to say, the behaviour of some of the rulers here in the past has not really helped to dispel the conviction that aid to Africa will be wasted, or worse, stolen.' There was a murmur of agreement from the floor rather than dissent. Many of them had struggled with the problem for years.

'However, my friends, we *do* have enough money to fund about 80% of our normal tasks, at least for the next year, so there should be no let-up in our efforts. I would now like to ask Ayo Kipkemoi, from Kenya, to tell us what his sub-committee has distilled from the general economic situation.'

'Thanks, Michael. Well, as you can imagine, since last year's conference things have deteriorated further. Our dependence on providing raw material rather than finished goods for the world has always been a bit of a trap. With the drop in world population and the general decrease in manufacturing and construction, the demand for iron ore and copper ore has collapsed. This affects South Africa, the Congo Democratic Republic, Zambia and Mauritania.

Nobody's hoarding gold any more, bad for South Africa of course, and Zimbabwe. And diamonds are neither being used so much for fashion or in machine tools, bad again for South Africa and Botswana – with thousands of miners out of work and many more drifting back, broke, to their own countries, causing more problems.

Oil, too, is not needed as much, so the price is on the floor. The effect on Nigeria, especially, has been devastating and has caused major unrest. Not just riots, but Boku Haram's thugs have used the crisis and the perceived weakness of central government as an opportunity to revive themselves and resume their murderous activities.

As to exporting food, most staple foods are now, of course, desperately needed at home. Some countries are still earning a little foreign currency. For instance, Ethiopia and Uganda from coffee, and my own country Kenya, from tea, of course. But our cut-flower market to Europe has gone, as has Zimbabwe's. And neither Zimbabwe or South Africa probably ever envisaged that the demand for tobacco would go down so sharply – for falling population reasons, of course.

I can personally vouch for the fall in tourists; many like to combine beach holidays with looking at animals. But we have virtually no interesting animals now, and in the northern hemisphere they've got beaches, empty beaches, galore.

So, a pretty dismal picture economically, and one which isn't going to get better. Most Africans, as the population reduces, are heading back to subsistence existence, I'm afraid. As Sir Michael said, we, and other charities, are needed more than ever.' He sat down, grim-faced.

The next item on the agenda was food. This was presented by Jakob van de Merve, a South African, very well liked and respected in his country, and also by the delegates.

He too provided a bleak picture. Africa had become dangerously dependent on food imports, especially since some countries years ago had forced out their productive white farmers. Even Zimbabwe, which used to export food to four neighbouring countries, was now dependent on food imports. And with the collapse of its own dollar-earning exports, it had little money to pay for anything.

Jakob reported that other countries like the US, France and Britain had helped with the import of live cattle and bull sperm for artificial insemination, and there were now some cattle herds slowly building up on the continent, although some of the cattle breeds were a little strange – American longhorns, for instance, but they might thrive with luck, providing the insect problem didn't get worse.

For coastal countries there were still fish, but with the threat of starvation looming worldwide, both local and foreign boats had begun to recklessly over-fish, and stocks were plummeting. African countries, he said bluntly, might have to defend their waters by force.

Many animals, at least mammals that had once swarmed over the plains of Africa, were dying out, as had their predators. Some rare breeds, bizarrely, had been saved from extinction by artificial insemination with their sperm preserved, thanks to celebrity charities like that of Leonardo di Caprio. But that didn't help the food situation. Nobody had thought to create a sperm bank for antelope, impala, zebra and wildebeest. Why would they?

Apparently, so desperate were some people for meat that they were even shooting the vultures feeding on the last carcasses and even netting the crocodiles in Lake Kariba and in the rivers just to eat them.

Van de Merve concluded by saying that Africans would have to go back to a vegetable staple diet and would need nutrition and diet education as a matter of urgency.

There was nothing in his presentation that surprised the delegates, but it was still all pretty depressing. Even more worrying was Professor Alami's presentation on the health picture.

Ebola had broken out, affecting seven countries so far. The problem was, of course, that unlike the 2014 outbreak, no task force of expert foreigners were now coming to help. Routine health care was also deteriorating – partly because of the shortage of young nurses and doctors. With patients getting older, systems were not working and more and more patients were dying.

Insects, without mammal predators either on the ground or in the air, had built up alarmingly. And the breakdown of mosquito and tsetse fly control meant that malaria and sleeping sickness were becoming a real problem, as was Dengue Fever. Even plague had been detected in parts of Ethiopia.

All this meant that the African population was falling rapidly – and far more quickly than in other parts of the world.

As they broke for lunch, Joe once again thought about the Havens. Did any of these countries have them? Did any of the people here even know about them? And what the hell was going to happen to his beloved continent, once the cradle of all human life?

Bristol, England

Anna picked up the phone.

'Hi'.

Her best friend Judy, obviously calling to make last-minute arrangements for the Glastonbury Festival. Both of them had been looking forward to it for weeks.

'Look, I'm awfully sorry, but I don't think I can come'. A pause. 'Just don't feel up to it.'

'Why?' Anna was hugely disappointed. 'What's wrong – are you ill?'

'No, just feeling really rough. Absolutely awful. Bad time of the month. Much, much worse than usual.'

Anna was amazed. 'Judy, I can't *believe* I'm hearing you! And if I am, you must be the only girl on the planet who's going through all that. For God's sake, Judy, get a life, and for goodness sake ask your doctor to give you Progestogen. I get injections every three months, and I haven't had a period in years. What's the point of them, if none of us will ever conceive?

Look, I'll call you tonight to see if you're any better.'

She slammed down the phone, feeling guilty, but also thoroughly irritated. Who else could she ask at the last moment? Damn!

Moscow

Ivan Baranov knew he was getting old. Every day his body had been reminding him more and more, and the pills were working less and less. It was eighteen years since he had been 'volunteered' at that conference in London for the job of keeping the Havens secret. And he had been sixty then, for goodness sake! For some time he had realised that he must find a successor. The flying was getting him down and increasing his aches and pains, and he was beginning to long for retirement at his dacha outside Moscow.

He had long since decided that his successor should be Russian. It was not just that the hand-over would be more efficient if they both spoke the same language. It was also a question of attitude. They needed someone steeped in the concept of *maskirovka*, but also who was genuinely ruthless. He had been having some trouble with his colleagues, especially the Western ones, about the need to eliminate any chance of leakage of either information or people. With the Chinese he had no problems at all. They had dealt very swiftly with a couple of families who were homesick and who thought that they might escape the claustrophobia of their Haven.

He had drawn up a shortlist, including a promising ex-Stasi guy from East Germany, but he still favoured a Russian. And who better than Vladimir Petrov, the man who had been in charge of the Russian programme and who had put down that salt-mine problem? All very quietly dealt with.

There was a knock on the door.

'Come in, Petrov.'

Washington, D.C.

Ann Hearst had called together a small group of leading scientists to try and assess the biological situation of the world, what kind of future to expect, and how to prepare for it. All of them knew about the Havens and were among the lucky few who were free to come and go to them, and whose families there were able to reproduce.

Professor William Fenton opened the discussion.

'One important thing we've been noting is that global warming, the big threat in the past, has stopped in its tracks and is, in fact, reversing. The reasons are fairly simple. First, the emissions of greenhouse gases have gone right down. The world's population has halved, and economic activity has gone down by more than half. There are far fewer cars and trucks on the road, far fewer factories operating and fewer cattle producing methane gas.

Second, the world's ability to absorb carbon dioxide and the other gases has gone up dramatically. On the one hand, human settlement has retreated. One example – the Brazilian rain forest is taking back land once cleared for agriculture and cattle-raising. Another reason is the steady loss of mammals and the way they ate both seeds and plants. I know there are many left, but sadly, they are all steadily declining.

Within a couple of years after the plumes, you'll remember, we began to lose the smallest ones – mice, voles, shrews. After five years, it was rats, rabbits and hares. A decade later, the deer began to disappear, along with monkeys, wildebeest, zebras, wild pigs, peccaries, tapirs, llamas, kangaroos and warthogs.

And now there are hardly any camels, elephants, giraffes – except for a few in zoos.

With the removal of the grazing of these animals, there has been a huge increase in woodland generally – forest, scrub and jungle – all absorbing carbon dioxide.

From that point of view, I suppose, our limited human population may in some ways have a better world, but it will be far less interesting as far as animals are concerned.

We need to pay attention to the four categories of creatures that are thriving. Let me ask the experts to report. Dr Troughton, over to you to tell us about fish.'

Troughton stood up.

'Well, fish are doing very well. They used to have four types of predator. First, us humans. Even though we desperately need fish for food, fishing activity has actually gone down as the human population has reduced and aged.

Then, of course, all their mammal predators have begun to thin out – seals, dolphins, whales, killer whales and porpoises.

Third, other bigger fish. These have gone up, but not enough to stop a general rise in fish numbers.

Fourth, birds. They are thriving too, but the slight increase in plunging birds like gannets, boobies and pelicans at sea – and kingfishers and heron on land – are not enough to dent the fish population. And eels are doing well, due to the demise of otters and mink.

So, from sardines to sharks, fish are pretty much okay.'

He handed over to Sabine Trott.

'Birds. As we've heard from Alistair, birds are doing very well. In the wild, they've lost many of the predator mammals that used to keep down their numbers by eating their eggs and their young. Creatures like foxes, polecats, mink, racoons, rats and squirrels.

And as for humans, with the demise of their other pets, especially dogs and cats, and the lack of children, there's been a big increase in birds as companions – canaries, budgerigars, goldfinch and parrots.

Pigeon racing has come back as a sport and, if anyone wanted to go shooting grouse there might be plenty of them.

DONOUGH O'BRIEN & LIZ COWLEY

More seriously, birds as food have become ever more important. Chickens mainly, with many kept domestically, for home egg production. But turkeys are useful for their bulk, and geese and duck have become more significant. Even ostrich farms have come back.

We have one serious worry. Although there are fewer pigs for cross-infection, we're anxious that greedy producers will try to churn out too many birds and keep them in poor conditions. An Avian Flu epidemic is the very last thing a hungry world would need. That's a real threat.'

She handed over the podium to Dr Robert Starkey to discuss invertebrates.

'Many people don't think about invertebrates a lot. But we'll have to watch the inevitable huge rise in insects. While they're still being eaten by birds, of course, mammals used to eat many of them. However, we must remember that bats were equally important in eating vast numbers of insects. We've had many problems with increased insects meaning increased disease, especially in Africa, and the lack of control of mosquitoes and tsetse fly has been a major nightmare.

On the plus side, bees in the wild are doing very well because there are no badgers or bears to attack their nests.

Other invertebrates that people don't often think about so much include worms. Earthworms are benefitting from the lack of moles, for instance. Molluscs, like slugs and snails are also doing well due to lack of small mammal predators.'

The final speaker was Alfred Barlow, their reptile specialist.

'The situation for reptiles, I have to report is patchy. The crocodiles and alligators that eat fish are in good shape, like caimans and gharials. But those that relied in the main on mammals are in trouble. Among the snakes, pit vipers such as rattlesnakes, moccasins and bushmasters, which relied on their ability to track small mammals in the dark, are all dying out as their prey dies out.

The big constrictors are also having a bad time. We've even had disturbing reports of humans being crushed and eaten by anacondas and pythons obviously desperate for food.'

After the specialists had finished, a Russian Professor brought up another subject.

'It's also extremely important to point out that certain communities have been very badly affected by the devastation of mammals. I suppose we don't often think of reindeer, except possibly at Christmas. But there's a swathe of territories from Finland to Kamchatka where these animals constitute a vital source of food and transport. The situation in such places is getting serious.

Similarly, the camel is still important for the Bedouin, and all through the Arab world and right into Central Asia. That's another crisis in waiting.

And South America's only transport in the mountains used to be the Llamas, and they've now gone, as have the Alpacas which used to provide food and clothing. Such communities are in real trouble.'

The meeting concluded that the lack of mammals was having major effects on other wildlife and on the landscape of the world, that there were almost certainly threats that they may not have been foreseen, and anything new should be reported at once.

Kostinbrod, Bulgaria

The health inspectors stopped their vehicles outside the vast and tatty building. A scruffily dressed guard stood at the gate in a nondescript uniform, at first surly and belligerent and refusing to let them in. Then, he noticed the police and at last realised who they were. He opened the gate – and promptly ran away. They swept into the parking lot, dismounted and donned masks and gloves, and then cautiously approached the nearest entrance door.

The sight inside appalled them. And the stench! They knew that there were around a million chickens under one roof in this gigantic building, but they did *not* expect half of them to be dead or dying.

Swiftly they sealed off the whole complex and sent teams out to block the roads and set up a quarantine zone about three kilometres out. Then their police colleagues tried to find the owner. Questioning a couple of frightened employees, they discovered that he apparently knew he had a serious Avian Flu outbreak, but had done nothing about it, trying to cover it up – and forcing his staff to do so.

After only a few hours the police traced his big BMW to a house in Sofia, where he was found with his mistress and hauled off to jail.

The clean-up squads eventually disposed of the vast piles of dead chickens, but the flu had spread, and total loss to the Bulgarian poultry population was nearly three million – all the more devastating with the lack of cattle, sheep and pigs for food.

The exhausted Chief Inspector thought about the wider risks.

'Mind you, this is small compared with the huge outbreaks in China and Vietnam. Let's hope it doesn't get even worse.'

CHAPTER TWENTY-ONE

Camp Pendleton, California

Captain Patricia Hearst, USMC, stood at attention in front of her Commanding Officer, Lieutenant Colonel Lewis Puller.

'At ease, Captain.'

Puller then became much less formal. He turned to his Master Gunnery Sergeant, who ran his office. 'Gunny, can you leave us please?'

When he had gone, Puller said 'Sit down, Trish.'

She sat in front of his desk. He leaned forward.

'Now, I have to tell you something completely secret. You are not to breathe a word of it, not a word. Do you understand?'

She nodded.

'You're going to be re-assigned to a place in the Rockies somewhere. Even I am not allowed to know where it is precisely. It's called a Haven, and just after the meteorites eighteen years ago, when all men went infertile, this place and others were set up to create new populations. Apparently they had the sperm and the advanced techniques to make it work.'

Tricia was conscious that she was gaping at him, with her mouth open. She could hardly believe her ears.

'I know that's pretty amazing. But there's more. We think that all that meteorite and plume stuff was no accident. We're under threat. And, you may not believe it – I didn't at first – but the threat is from space, from what we'd call aliens.'

Tricia frowned. 'Seriously, Sir?'

Puller nodded. 'I know it sounds whacky, but I assure you we've had their recon ships under surveillance for years. But we can't let them know we're on to them. That's why we've had to let the world appear to be ageing and dying, and to keep the Havens a total secret.' For a moment, he allowed her visible shock to sink in.

'Now, to explain what your assignment is all about. To have armed forces ready for the worst, we've had Army and Marine detachments in these Havens for a long time, with instructors who are now, of course, in their fifties. But the children of the first mothers are now mature, and the new Marines and their officers and non-coms need much more modern training from the outside. So we want you to go there with a small team as Training Officer. You'll be one of the few people who can go in and come out again. And we may need you to visit the other ones.

So, you'll leave in a week. That okay with you?' He was pleased to see Tricia nod, but only slowly. Of course, it was a massive shock to take in.

'By the way, let me ask you something. Before just now, had you ever heard about the Havens?'

'No, never.'

'Not from your mother?'

Tricia looked puzzled.

'No, why should I?'

'Because she invented them. She's pretty well in charge of them.'

It came like a thunderbolt. Her Mom running the Havens? So that's why her mother had been travelling so much, and never seemed to be around, sometimes out of communication for weeks at a time. Why had she never said? Obviously not allowed to. It must have been an impossible burden. Unimaginable. But it explained so much.

'She never mentioned that to me, Sir. I always thought she was a geneticist, trying to help the food problem. That's what she always said.'

'Well, I must say I have to commend her security. It's only now that I've been able to tell you. And only now that she can.'

He stood up and shook her hand.

'Dismiss, and good luck. And, by the way, you might meet some nice young men!'

Tricia hardly heard his last remark. She was still in shock.

Officers' Mess, Hope Haven

'Hi. I'm Tim, Tim Harvey.'

The young officer who had sat down at the bar was very big and tall. He wore the silver bar of a full Lieutenant on his collar, but was probably a little younger than her.

'Tricia Hearst.' She shook his hand.

'Have you just got here?' he asked. She obviously had, he thought, because he had not seen this attractive Captain before, nor anyone bronzed by the sun – the real sun – for ages.

'Yep, just come from the outside, California. I've been assigned as Training Officer, new weapons and tactics and so on. Have you been here long?'

'All my life. I was one of the first to be born here. From a Corps family too. My father is one of the old instructors. He's finding it a bit tough now, at his age. By the way, would you like a drink?'

Tricia realised that Tim was not a 'chilman'. He would be like a normal man. With a shock she also realised that she had never actually met one. At twenty-six, she was something very old-fashioned – a virgin – like all her friends. And to whom any men other than chilmen were excessively rare.

She accepted a Coors and looked at him with ever more interest. He was very good-looking, seemed very polite, amusing and pleasant. And he was *normal*. She literally felt her body stir.

As they chatted, they seemed to have a lot in common and an instant rapport. But she had two vague worries. Surely this guy must be very in demand with all the girls around here? And if Tricia was somehow going to be in command of him as a senior officer, any flirtation would be against all the rules.

But one worry went away at once. He revealed he was in charge of the Motor Pool, the Marines' vehicles, and would not be part of her infantry training courses.

He looked at her, holding eye contact for several seconds. Much longer than one would normally do with a stranger.

'Trish, would you like to have dinner?'

Maybe the second worry was going away.

Washington, D.C.

Charles Koenig had taken the opportunity to visit his old mother in Washington – ninety now, and living quite happily in her home with a permanent carer. At least that was a relief.

It was after supper that he got a call on his cellphone.

'General, Sir. We've just had a call from the Keck Observatory in Hawaii. They regularly sweep their sector of the sky for us with infra-red to see if there's any change.'

'Sure, I know.'

'Well, sir, they say that the three drones that disappeared, apparently malfunctioned, have been replaced. And in exactly the same position in the sky.'

Koenig exhaled a breath. 'Well, I'll be *damned!*'

'I knew you'd want us to check to see if the other two drones have been replaced too. But we'll have to wait a few hours for the earth to rotate for the Dome C and Tenerife observatories to have a look.'

Koenig thought quickly.

'Excellent, Munro. And ask them all to look for something bigger, further away in space. There has to be some kind of mother ship. It may have come and gone, but they may catch a glimpse of it. Report as soon as you can, please.'

Well, well, he mused. The bastards can count. And they're methodical. 'Never underestimate your enemy'– he reminded himself, one of the oldest rules in warfare.

PART THREE

CHAPTER TWENTY-TWO

Munich, Germany

Petra knew that she had been right all along. That strange woman – she had given her the code-name 'Ingrid' – had surfaced again. But this time she had made contact by dropping an envelope through the letterbox at the office of *Schwabinger Beobachter*.

They had met just once, but that was enough. 'Ingrid' had told Petra how she had been recruited by a 'scout', how she had given up her life to go to a Haven because she desperately wanted children, revealing exactly where it was located and how it was disguised. 'Ingrid' then revealed that she had failed in her attempts to conceive a child, and had then been horrified to realise that she could not leave the place. Years then stretched away working as a teacher to other people's children. Every month that passed she missed her family and friends in Munich more and more.

At long last she had managed to escape and was now living with an old friend outside the city. She told Petra that she literally feared for her life, and that there were some kind of security people searching for her.

Petra had interrupted, 'I've met the Nazi bastards.' She agreed never to reveal 'Ingrid's' real name or location, but promised that she would blow the story soon. The very idea of such a place deeply offended her liberal upbringing, and she was now made even more determined by the high-handed attitude of those men who had visited her. She knew, too, that they had later tried to ruin her. Her brewing friends at Lowenbrau and Hofbrauhaus had been visited too, and told to withdraw their advertising from the paper. But they were such good friends that they had agreed to halt their advertising for a while while sending her a secret subsidy. So her newspaper had just about managed to keep going.

Petra had indeed driven up the autobahn with Hans and turned off to where 'Ingrid' had said the Haven was. She could not get really close to the old mine in the forest, but they saw enough to convince her that 'Ingrid' had been telling the truth. And with a long lens, Hans had photographed it too.

She wrote up the story herself, on her own PC. She was sure that those Stasi, Gestapo bastards wouldn't touch her once the story blew.

Paris, France

'It can't go on.'

Ann had needed every last drop of courage to admit this to the annual meeting of world leaders, which in rotation was being held in Les Invalides in Paris.

'The purpose of the Havens and the secrecy about them has to come to an end. They were our only hope twenty-three years ago, but some vitally important things have changed. Let me list them. First, the world situation is getting worse and worse. As all of us know, morale is at rock bottom. And why wouldn't it be? The riots and other disturbances round the world are just the tip of the iceberg.

Second, morale *inside* the Havens is slipping, or to be more precise, plummeting. Once the initial excitement of being the only people to have children wore off and then the challenge of bringing them up lost its novelty, the claustrophobia of being cooped up there, apparently for ever, has built up. People are now trying to escape as if from prison camps. And they are going to start to succeed.

Third, we can't keep a lid on the story any longer. It's nothing short of a miracle that we've managed to do that so far. Baranov's German team now tell us that at least one newspaper there is planning to blow the story. We can't start liquidating whole newspaper staff and their families.'

Someone thought they heard Baranov mutter something like 'More's the pity' in Russian. Luckily, the simultaneous translators did not pick it up.

'But the fourth reason we can't continue like this is the key one. With death by disease and medical neglect much higher, the world's population is now even lower than we thought it would be all those years go. Soon the sperm we've built up in the Havens will be redundant – because the number of women of child-bearing age will be far too low, and the relatively small number of women in the Havens can't make up the shortfall. We now realise that if we wait even another ten years, there won't be enough people to *run* the world, let alone defend it.'

She took a deep breath and looked at her audience.

'So I would strongly recommend that we take the risk and make an announcement by newspaper – of course not television. This should reveal that the Havens exist, that there *is* now enough sperm for the remaining women in the world under thirty-five, and that we'll be providing the expertise and the fertility clinics.'

'But won't there be real anger,' asked the President of Italy, 'about how the

Havens were created in the first place, and how the sperm has been kept back – bearing in mind that the general population doesn't even know about our potential enemies?'

'Clearly, that's a massive risk. And we'd have to be prepared for that. So this is also the time to tell them about the alien threat and to convince them that, on balance, our decision years ago was the right one, indeed the only one. But we'll still need to buy time. So another part of the message is that we should try to hide the presence of new children as long as possible.'

'Will that work?' asked the Spanish Prime Minister, doubtfully, echoing the sentiments of many in the room.

Ann paused.

'Probably not for long. But I think we can count on their drones not being able to pick up a woman pushing a pram from that height. But they may well be able to spot a complete playground. And schools starting up again. That's certainly a very big worry.'

The President of China raised his hand.

'What about Africa and South America? Weren't they really short of Havens there?'

'Correct, Mr President. We have less than a quarter of what was needed. So the sperm will have to come from other races, mostly white. Ironically, we may end up with very few black people in Africa.'

There was protracted silence while the meeting absorbed this strange and sad concept.

'What should be the timeframe for this, Ann?' asked the US President, Ted Hagen.

'I think about a month. We need to prepare the communications perfectly, to avoid civil unrest, and, more important, we need to be *seen* by the public to be providing the means to conceive children *immediately* – with pictures in the press of women entering clinics, announcements of pregnancy successes and so on. Ideally, there should be a powerful 'feelgood factor' that should help overcome, or at least make a dent in resentment. And perhaps national days of celebration. Maybe a 'Baby Day'?'

'And what about the military in the Havens?' asked the British Prime Minister.

'They should leave the Havens as quietly and carefully as possible. No columns of vehicles, no sudden air traffic and virtual radio silence. They should take up new positions as secretly as possible and continue their training.'

The subdued meeting took a vote. By a clear majority, the world's leaders decided to eliminate the Havens. It was almost a relief. The only way to save the human population they may have been, but a moral concept? That was another matter entirely.

Ann left the meeting in a strange mood. The Havens, her Havens, had been a success, but also a sort of failure. Now she was not sure if she was proud of them – or ashamed of them. It was almost as if she were carrying the world's weight on her shoulders, as in a way, she was.

Munich, Germany

Petra stared at her screen in disbelief. She was looking at an urgent government news release from Berlin. To her horror and shock it had revealed the Havens. It had even named the south German one in her story! She was so overcome with anger that she skipped over something about aliens in space.

All her dangerous work of the last few weeks, the risks of meeting 'Ingrid', the withdrawal of her advertising, the mental anxiety – all for nothing! She was not to know that she was, in fact, one of the reasons for the revelation to the world about the existence of the Havens.

And it was scant compensation that the two brewing companies went back to advertising in her paper.

Something even more ironic and annoying came later; a prize from the German Newspaper Association for showing restraint in 'not revealing the story.'

Hope Haven, Montana

Doctor Rachel Leibovitz, forty-four, but feeling ten years older, was sitting at her computer plagued by serious concerns as the Clinical Director of Psychiatry at the Montana Haven. Requests for anti-depressants had been rocketing over the last decade, mostly among her many female patients, and not just the unfortunate ones who had never been able to have children, or even worse, those who had gone through the agonies of still-births. And suicides, tragically, were not even uncommon any more. She had learned to spot the early warning signs only too well, as could her colleagues, although incidents of such despair were rarely widely reported, let alone in the *Haven Herald*, the daily paper, presumably to keep up public morale. As if all that were not bad enough, there was now a fast-growing lobby group for a clinic like Dignitas where people could have an assisted death.

Havens may have been the only way to take the world forward in such desperate circumstances, she conjectured, but she was increasingly unsure and uneasy about the moral implications and the inherent inhumanity of such a divisive concept – in effect, imprisoning trusting people indefinitely while ignoring millions of others who wanted children; and she had many times confided this to her husband Aaron, and to her best friend, Ann Hearst, both of whom she knew shared her serious and growing doubts and moral misgivings.

Now, reading the *Haven Herald*, she felt a huge surge of relief at the sudden and totally unexpected news that the whole scheme was coming to an end, while shocked that she, or as far as she knew, any of the clinic's staff had not been consulted. Had Ann Hearst had anything to do with this? Quite probably, she thought. But the upheaval, she knew, would be massive, leading to a mountain of new problems once her many patients were released to a critical and unbelieving outside world, whose millions of inhabitants had been denied the possibilities of reproduction. There would be huge, and perhaps catastrophic moral and physical repercussions. An unimaginable backlash.

But going through the announcement once again, it was as if a great moral weight were being lifted from her conscience, allowing her to feel like a human being again. 'Thank God' she whispered under her breath. It had to be right, even if there were millions out there who, once the news was out, would be horrified that the Havens had ever existed – and would never be able to forgive those who had inhabited or condoned them. But even if there were violent unrest in the world amongst all those millions who had never realised that Havens existed and had never been able to have children themselves, it was surely better to admit what had been happening rather than carry on this experiment in an inhuman, unnatural and increasingly troubled environment.

She ran her hand through her once lustrous but now thinning hair, sadly remembering that her formerly thick, shiny tresses were what had first attracted Aaron, her husband of thirty years, when they were both young medical students at a college lecture in Tel Aviv, when he was sitting in the chair behind her. He had always told her that her hair was what had made him fall in love at first sight, but had not done so recently, and the reasons were all too obvious. Recently, she had been losing almost as much hair as hope. Even the name 'Hope Haven' now felt hollow.

No longer did he sing his favourite song –'Boys of Summer' by Don Henley of the Eagles – 'I can see you with your long hair flying and your sunglasses on.' It all seemed such a long time ago. Like another world, which of course it was.

Her thoughts were suddenly interrupted by a loudspeaker announcement in the main Plaza outside – a Radio Hope broadcast to the Haven – and she hurried to the window. All at once, the Plaza was filled by more and more people flocking out to listen to the news that the Haven was closing, first in silence and stunned disbelief, but then with shouts of joy almost as if a war had ended. At last, all of them were free, though not of the moral implications of all that they had been through.

They would never shake off fierce criticism for the rest of their lives from the millions of childless couples they had left behind them.

CHAPTER TWENTY-THREE

Washington, D.C.

Major Patricia Hearst was back in Alexandria with Tim. It was her favourite kind of weekend – just the two of them with Ben, with nothing planned.

Suddenly the phone rang. Her mother.

'Hi. I've just heard from Charles Koenig. There's been a change. The Keck Observatory people have just told him that the drones have been joined by other ships.'

'Oh, my God.'

'Much bigger ones, and checking with the other observatories, we've now counted nearly nine hundred of them.'

'Christ!'

'We think something's about to happen. I'm sure you'll get orders soon, but I thought I'd give you a 'heads up' in advance.'

'Thanks, Mom. I wonder why they're doing it now? Another ten years and the population would really have been depleted.'

'Who knows? They may have problems of their own.'

Tricia thanked her mother again, and headed for the bedroom.

Tim was surprised to see her emerge in uniform.

'What's up?'

'I'm sure you'll get a call soon, but I think things are happening. You may need to get Lucia here to look after Ben, and get down to your vehicles.'

10, Downing Street, London

It had to be something really important.

Why else would eight of the world's leaders meet in London to make a television announcement – and an international one? All over the world, people crowded into bars and cafes or else made sure they were home. All day there had been trailers on the broadcast, not only on TV, but radio and the vestiges of social media that had survived the turbulent past twenty-three years.

When the broadcast came on, millions of viewers saw that the news conference was chaired by the US President, Ted Hagen. He was flanked by the leaders of Russia, India, Japan, China, France, Germany and Great Britain.

'My friends,' he started, and the simultaneous translators repeated his words in their own languages, while his words began to march across the bottom of the screens.

'I have something very important to reveal to you tonight. You all know of the mysterious meteorites of thirty years ago and the vapour plumes they caused, with the devastating results that have blighted all our lives and appeared to doom our world.

And as you all know from our previous announcement three months ago, the leaders of the world realised that it was not just a cruel act of nature. Rather, it was an act of aggression, and the type of aggression we all used to joke about, or make movies about. What we called 'aliens'.

Ted Hagen paused.

'Soon after the meteorite attack, the US space station of that time was struck by what appeared to be an unknown spacecraft. Nothing showed up on radar, but with infra-red detection, our people then checked space to find that nearly 300 of these craft were hovering in orbit about 350 kilometres above the earth. They thought, and we still think, that they are watching us – and working out when our population would be so reduced and our people so elderly and weak that would be safe for them to attack.'

He paused again, knowing his announcement was momentous.

'Just recently, over 900 craft, and much bigger ones, have assembled above us up in space.' He waited as a picture came on the screen.

'Here is an infra-red image of one of them. While we're pretty sure the smaller ones were unmanned drones, we suspect these much bigger ones may have the ability to launch things towards us. So, we must all be ready.

As we also told you, twenty-three years ago, doctors were just able to save enough sperm to start breeding children by artificial insemination – but then only for a limited number of women. 'Havens', as they were called, were created, hidden away in many countries, and certainly all the ones represented here. There, new military forces were created. You will have met young people coming out from these Havens and to your aid. They are fit, have weapons and are highly trained to help us to face whatever is coming.

I know that many of you were shocked by the decision to breed such children – now adults – secretly, but it was the only choice. Our only hope of saving Planet Earth. I was not one of those children, and was born just a few years before the meteorites had struck. But, like most of you, I have not been able to have children, so I can more than sympathize with your predicament.

But now we are working at full strength to make sperm available to all the women who want it. And I hope that no cultural or religious barriers will stop you doing so. We need new generations.

But we're sure now that we are under threat.

Let us now put aside our shock, our anger, our resentment and devote all our energies to resisting what new threats are coming and rebuild our world.'

Saint-Omer, France

The old chateau near Saint-Omer had been chosen long ago as a good location for a military headquarters to co-ordinate military activities between Britain, France and Belgium. It was forty miles from Lille and close enough to Calais, where the Channel Tunnel had been re-opened to move tanks and other heavy equipment to France.

For several days an invisible battle had raged 220 miles above the earth, with satellites firing laser weapons attempting to destroy the larger enemy ships that had recently appeared. In many cases, it seemed sufficient not to destroy, them but just to de-stabilise them. They would topple out of position, drift lower and get caught in the atmosphere, quickly burning up with the friction.

But enough survived to launch their cargoes and thousands of small specks of light streaked through the sky at night. Observers reported that the disruption had worked and that many fell uselessly into the sea, although quite enough of them ended up on land. All available media had warned the public not to approach anything that had fallen, but to report it to the police.

Military forces from the Havens had now been fully deployed, working with the elderly personnel who were the remnants of national armed forces in all the various countries involved.

With reports of smoking globes being found all over the Pas-de-Calais, the combined military team had helicoptered its biological expert, Professor John Akeroyd, to find out exactly what they were up against. By the evening, he had returned from the field, and in the old dining room of the chateau he gave his report.

He turned on a projector and wi-fied it to his tablet.

'We found a number of spherical containers, broken open.' He touched the tablet. 'Here's a picture of one of them. They had thick walls, and were insulated. Both materials we don't recognise. That explains how these survived while the drones didn't. We brought back one for your people to study.

We noticed one thing. Whereas we use parachutes to slow down anything we bring back from space, these domes have a lattice-like air brake, a bit like Stukas and Avenger dive-bombers in the Second World War. It means that these domes can hit the ground just slowly enough not to smash up anything inside.

Each globe had opened itself on impact, and in them there were 38, yes, precisely 38 eggs. They are translucent, 10cm in diameter – about the size of a boule ball. We bought four back – and destroyed the rest with a flame-thrower.

Many of the eggs were empty by the time we got to them, but we recovered some intact and removed the live creatures inside. They are about nine inches long, a mollusc very like our domestic garden slugs, with a well-developed radula, a sort of tongue armed with very hard teeth. They don't have eyes on stalks, but two large ones on the bodies. We're dissecting some of them now to find out more.

As you may know, our garden slugs burrow down very easily into the soil to escape predators and to keep cool, their moisture content being critical for their survival.

So we think that nearly all these things, where the ground is soft enough, have burrowed and disappeared. They probably only come back out at night.

If they land in the sea, they won't survive. Nor in hot or hard desert. We're already finding lots of corpses. But in soft earth, marsh land, forests, jungle and cultivated farming areas, they'll burrow and thrive.'

'How big will they grow?' asked General Corbett, the senior British officer and commanding Allied forces the Pas de Calais area.

'Judging by the relative size of the just-hatched babies, General, the adults will be huge.'

'How huge?'

'About four feet long.'

'Good God!' The General was visibly shocked by the thought of such creatures. 'Then, we'd better be ready for anything. Inform London, and put out the word to try to destroy as many eggs as possible before the creatures burrow to safety. Warn everyone that the real problems will come in a few weeks.'

*   *   *

At least they knew what to expect. Any eggs found intact were destroyed by groups of citizens, many hysterically angry and convinced, rightly, that the creatures were something to do with their doomed world. Sometimes the eggs had been found by following flocks of birds big enough to break into the eggs and fly away with the slugs, but that was scant comfort.

Soon there were sightings of adolescents, a foot to 18 inches long, now not only disgusting to those who hated such things, but gradually becoming dangerous.

Would the adults really grow as big as they feared?

Liphook, England

'Sit down and eat, darling!' Delia Collins started to spoon out the last of the month's meat rations on to two plates.

'I can't,' said her husband. 'I've just seen something horrible in the garden.' He looked up from his wheelchair. 'You ought to go and see it.'

'What? Well, I can't go now. It's time to eat. Now please get your chair up to the table. And eat all of it. We get little enough meat as it is. And you're getting too thin. '

'But it's frightening.'

'What's frightening?'

'The thing in the garden. Sort of like, well, a huge slug.'

'Oh darling, don't be pathetic. There are thousands of slugs in the garden. They're everywhere. Grow up. You're seventy, not seven.'

She started to spoon out the stew. 'Now do shut up, please, and eat. If you don't put on weight, you'll get even frailer. And I'll be blamed by Doctor Fenton for not treating you properly.'

Her husband looked stricken. 'But you've got to go and see it.'

She suddenly noticed that he looked terrified. Pale, wide-eyed and suddenly ten years older than his years. What on earth had spooked him? Perhaps she ought to have a quick look.

There, on the lawn, was a horrifying sight. Worse, there were now two of them.

Rushing back inside, as fast as she could, she locked the French windows, her heart pounding. What on earth were they? And what to do? Phone the police? They'd never believe her. And anyway, there were so few police these days.

Dithering, and overcome by blind panic, she suddenly heard the sound of breaking glass.

St Omer, France

Professor Akeroyd had just returned from the field, and was reporting to the military group.

'Well, we've found an adult. I just managed to stop one of your over-eager Paras, Colonel Castries, from destroying it with one of the yellow-tipped shells.'

Castries smiled and shrugged.

'He then did manage to kill the thing – with about thirty shots. And I put a rule alongside it to show its dimensions. It's what we expected.

Very big, about four feet long, or one metre twenty. Probably weighing about a hundred kilos. As you can see, it has indeed turned out to be just like a giant slug. We've brought it back in a body bag, and my people are conducting an immediate autopsy down below.

It appears to have most of the common characteristics of keelback slugs, what we call 'Limacidae', apart from its immense size, which will scale up its appetite and more importantly, its speed of movement. Its two very large eyes remind me of another mollusc – the octopus with its excellent vision.

Garden slugs, the ones we all know, can travel at 0.03 miles an hour, or nearly 0.05 kilometres, which may surprise you, but the Limax, which is what I've called this thing, is a hundred times bigger. So it can probably travel at more than three miles an hour; about the speed of a slow human walker.'

He paused, knowing the effect of his words.

'Another thing we must note. As you know, slugs spend a long time underground, burrowing up to two feet, especially when hot, largely to protect their considerable water content. The Limax, unfortunately, can certainly burrow much deeper. So it may be difficult to detect from the air during the day. If it's like its miniature brothers, it will be a remarkable and efficient burrower and not leave easily detected earth piles, unlike, say a mole.

Like all slugs and snails, this one has what is called a 'radula'. That's a sort of tongue covered in teeth, made of the hardest substance in nature. They normally just use the radula to scrape off matter from rocks or cut into leaves. But then there's the 'ghost slug', discovered in Wales, the *Selenochlamys ysbryd*. 'Yspryd' means ghost in Welsh, because it's white and lives underground. But the unpleasant thing is that it's a proper predator and uses its radula to kill and eat earthworms. A giant version of that would be really dangerous for anything that could not get away fast enough, or was trapped.' He saw one of the women visibly shudder.

'Such creatures would probably only do well in places where there's plenty of rainfall, but that is, very unfortunately, where a lot of our surviving populations are.'

He paused. They all heard the sound of explosions in the distance.

'So, what can we learn from our normal slugs? Many pesticides are well-known, of course. One is common salt, which kills them by drying up their water content. Extensive salt water spraying, if you can organise it on a large enough scale, may be an answer, but not if they've gone to ground. There are other methods, many with downsides. For example, heavy chemical use may make the ground infertile for years, although in this crisis that may not be important. It would mean extensive evacuation, but we may have to evacuate anyway.

Another piece of bad news is that they breed prolifically, and they're hermaphrodites. If they mate, and they may have started, it means they can each produce eggs – and 30 to 100 at a time, several times a year. With no real wildlife left, they'll have no predators – except birds and us. And with that quite high speed they could arrive fast and unexpectedly especially in the dark, and as omnivores, they could devour anything that couldn't get out of the way – horrifically, the old, the frail, the injured.'

Jane Lomax, a young British Major, interrupted, waving a piece of paper.

'You're right Professor, in your assessment. We're just now getting reports from all over – France, Belgium, Holland, Germany – everywhere. These horrible things, just last night, climbed up the side of buildings, even very tall ones, breaking in and eating everything and far worse, *everyone* they found.' The room was shocked into silence.

The Professor was about to respond when the Military Policeman on the door knocked and let in a figure in a white coat.

'Morning, everyone.'

'Ah, here's Dr Hugh Synge from Cambridge. Have you got anything, Hugh?'

'Yes, we certainly have.' Synge took a chair at the table and started to explain his findings. 'Key things: its large radula is covered in teeth half a centimetre long. More important, the creature has a brain. Not a huge one, but in bodyweight comparison terms, slightly smaller than a dolphin's, or the same as an octopus. That may indicate certain things. For instance, it may be able to communicate in some way and work as part of a team. Exactly like killer whales work together hunting and dolphins herd fish. Some jellyfish too, are team workers.'

'So,' said General Robert Corbett, the senior British officer present, 'we know they can gather and herd together and they certainly show evidence of a sense of purpose. We'll have to deal with them.

But whoever planned this must have assumed we'd already be either gone or be completely enfeebled. After all, if you were designing an ace weapon or species to defeat us, you wouldn't have tapped in a maximum speed of three miles an hour; with main armament a sharp tongue.

So there has to be involvement by something else, something *much* more sophisticated, able to plan and execute the attack in the first place.'

'That's for sure,' added Air Commodore Harry Wilson, the RAF liaison officer. 'These slug things didn't fly sophisticated vehicles across space. Not exactly Biggles types, are they?'

The reference to the 1930s children's books about a mythical British pilot was largely lost on the group. But General Corbett smiled. He *did* remember Biggles, although it certainly wasn't a time to muse over his boyhood flying hero.

'So, we have to believe that something else greatly superior is still up there,' he continued. 'Maybe these appalling slug things are, well, like mercenaries, expendable thugs sent ahead, probably too early, to do in the world before the *real* action from the clever ones starts. That's a *truly* frightening thought.'

CHAPTER TWENTY-FOUR

London

Ann and the others in London were trying to analyse the reports pouring in from all over the world. Four weeks ago, despite the disruption they had been able to achieve in space, egg containers had landed everywhere. In the sea, they were obviously wasted, as well as in the freezing snow of the North and South poles. If they landed somewhere hot like the Sahara they did not survive, and that also went for places that heated up during the day like Spain, Texas or Turkey. Anywhere, too, where the ground was too hard or too rocky for the creatures to dig down and bury themselves for protection. But of course, that still left huge areas of the world where they could survive, flourish and breed.

'Now that we know for certain how large they can grow,' said the USAF officer, 'our air forces are rushing ammunition and special weapons to our forces. One obvious and economical method is the use of salt water, especially sea-water, which they seem to find deadly. Near the sea or in seaports, we could suck up sea-water and simply use a long system of pumps and hoses. Further inland, normal fire engines would work, or in much greater numbers, modified road tankers equipped with high-pressure pumps.

Our army friends are looking at modifying old flame-thrower tanks to project saltwater. There won't be many of those, of course, but they would give perfect protection for the crews. But we can retro-fit vehicles to have the same effect. We all kept plenty of tanks secretly, but salt-water launching ones are going to be much more useful than ones firing guns.

Then further inland, we propose using the planes we normally use for fighting forest fires. But even then there are problems. First, to make it work properly, the targets can't be too far inland for the planes to be able to make enough worthwhile round-trips from the sea.

Another issue is that the planes may be in the wrong places, only in climates and economies that used to find it worthwhile putting out fires at quite a high cost. Finally, pilots. It's really skilled flying. It used to be retired naval and air force people who did that, but they may be too elderly now. So, we may not have enough pilots for the tankers. We do have other aircraft with pilots that can act as lead planes, or 'bird dogs' as we call them. And we also may be okay for helicopters, but they don't really carry enough water.'

'Would that go for crop-dusters? asked Ann, remembering her childhood days on the farm. 'There must be hundreds of them around.'

'Yes, and we may end up using anything we can get hold of. And with land-based planes, we can strengthen the salt content, which may make up for the lack of load.

But, let's look at what we've got in the way of regular tankers.' He checked a long list. 'Lots still in the USA, mostly in the south or south west, some in Canada, and in the Mediterranean, and the Russians have got plenty of Berievs and some Ilyushin-26s. We'll have to check with the Far East commands. All sorts of planes may have to come out of mothballs, even the old Boeing 747. That could carry over 20,000 gallons.

In the meantime, for the men and women on the ground, they should use the special yellow-tipped shells that we developed to explode inside a large, soft body. If they have to use conventional rifled bullets, they should aim for the eyes and the mouths of the things. And small reconnaissance drones will be useful to get them at in accessible places.

I'm sure we'll all learn as we go on – and everyone should keep other countries informed about any new developments that seem to work.'

Saint-Hippolyte-du-Fort, France

Alphonse Duran was bored out of his mind, even more bored than he would have been sitting at home on a Saturday.

He had been sitting beside the old mining road since about eight this morning. Dressed in his bright orange jerkin, his rifle beside him, he was waiting to try to shoot a 'sanglier' or wild boar. There weren't, of course, many of them in this deeply wooded part of the Cévennes region. Like all mammals, they had nearly all died out. But the various hunters' associations had retained some sperm and then had done something they did several decades ago – cross-breeding with pigs and thus doubling the birth-rate. So there were enough to keep the sport going in a rather feeble way, and the meat was a valuable bonus. They even had enough dogs now, although they were a curious lot. All rather classy types that had been saved by their sperm being frozen for dog-breeders.

About three tedious hours had passed. He wondered why everything had gone rather quiet. By now he surely should have been able to hear the dogs of his friends coming towards him, hopefully driving a boar through the woods towards his gun. They normally made a hell of a din, with the tinkling of the bells on their collars, and their excited yelping adding to the shouting of the hunters. But all was silence. Very curious. Surely he was in the right place?

Suddenly, a boar broke cover from the bushes in front of him, and so fast that he had no time to reach for his rifle, let alone release the safety catch, aim and fire. No bloody warning at all! How annoying.

He picked up the rifle and resolved to be more alert. And ten minutes later, sure enough, he saw something black through the bushes that certainly looked like another boar. Except that it was moving very slowly. But Alphonse wasn't going to be caught a second time by something that suddenly rushed across the road before he was ready. 'Ah, non!'

So he released the safety catch, took careful aim and fired. The crash of the shot echoed round the valley.

Extraordinary. The shape kept moving. He was sure he had hit it. The range was only about thirty metres. And with *his* Mannlicher 270? Damn it. His friends certainly didn't want the wretched chore of having to track a wounded boar all day across these hills. It was not just respect for the animal. It had a lot to do with the value of the meat.

Frowning, he ejected the cartridge case, slid forward the bolt and shot at the object again. Again the thing kept moving towards him.

Then it broke through the underbrush and the horrified Alphonse saw what it was. And there were two more behind it. Black, amorphous, shiny. What the hell were they? One of those things on yesterday's TV news?

Trying to calm his nerves, he stumbled off towards his old white van, started it and set off down the hill, much faster than he knew was safe. Round a sharp bend there were two more of them on the road, big enough to send the little Peugeot off the mountain if he hit them. But he braked violently, swerved on to the verge and just managed to get past them.

Being Saturday, the 'Café de la Bourse' in the centre of town was crowded when he burst in. He shouted out what he had seen, 'Les grandes limaces!' But to no avail. Everybody laughed and went back to their Bezique or their gossip. Alphonse was known to drink a bit, and he certainly grabbed a large cognac now. Nobody seemed to want to listen to his outlandish story.

Then, after a while, somebody behind him said that it was a bit strange that André and Michel hadn't turned up from the woods. They always did. They *always* had lunch here after hunting. Where *were* they?'

And only a second later, everyone looked up. A puzzled silence. The siren on the Fire Station roof had started to wail.

It only ever did that if there was a *real* emergency.

Montpellier, France

The double railway track for the TGV from Lyon to Spain seemed to be working quite well as a barrier. Jean-Baptiste Eblé did not know if the old gardener's trick of scattering eggshells to deter normal miniature slugs and snails was working, in this case against their monstrous cousins. Perhaps the sharp stones of the rail track's ballast were uncomfortable for them, and made them use up too much water to make extra slime. Anyway, they seemed to be reluctant to cross the tracks, and skirting them, instead their black masses were trying to crawl south towards the airport by using the road bridges. So it was at the bridges where he had stationed his Gimaex salt-water fire engines.

The 'Sapeurs Pompiers' of France were legendary figures, and rightly proud of their calling. They not only put out fires, but were the ambulance crews as well. And they bore military ranks, like Jean-Baptiste – a Captain. Of course, most of them were quite elderly now, with just a sprinkling of 'chilmen' who had made the physical grade.

From the direction of the city of Montpellier, to where thousands of locals from the hills and woods of the Cévennes had been evacuated, Captain Eblé could hear continuous explosions, along with a couple of really huge ones. Those must be those big fuel-air bombs that he had seen being loaded on to aircraft, he thought – explaining why it was important not to abandon the airport. While, of course, there was no more Ryanair airline traffic, the place was a hive of military and air force activity. And that was being supported by those new Haven people; fit, competent young men and women, many scarcely twenty years old. Their only problem was sunburn. They had arrived from wherever they had been in the Massif Central looking very pale, and some of them were now painfully red.

They had proved very helpful when they ran the salt-water tanker columns up to the city. When the mid-day heat had forced most of the creatures to hide, a column of water tankers, escorted by armoured vehicles and aerial water-bombers, ran the gauntlet to deliver salt-water to the defenders of Montpellier. Jean-Baptiste had taken part in this the day before. The drill seemed well worked-out. They had set off behind a bulldozer with makeshift armour welded to its cab. Helicopters went ahead with bags of salt water that they released on the road ahead. The bulldozer then scraped the dying slugs off the road, so that the column could keep going at a steady 15 kilometres an hour. Only occasionally did Jean-Baptiste's fire crew have to squirt salt water at encroaching slugs. And the soldiers seldom had to shoot at anything.

In Montpellier, the military, strengthened by these young people, seemed to be holding their own. The slugs did not seem to like built-up areas, perhaps realising their vulnerability in the heat and on hard surfaces. Quite a few inhabitants of the town or the surrounding area wanted to get out. So they were loaded onto buses, armoured with steel plates, and came back with the column.

Radio traffic told the story of similar columns getting through to Nîmes and smaller towns like Anduze, Saint-Hippolyte and Ganges.

All day and night aircraft roared over their heads. Some were those yellow Sécurite Civilé Bombardier fire-fighting planes that scooped up sea-water from the étaings nearby. Other planes had to be loaded from tankers at the airport's military facilities. They would be using the same mixture that he did – salty sea-water – but with any added salt they could find, like the winter road gritting store, which was unfortunately pretty small due to the relatively warm winters in Languedoc.

They had been warned that night times would be the worst. Many of the slug things hid in the day, and it was only at night that their terrifying numbers were revealed.

And now night was falling. The generators hummed into life and the big arc lights came on. The fire engines were started up, so their pumps were ready. How long would it take to get electric fences? But Eblé had heard that, in the north, the creatures had burrowed under them. But they *might* not be able to do that in the hard, sun-baked soil of this region.

Two truckloads of French Haven troops came to a halt. The young soldiers were carrying some strange-looking weapons that he had never seen before. He greeted their commander and soon the soldiers spread out on the bridges to support the fire crews.

His radio crackled.

It was the 'bird dog' spotter plane. The things were coming.

'Stand by everyone. Watch your front!'

Suddenly Eblé looked to his right, to the east. There was a strange rumbling sound – and bright lights. Coming down the line, travelling very slowly, was a train, headed by a diesel locomotive pulling six tanker waggons. Each mounted a big searchlight and a water projector, and their crews were spraying the far side of the track with long jets, obviously of sea-water. Each one probably contained 60,000 litres, thought Eblé. Huge firepower, or rather water-power.

With its windows protected with steel shutters, the diesel ground past him hauling its deadly train and trundled on towards Béziers. Hundreds of sinister black sinister shapes lay writhing and dying on the other side of the tracks, a sight straight out of a horror movie.

An armoured train, a veteran weapon indeed – now *that's* lateral thinking when you need it!

He smiled and faced his front again.

Jinshanling, China

'Move 200 metres to the left, Sergeant.'

Staring into his night-vision binoculars and talking on the radio, the Lieutenant was standing on the Great Wall of China not far from Beijing. Interested in history, he knew that the Wall had served many purposes – its main one being to try to keep out the Mongols centuries ago. He also knew that far from being a mere 8,000 kilometres long as had once been thought, it had been found to be much more complicated and three times longer: a deserving 'wonder of the world'.

But now the sections of Wall served another purpose. All over China, tens of thousands of troops and civilians were driving the giant Limaxes towards them. The civilians were mostly about fifty years old and the soldiers were a mixture of the elderly from the old People's Liberation Army, along with 'chilmen' born thirty years ago and much younger men and women who had emerged from the Chinese Havens. The technique they were using was the only one possible in these rocky, wooded hills, and they were doing it at night when the odious creatures were moving, rather than hiding from the heat. Many weeks into the job, he and his comrades were still repelled by the sight of them and the knowledge of what they could do – indeed had done – to so many frail humans.

They walked slowly forward in a long line, close together. Three civilians to each soldier. The civilians had powerful torches, axes and scythes, while each soldier was equipped with a torch, a spade with its edges sharpened and a dual-purpose assault rifle. Every few minutes, a man or woman would cry out. The closest comrades would then converge and they would smash the clusters of eggs with their spades. Every few minutes, too, would come the sound of a shot. An adult had been found and a soldier had destroyed it with a single one of the highly-effective explosive yellow-tipped shells that the Americans had given them.

It was the only way to get rid of them. No vehicles could get up into the rocky woods to be close enough to use salt-water projectors, and anyway the salt-water was far too heavy for anyone to carry in any quantity.

If the creatures reached the Wall, they became easily visible to the sentries lining the top of it. There, he and his comrades *could* use salt from the storage tanks that had been helicoptered in and placed at regular intervals.

The young Lieutenant was sweating from running up and down the Wall, directing the searchers by radio. But he was delighted to be free from the claustrophobic atmosphere of the Haven where he had been for over 20 years. At last he was doing something that he was trained for. And who would have thought, he mused, that the Wall would *ever* be used for a military purpose again?

Next to him, an even younger Second Lieutenant was looking at a screen slung round his neck. He suddenly exclaimed. Buzzing away in the distance, his small drone's infra-red camera had spotted something on the left of the line of searchers.

He looked through his binoculars and realised he needed to make an adjustment. He pressed the transmit button on the radio. 'No, Sergeant, further still to the left, please.'

CHAPTER TWENTY-FIVE

London

The BBC evening TV news had just started.

'The government announced today that burial of bodies in Britain will shortly be illegal. Near Leeds, where the Town Council had assured people that Limaxes had been cleared, it has been discovered that they have been entering graveyards and have cut their way into the coffins of six recently-deceased people, with immense distress to family members.'

A tearful woman was now being interviewed.

'It's terrible. We went to visit my father's grave, and it was all ripped open. And all covered in that filthy slime.' She wiped at her tears. 'Horrible. Why can't the government do things properly?'

The announcer came back on the screen. ' This is not the only evidence of the latest results from the Limax invasion, which the military is trying to resist. Cremation will be mandatory from next Monday. In the meantime, the public is reminded to report any sightings, and not to approach adult Limaxes unless accompanied by armed soldiers.

In addition, anybody living in houses bordering graveyards should be specially vigilant.

In London, the District Line and the Bakerloo Line were again disrupted by Limaxes getting into the tunnels and being electrocuted on the line. As the bodies are very heavy and probably poisonous to handle, the RMT union is asking for military support or they may take industrial action.'

Ian and Laura looked at the television in horror. Never mind the problems on the tube, what an appalling thought – those revolting giant slugs raiding graveyards for human corpses, with tongues strong enough to saw through wood to reach them. It was horrifying enough that they were able to kill – and eat – live humans, but unimaginable that they could also seek out the dead.

They had been looking forward to seeing the old John Wayne western 'The Searchers' that was coming on after the news, but neither of them was now in the mood to watch it. Or even to have supper. The very business of eating at all would feel grisly after such a ghastly announcement. Did people really have to know about things like that, Laura wondered, quickly realising that they did. People were dying all the time. Plans had to be made for, if not burials, cremations. And who would ever want to be buried now? And come to that, who ever would want to visit family graves or walk around a churchyard – or be a grave digger, come to that?

'Sorry, but I can't watch this.' She went to the television and switched it off. 'And I suddenly don't feel hungry either.'

'Nor me,' said Ian. 'I don't know about you, but I feel like an early night. Better close the steel shutters.'

Laura shuddered.

Bielefeld, Germany

'What we're goin' on with now,' said Sergeant Shannon in the curious way the British Army sometimes spoke, 'is removin' the main armament.'

It was the middle of the night and they were working on a Challenger tank in the German Army's workshop in Bielefeld. There were seven other British tanks in this cavernous place, all with teams working on them. And about ten German Leopards, with equally busy crews. The noise was deafening.

'Why *are* we taking the gun out, Sarge?'

'Don't you *ever* pay any attention, sonny? I sometimes tink that feckin' chilmen are thicker than feckin' Welshmen.' As he was addressing Craftsman Jones, the Sergeant thought that this was a hilarious double Irish joke. Not surprisingly, Jones did not.

'I'll tell you why the officer told us to take the big gun out. 'Cos its useless against those feckin' black, slimy feckers. We'll be puttin' in that salt-water thrower ting in instead, and hooking it up to that tanker trailer.. And when we've done that, we'll take out the Browning, 'cos they've found that machine-guns are feckin' useless too. An' we'll replace it with that little gun over there – the one that fires them yellow shells.'

The hapless young fitter tried to argue.' But...'

'But nuttin', Jones. If you'd get a feckin' move on we could do this tank before breakfast.

BETTY, BRING THE GANTRY CRANE OVER HERE!' he shouted to the big REME Corporal. She promptly hit a switch.

'And thank the Lord we're not Yanks. I'm told they got hundreds of bloody great Abrams to change. At least our Army went broke and has hardly any tanks.

Now, let's get a move on. They need these quick.'

Spokane, Washington state

The siren had been going for an hour now.

The city of Spokane was gripped with real anxiety. Everyone knew about the Limax invasion from the national television – now government-run, of course. It was their only source of news. Long gone were the six TV and twenty-eight commercial radio stations that they used to listen to.

Several of the sphere things they had been warned about had been sighted, and in Manito Park an adult Limax had been found and killed – with great difficulty. Its revolting radula tongue armed with rows of sharp teeth had been pictured in the *Spokesman-Review*, their local newspaper kept going by donations.

Like all cities, Spokane was now a shadow of its former self, down from 200,000 to just 50,000 mostly elderly inhabitants. Half the houses stood empty. But it was still important, the second largest town in Washington state to Seattle.

The night before, the Mayor had called an emergency conference with Council Members and his staff after his own telephone briefing from the state Governor. Apparently Spokane and its suburbs were especially vulnerable. Its mild summer climate on the plateau between the Cascades and Rockies meant that the Limaxes did not have to hide from the heat in the daytime. And its depleted population in the surrounding countryside meant that many of the creatures had landed undetected, and with the time to breed undisturbed. Old mine workings would be perfect places for that.

Suddenly, the city appeared to be isolated, too. All traffic had stopped yesterday on Interstate-90, and even on the smaller highways and roads leading into the city. The railroad, the BNSF, had suspended the long freight trains that normally passed through several times a day, and the two *Empire Builder* passenger trains had not run for several days, each kept back for safety in Seattle and Chicago.

For hours panicky people had been streaming in from the suburbs, and their cars now clogged the Downtown area. Surely big buildings like the Davenport Hotel and the Fox Theater would be safe?

The reason for their panic was pretty obvious. The big, black Limaxes were pouring out of the countryside and seemed very difficult to stop. Police in South Hill and Comstock had radioed in saying that their shotguns, rifles and pistols seemed almost useless against them. Bullets went right through, and the creatures just kept going. The police had managed to kill a few before retreating, but only after a huge expenditure of ammunition. It was the same with the Air Force people out at Fairchild. After a losing battle, they'd had to abandon the Base and retreat to the city like everyone else.

What seemed to work in Seattle and Everett, the Governor had told the

Mayor, was salt-water, sprayed from fire hoses. That was all very well near the sea thought Spokane's Fire Chief, as he frantically tried to get his crews to mix up enough salty water by using the salt stored for the roads in winter. But with Spokane's mild climate, they probably wouldn't have enough of that – and not enough fire engines either to be in several places at once.

In desperation, the Mayor had called everywhere he could for help. Where the hell were those Haven people the President had mentioned in that recent broadcast?

*   *   *

Like the city, Spokane's Sacred Heart Medical Center was also a shadow of its former self. Long gone were the 4,000 staff, and long gone too was the Children's Hospital. After all, there had been no children in Spokane for twenty years.

Now there were only about 400 patients, looked after by 150 rotating staff. All the staff today were tired. Early that morning, the night staff had been advised not to leave and no day staff had yet arrived to relieve them.

They had all heard the siren and the nearby sound of gunshots, and then the calls had started coming in. But none of the ambulance crews out on calls dared to try and come back to the hospital to deliver patients. The paramedics manning the vehicles would have no alternative but to try to deal with their patients as best they could. With the roads and highways empty, at least there had been few of the normal traffic accidents – only one or two from drivers trying to escape the slugs.

The watching staff saw the first of those horrific creatures moving steadily towards them below the trees in front of the hospital. Trying to keep calm, the Director quickly ordered all doors to be closed, locked and barricaded with anything to hand – gurneys, cupboards, filing cabinets, boxes of materials and food trolleys. Everyone watched the approach of the Limaxes with mounting anxiety and fear.

And the fear sky-rocketed when they suddenly realised that the creatures could climb. Climb buildings. And as high as they wanted to. Worse than anything in a horror movie.

The noise of breaking glass on the second floor and the screams of a nurse sent the place into turmoil. Those screams had come from a geriatric ward. Desperately a team rushed in, to be met by the appalling sight of two Limaxes breaking their way in through the window. While some of the staff started hitting them with anything they could, including that floor's only fire axe, the rest grabbed the beds full of uncomprehending old patients and wheeled them out and down the corridor. There, the staff barricaded themselves and their patients into one large room, blocking its windows with mattresses. The same thing was happening on other floors of the hospital, but only eight rooms had been secured.

From one of them, above the hubbub, the Director tried to telephone to call for help.

The lights suddenly went out and one of the nurses screamed before controlling herself.

The emergency lights flickered on. In each room the senior doctor or nurse frantically tried to assess the situation and how long they and their patients could stay barricaded in. In some rooms there was water. In others, the lunch trolley had just been delivered, so there might be sufficient food – for now. But many patients were due for medication and the pharmacy was now out of reach.

The Director tried to talk to the various rooms by telephone. Only some of them answered.

There was almost no sound from outside, only that distant wail of the city's siren. Until all at once, in one ground floor ward, the staff distinctly heard an eerie chewing sound from the other side of a mattress blocking a window.

*   *   *

Suddenly, a distant, but very large explosion was heard – even with the mattresses acting as buffers on the windows. Then there was another, a minute later, and rather closer. The sickening chewing noises at the windows abruptly stopped.

All over the hospital, the staff moved as close to the covered windows as they dared straining to hear what was going on. Could they be blowing up the city? The power plant? There was no way of knowing, and nobody was going to remove a mattress to take a look.

'Hang on' said a male nurse, 'I'm sure I can hear a helicopter, in fact, maybe more.'

Then, they all could, and there were many more explosions now. Smaller, and quite frequent. But there was no shooting, no automatic fire. Then the beat of the rotor blades got louder.

'I think one's landed at the Helistop.' said the Director over the loudspeaker system. 'Nobody move. We don't know what's going on.'

Now, there were more small explosions, and they were going off in the building itself.

'Is there anybody in there?' came a loud and authoritative female voice. 'Show yourselves!'

'Yes, yes! Doctors, nurses, patients!' shouted the Director. 'We'll open up'

They dismantled the barrier around the door and finally looked out. There was a tall and powerful looking woman in full military gear, surrounded by Marines.

'Hi, I'm Major Patricia Hearst, United States Marines. I figure we got here just in time. They were all over your hospital.'

The Director introduced himself, stumbling through his effusive thanks, and then looked around. The corridor was littered with pilesof black sticky stuff that he took to be the remains of the Limax slugs. He glanced at the Major with astonishment.

'We take them out with special little shells,' said Tricia. 'They blow up when they're just deep enough into their bodies.' That would explain, the Director realised, why there wasn't the usual sound of battle, automatic weapons and all.

'Takes a long time shooting 'em one at a time. Mind you, we were able to use a fuel-air bomb or two where they clustered really deep to the south of the city. You may have heard the bangs.' The Director nodded, struggling to take in the scene.

'We came from a Haven, the one in Montana. You may have heard the President talk about them. Came as quick as we could, only took a couple of hours flying from Glacier Park, but then we had to clear I-90 to let the tanks through to the city, and there were other people to be rescued in Spokane.

Now, I'm going to leave a squad with you and I want you to send some of your people as guides to go with the Marine teams and search every last damn inch of this hospital. Leave nothing to chance.

They may look like overgrown slugs, but they've got brains of sorts, and they're as cunning as they are revolting.'

CHAPTER TWENTY-SIX

London

Only about half of the world's leaders had been able to come to London. Many were really struggling with problems in their own countries, and felt they couldn't leave. So the meeting was expanded by video conferencing.

Ted Hagen, the American President and Chair of the meeting, made some opening remarks.

'The attack of these slug creatures, the Limaxes, is in many ways very puzzling. Against a well-organized defence they're largely ineffective – slow and vulnerable. Of course, our own counter-attack in space disrupted their launches sufficiently to make many of their globe containers land in useless locations – the sea, the desert and the snow. Thus they can be, and *are* being, eliminated in *most* of the world.

We have to conclude that something compelled this enemy to launch years, or even decades, too early. Logically, the Limaxes should have arrived on a planet devoid of any effective opposition – rather like an army of garbage men – just cleaning up.

Whether they detected the Havens and their children, or whether they had their own issues that forced their hand, we don't know. My own fear is that after this comparative failure, they'll be back.

I'd now like to go round the room, country by country, for your reports.'

Each country then reported its progress, most of which was steady and improving. And unsurprisingly, those countries with determined leadership, enough Havens and a high population-to-size ratio were doing best.

However, Australia's Prime Minister, via satellite, revealed that with low population and a huge land mass, they were struggling. With most of the population in the coastal cities, the vast 'Outback' had yet to be tackled – although a lot of it, she speculated, was probably as inhospitable to Limaxes as it was to humans.

New Zealand then reported that they could have been even more vulnerable, except very few container globes seemed to have landed there.

As to the United States, Ted Hagen reported the situation himself.

'Well, you have to understand that America is a rather special case. Incredibly, the population, even if reduced to about 160 million, still owns about 100 million guns. And they have reacted to these slug things with fury. They are the symbol of what has taken away their manhood. And for the hunters, what removed their weekend prey.

So Americans have not waited like others for the army or the Haven people. No, they've gone right over on to the offensive. Nor have they sat passively in the towns to await events, they've gone into the woods and mountains with murderous intent. All over America they're streaming out in their thousands in cars and pick-ups, and going off to hunt Limaxes as they once did deer and moose – except this time with real hatred.

After all, people who wiped out millions of bison just to starve the Sioux and Cheyenne to help the railroads, are hardly going to hesitate with the Limaxes. And sadly, the National Rifle Association and its ridiculous interpretation of the Second Amendment about the right to bear arms has this time been proved right.'

Some of his listeners were aghast. But many others nodded in approval.

'However, they may be enthusiastic, but we need people to be methodical. Methods which might suit a Saturday trying to shoot reasonably harmless deer are not going to work against thousands of creatures which are real enemies, intent on our destruction. We'll need to get the army in, divide up territory into blocks and carefully sweep them clean. A long, tedious and dangerous job.'

Canada then reported that it was doing quite well, with less people, less guns and harsher weather.

China, still with a huge number of people and a well-organised Communist central government was methodically combing the country. Russia's new government was less well organised, but was gradually getting on top of things.

India and Pakistan had stopped quarrelling over Kashmir and had collaborated against the common threat, as had North and South Korea.

While Muslim countries had initially rejected artificial insemination on religious grounds, in the Middle East, populations were generally safe, and being mostly desert, the Limaxes had never even started to flourish. Western European countries, with their high populations and good infrastructure had largely eliminated the Limaxes, although occasional outbreaks were still being reported.

The meeting turned to the two huge problem areas that remained. Ted Hagen revealed that one of them, South America, would be covered by a special video presentation from Brazil scheduled for twelve noon. There, they were informed, was a tragedy waiting to happen.

Africa, with its very few Havens and wracked with disease and starvation, was also a special case. Hagen revealed that Sir Michael Bevan of AfricAid had approached him. AfricAid was probably the only vehicle now able to get help to Africa, although it would need troops as back-up, and the meeting voted extra funds for this charity and its work.

At exactly noon, as previously arranged, Angelina Rossi, the President of Brazil, came up on the screen, wearing a sombre black suit and flanked by a scientist.

She spoke slowly and gravely, and in excellent English.

'Good morning to you all, and thank you for taking the time to listen to us in Brazil, especially as the message we have today is of world importance. We know you have grave problems all over the world, although we're pleased to hear that you are gradually solving them. However, in our continent, the situation is extremely bad, and especially here in Brazil. It is nothing less than perilous for us all.

As we all know, the Limaxes are likely to be less effective where it is hot and dry, where it is cold, or where the land is hard. But here, unfortunately, we have almost the perfect place for them to survive and to thrive, and to hide and multiply. I refer, of course, to the Amazon Rain Forest. And this vast area, I cannot stress enough, is not just a Brazilian problem, but a world problem, something that affects each and every one of us on our planet. Let me ask my chief scientist, Professor Callisto de Souza, to explain why.'

A silver-haired man with glasses took over. 'Good morning.

It is my duty to tell you that the Limaxes have done only too well in the rain forest, an area covering 400,000 hectares of our continent, the size of the whole of Europe.

The land is soft, they have no predators, and the weather is warm and moist, ideal conditions for rapid breeding. As a result, they have multiplied prodigiously, despite our unflagging effort to keep them under control. Huge resources have been poured into our programme of control. But we only had two Havens, and like everyone else, our population is reduced and ageing.

Protecting our coastline cities has eaten up many of our resources, and I'm glad to report they are making good progress with salt-water systems. But Brasilia, our capital inland, is under siege and virtually cut off. And in the rain forest we have had to rescue whole communities – big and small – from a jungle now swarming with more and more Limaxes.

That brings us to the second crisis. There are so many of these creatures that they're quite literally eating the forest away. And the situation is much worse than it was before, when the logging companies were felling trees, and the farmers were clearing swathes of forest for cattle breeding. My very sad estimate – and that of my scientists – is that we will lose a further 10% of this precious area in just a few months if we don't get any help.

Let me explain why outside help is so vital. As our President has said, it is not simply a problem that affects Brazil. It's one that affects everyone, and everywhere in the world. And why? Because the rain forest and its health are vital to our whole planet, indeed what you could call the very 'lungs of the world'. Without its unique ability to absorb carbon-dioxide, we'll get a sharp increase in global warming – a problem that many of us probably thought had gone away. Let me explain further.

The Amazon rain forest covers one billion acres. If it were a country, would be the fifth largest in the world. It is a vital carbon sink. A few years ago, a 20% deforestation of it was estimated to add to the air the same amount of carbon dioxide as all the cars, trucks, trains and ships in the world put together. We learned our lesson and stopped the reduction of the forest. Borneo, Sumatra and the Congo Basin did not.

But if the Limaxes are now able to eat it down to nothing, the additional greenhouse effect would be huge. Temperatures would rise about 4%, and that means sea-water levels rising several metres and drought devastating the world. They must be stopped, or the consequences will be catastrophic.'

President Rossi came back on the screen. 'I, we, and our continent appeal to you all. We are asking our friends in the world to divert more of your people and resources to come to our aid and help us to clear our vital rain forest of these terrible creatures. We're doing everything we can, but we cannot succeed without your help. The very air you breathe is now under threat, and will continue to be threatened without assistance from outside. And it will go on getting worse.

Distressing though they are, I would like you to see some images of what is happening to this vital land mass, hoping that they may help to explain our plight.'

A series of grim images came on to the screen, one after another. Vast piles of Limaxes, almost like mountains. Shots of ravaged forest. Aerial views of huge devastated areas. Distressed inhabitants being herded on to trucks or boats. Villages destroyed. Exhausted aid workers. Crying mothers and children.

As the last piece of film went off the screen she concluded. 'Thank you for listening to us today.'

Ted Hagen, leaned forward and pressed his mike button.

'Thank you, President Rossi, and your team, for bringing this so vividly to our attention. We will debate this at once and come back to you.'

The meeting had not been surprised by this information, but any complacency after hearing about success elsewhere had been eliminated.

Ted Hagen spoke up.

'Of course, in South America we're probably not just talking about Brazil. There'll be

other countries there with the same climate – Colombia, Ecuador, Venezuela.' He paused.

'I have a proposal: that we create a form of national service, or draft, and send as many people and as much equipment as we can spare to South America, say for three month stints. It will take tens of thousands, many years and billions of dollars. But it's the only thing we can do.'

Chapter Twenty-Seven

Amazon River, Brazil

Her heart pounding, Maria had just made it to the jetty in time, her whimpering children clinging to her in fear. The whole north bank of their Amazon tributary now seemed to be swarming with the horrible things.

Thank God! Her husband Antonio and his little boat were at the end of the rickety little jetty, his outboard running. She stumbled down towards him and handed over little Florencio and Madalena, who had begun to scream at something. She looked back. Two of the black monsters had slithered out from the green jungle and down on to the wooden jetty.

'Vamos, Tony! VAMOS!' she bellowed at Antonio, jumping in as he fumbled with the line.

The little boat stuttered away – just in time. One of the things got really close, but with a sudden cracking sound, it broke through the edge of the rotted, dilapidated woodwork, and slid into the water.

A sudden flurry and surge of swishing water told the terrified couple that the piranhas had found something to eat.

Out in mid-river they stopped and drifted, the motor idling against the current, wondering where to go. The South bank? Where on earth would be safe?

Suddenly, above the noise of the outboard, a steady roar came from down river. Into view came several big, powerful boats full of armed men. One looked like a fire-boat. Hovering above them clattered an army helicopter pointing bright lights downwards. The convoy swept past, with a couple of the soldiers, foreign-looking ones, waving to them, as they rocked in the wake.

Perhaps somebody was at *last* paying attention to this accursed and forgotten spot?

Punta Loyola, Argentina

Capitan Antonio Ramos was the Port Commander of Punta Loyola in the Santa Cruz province of southern Argentina. He was at his desk trying to work out if any of his remaining sailors could be spared to be sent to the city outskirts to help the fight against the Limaxes.

A Petty Officer knocked and entered.

'Sir, two British ships are at the harbour entrance, a destroyer and what looks like a fire tug. They've requested permission to enter. It's strange. The officer on the radio spoke fluent Spanish and was not British – obviously Argentinian.'

The Commander was amazed. Why were the British here? We were fighting them not long ago. And with Argentines on board? He reluctantly gave his permission and then quickly walked to the quayside himself. Another surprise. Both ships flew two flags, the British White Ensign and the sky blue and white one of Argentina. What could *that* mean?

Once the two ships had made fast, he presented himself at the gangplank leading to the destroyer. He was again surprised. The British Captain saluting him was accompanied by army officers. They wore mottled camouflage uniforms and with distinctive blue and white Argentinian patches on the sleeves. One of them, very young, saluted and then put out his hand.

'Buenos Dias, Señor Commandante. I am Capitan Suarez. We're here to help, and there's much to discuss.'

Russia

General Ivan Baranov felt all of his seventy-four years as he sat in his study, drinking. He had become bored with state television, which had recently become ever more tedious, and no longer enjoyed Russian opera.

His dacha was sixty kilometres outside Moscow, quite big and spacious, and full of memorabilia of his career. But it was not a happy place. His wife had left him years ago, declaring that the handsome and hopeful young man she had married had turned into a monster. And they had never had children.

So the house was empty, and felt empty. His only visitor was Taina, his cleaning lady, and for some reason she had not turned up today. When the Russian government had refused to go on paying for a security detail 'because of the economic situation', he had privately paid for a team of his own men. But the one on duty during the afternoons, Sergei, was pretty useless – not only old, but usually drunk or asleep most of the time. It was high time he recruited a replacement, but everything seemed so much effort these days.

Some of his old comrades were still alive, but he would not exactly call them friends. And they never visited or rang to suggest a reunion. Perhaps, he sometimes thought, he should have kept going with that Haven secrecy project and not handed it over to Petrov. But then he remembered the awful travelling.

These days he certainly wouldn't be up to that.

Only very occasionally did he regret some of the things he had done in his life. And only occasionally did he wake from bad dreams.

Suddenly there was a strange sound coming from down the passage. Surely it couldn't be *them*? The local police had assured him that the woods had been cleared, and he had believed them.

He staggered to his feet, unsteadily. It was not just the painful arthritis, but the large amount of vodka he had drunk, even more than usual he quickly realized. He tottered to the gun cabinet and pulled out his Saiga-12 military shotgun. Then, opening the door very carefully, he looked down the passage.

To his horror, he saw poor old Sergei's body underneath at least six of the bastards, while others were sliding towards him. He closed the door, his heart pounding and thought for a moment.

He put down the shotgun.

Going to his desk, he opened the top drawer and pulled out his old Grach pistol. He checked it quickly, slid out the 17 shot magazine, and clipped it back in. He wouldn't need all those shots, he thought, sitting down in his comfortable old chair.

Just one.

Wiltshire, England

Cecily Laidlaw, a snowy-haired 80 year old, was watching the television evening news in her stone cottage in Hindon, in the picturesque county of Wiltshire in England. Her black cat, Abby, was purring on her lap as usual, keeping her pleasantly warm. But tonight, Cecily had noticed for the first time that Abby, her adored companion, needed help to get up there. At eighteen years old, pretty much like her owner, she was literally on her last legs.

Such a comfort had she been since Cecily's beloved husband, Gordon, had died. And no other cat would ever fill her place, even if she could afford one. After all, there were no more 'moggies' being born these days, and unlike her neighbour, Vivian Patten, she couldn't afford a pricy AI-born cat like a Persian or a Bengal. These days, cats born by artificial insemination cost a fortune, hundreds if not thousands of pounds if the breed were rare enough. And anyway, she had got used to Abby's funny little habits – exactly as she had those of her late husband, Gordon, and it was too late to start all over again.

Stroking Abby's still sleek and shiny fur, she envisaged them somehow leaving life together, having read somewhere that cats could sometimes sense their owners' eminent demise, and that they sometimes slept – as if to give comfort – on the beds of dying ones, and sometimes dying shortly afterwards themselves, as if the bond was somehow touchingly inseparable.

Suddenly the cat looked up, alarmed. Cecily comforted herself instantly that it was only because of the sudden crack of thunder outside, and that all her windows had been secured with steel shutters to keep out those dreadful creatures – the Limaxes – thankfully, a free service in Britain for anyone of her age.

Abby settled down again on her lap, readjusting her position, and the purring grew louder as Cecily stroked her.

Blessed Abby. What would she ever do without her? Life would be far less fun for her pet these days without any mice to catch, but she seemed content enough to eat and sleep, and hunt the lizards on the local allotment next door. Indeed, for her age, she was remarkably sprightly.

Cecily reflected, and not for the first tine, that life could be considerably worse, even with such dreadful stuff in the news. And Abby purred her contented agreement, suddenly turning upside down with all four paws splayed, obviously hoping to be stroked on her stomach.

CHAPTER TWENTY-EIGHT

London

The BBC television news came on at six o'clock with a surprise announcement.

'Buckingham Palace has just confirmed the exciting news that Princess Genevieve is expecting a baby, due next July. Let's go over to Buckingham Palace, and to Sue Barlow, our Royal Correspondent.'

The picture cut away to the front of the Palace and to Sue Barlow, heavily muffled against the biting December wind.

'Yes, Jim. This surprise announcement came to us only a few minutes ago. And there's even happier news. Now that everyone is once again able to receive artificial insemination from a donor, it might have been expected that the Princess may have done the same. However, I have some sensational news which I am allowed to tell you.

I can exclusively reveal that the baby's father *is* Prince George.

Years ago, we are informed, his mother and father became very worried about his enthusiasm for very risky, almost reckless sports. Some of our viewers may remember his skiing exploits as a teenager, and his feats on the Cresta Run.'

The television cut to library footage of the Prince tumbling down a slope during downhill racing.

'The Royal Family became increasingly anxious about the continuation of the family's royal line if he were badly injured, or even worse, killed. In 2026, he did *indeed* have a very serious accident and was put into an enforced coma for three days. During that period his parents took the unusual, but highly understandable decision to take a sperm sample. This has been kept frozen until recently.

We have been informed that the Royal Family did not want to try to use this while the rest of the world could not benefit from artificial insemination, nor when the Prince was fully engaged in his dangerous helicopter work in the Royal Navy, for which last year he was decorated with the Distinguished Service Cross.

But now that he has retired from flying, and now that every woman under 35 can have artificial insemination, the Palace has judged that the Princess should now be able to have a child. I've also been told that the Prince himself had absolutely no idea about any of this until a few months ago.

A wonderful piece of news for all of us this Christmas, and of course, for the Royal Family.

Jim, back to you in the studio.'

Kennedy Airport, USA

Two years of fighting the Limaxes had now passed, and except in South America and Africa, the fight was almost won. Now, in late December, Charles Koenig had called Ann Hearst to see if they could meet somewhere privately before the Christmas break, but not in one of the usual formal meeting places. They had worked out that the best one might be Kennedy Airport, where their busy schedules happened to coincide. And now they found themselves in a quiet corner of one of the few executive lounges still operating – that of American Airlines.

Arriving there early, Ann had glanced at the few newspapers, all now reporting the Christmas surprise of the 'miraculous' pregnancy of the British Princess Genevieve, thus ensuring the English royal line, as was the television news on in the lounge.

General Charles Koenig appeared, dressed in uniform, looked around and quickly spotted her. Still relatively youthful in appearance, thought Ann, and as enthusiastic and dynamic as he had been all those years ago when they had first met, when he had discovered the alien drones and she had thought up the idea of the Havens. It seemed like a lifetime ago.

'Hi, Ann,' he said kissing her on the cheek. 'How's things?'

He noticed with a tinge of sadness that time had taken its toll on Ann, but hardly surprisingly. The poor woman looked as if she had been bearing the weight of the world on her shoulders. Still attractive, but clearly worn out.

'Not great,' she responded. 'All's well with the family, but I'm sad about the Havens. They didn't *really* work as I hoped they might.'

Charles paused.

'I honestly don't think you should beat yourself up about that.' He put his hand on hers, allowing a rare moment of familiarity.

'You did your best. And back then, Ann, they were our only hope. Of course, after a while they became claustrophobic and difficult to keep secret, but that was *bound* to happen. But after all, they did work, up to a point. Without the young people from the Havens, we'd have been in real trouble. Frankly, I think you deserve a medal. However,' he paused, 'I wanted to talk about something else.'

Ann reached for her beer.

'Let me ask you something,' Charles continued. 'What do you think is going to happen next?'

Ann looked perplexed.

'You mean after we've been able to clear out the Limaxes completely, if we can do that? South America and Africa included?'

'No, I meant before that, I'm afraid.'

'Why?' asked Ann, although she knew instinctively where this was going.

'Well, think about it. Somebody, or something, flew sophisticated machines millions of miles, paused and then launched hundreds of poisonous missiles at us, most of them accurate enough to hit the sea and create the plumes. Then they carefully and precisely stationed 300 recon ships to watch us. A few malfunctioned, but they replaced them in exactly the same places in orbit.'

Ann nodded. She had been thinking many times along exactly the same lines.

'Then about 900 bigger ships arrive, and they launch thousands of Limax egg containers at us. We manage to disrupt them a bit, but they end up a scourge, albeit one we've just about managed to contain.'

Only just, thought Ann, vividly remembering her daughter's horrifying account of the action in Spokane and elsewhere.

'Well,' Charles continued, 'I figure that something made them launch that attack about twenty years too early.'

Ann nodded. 'I agree. 'We can only guess why on earth that happened.'

'Well, it may be that they rumbled our Haven system. Or perhaps whatever drove them to come here in the first place suddenly became more urgent. The Limaxes were *surely* not meant to come up against proper opposition – more likely they were intended to be a clean-up squad.'

'So, what's your conclusion?'

Charles sighed.

' Not a happy one, I'm afraid. My guess is that they'll be back. And if they're as determined as they seem to be, any new assault will be much stronger and more dangerous. We'll have to step up vigilance, not relax it. Complacency would be the biggest enemy of all.'

'And if they *do* attack again?'

Charles suddenly looked totally drained.

'I can only think of one last 'ace in the hole' that we may have. Luckily, nobody has tested a nuclear device for decades. It may just be that they don't even know we have atomic weapons. Why would they?'

Ann considered his words.

'You mean we'd have to attack them in space, before they could launch anything else?'

'Precisely. In the words of old movies, we'd have to nuke them.'

'Christ,' muttered Ann. 'You're probably right.'

Several moments passed.

'I think I need another drink' said Ann, 'perhaps something stronger. How about you?'

Verona, Italy

Four thousand miles away from New York in Verona, Sofia and Angelo were enjoying the best Italian wine they could afford in their little flat. They had just discovered, only two days ago in the Borgo Trento Maggiore, one of the city's main hospitals, that Sofia was pregnant with twins – and the ultrasound scan had shown a boy and a girl.

Angelo was surprised to find that he was every bit as thrilled and elated as his wife, even though he was not the biological father. For both of them it was infinitely better than remaining childless, and nurture he hoped, probably outweighed nature. He would pray for that in the cathedral tomorrow, along with thanking God for their double blessing.

It was all so different from last year. At last their faith in the Almighty had been restored. And by next Christmas, if all went well – and they would pray for that too – they would be a happy family of four, something they had always dreamed of. The thought was almost too much to take in. As Sophia picked up the two-thirds empty bottle to refresh her glass, Angelo put his hand tenderly over hers. 'Easy on that, Cara. I've got three of you to look after now!'

Connecticut, USA

Ann and Ted were delighted that Tricia and Tim and three-year-old Ben had decided to join them for Christmas at their wooden house in Connecticut. It was the perfect setting for a traditional Christmas, with beautiful views over a vast expanse of snow-covered lake and pine woods, and plenty of snow in the garden to make a snowman, and Ben could use a little sleigh safely on part of the snow-covered drive.

Ted had chopped down a splendid fir tree, now in their sitting room, the first Ann had decorated in twenty years, and she had asked the neighbours round for drinks on Christmas Eve, most of whom had returned now it was safe to do so.

Ted must have been lonely at the house, she often thought, staying for so long next to the deserted houses. He had never mentioned it or once complained about her long absences, nor the dangers he had evidently faced with the Limaxes – only revealing to her that his Winchester had worked well enough, providing he shot them accurately through the eyes. The thought horrified her, as did the area fenced off some distance away where he had hauled them off to be buried with his mechanical digger.

Now, at last, the family were all together in front of the cosy wood burner, watching the evening news on December 23rd. Ben was curled up on the sofa in his pyjamas and Santa Claus hat, happily drawing the illuminated Christmas tree. The whole family listened to the encouraging progress that was being made in eliminating the Limaxes all round the world, and the ambitious plans to help Africa and South America.

The news also celebrated the huge number of new births and a survey that had revealed that the favourite name for new-born girls was 'Hope' – at least in English-speaking countries.

But later on in the evening when Ben had been put to bed and the television was switched off, Tricia noticed that her mother had gone unusually quiet, not at all her usual positive self, and certainly not in the festive spirit of only an hour ago. Surely she couldn't be thinking it could all happen again?

'Well, I think I'll turn in,' said Ann. 'or I won't be in top form tomorrow.'

But Tricia knew that wasn't what was worrying her.

A frisson of fear swept through her as she realised she was too afraid to ask her mother what was going through her mind. And if she did, for the first time in her life, she knew her mother would spare her an honest answer.

CPSIA information can be obtained
at www.ICGtesting.com
Printed in the USA
BVHW031949111121
621385BV00001B/55